MONGOLIA AND THE GOLDEN EAGLE

An Archaeological Mystery Thriller

By Bradford G. Wheler

BookCollaborative.com
Cazenovia, NY 13035

BookCollaborative.com
PO Box 403
Cazenovia, NY 13035
BookCollaborative.com@gmail.com

ISBN-13: 978-0-9822538-9-2

Mystery, Thriller, Archaeology

PRINTED IN THE UNITED STATES OF AMERICA

Cover image by el_tazp

Interior design by Lorie DeWorken, MindtheMargins

Also by Bradford G. Wheler

INCA'S DEATH CAVE: An Archaeological Mystery

LOVE SAYINGS
wit & wisdom of romance, courtship, and marriage

GOLF SAYINGS
wit & wisdom of a good walk spoiled

CAT SAYINGS
wit & wisdom from the whiskered ones

HORSE SAYINGS
wit & wisdom straight from the horse's mouth

DOG SAYINGS
wit & wisdom from man's best friend

EIGHTEEN 6/10/71
The Poetry of John G. Hunter III

SNAPPY SAYINGS
wit & wisdom from the world's greatest minds

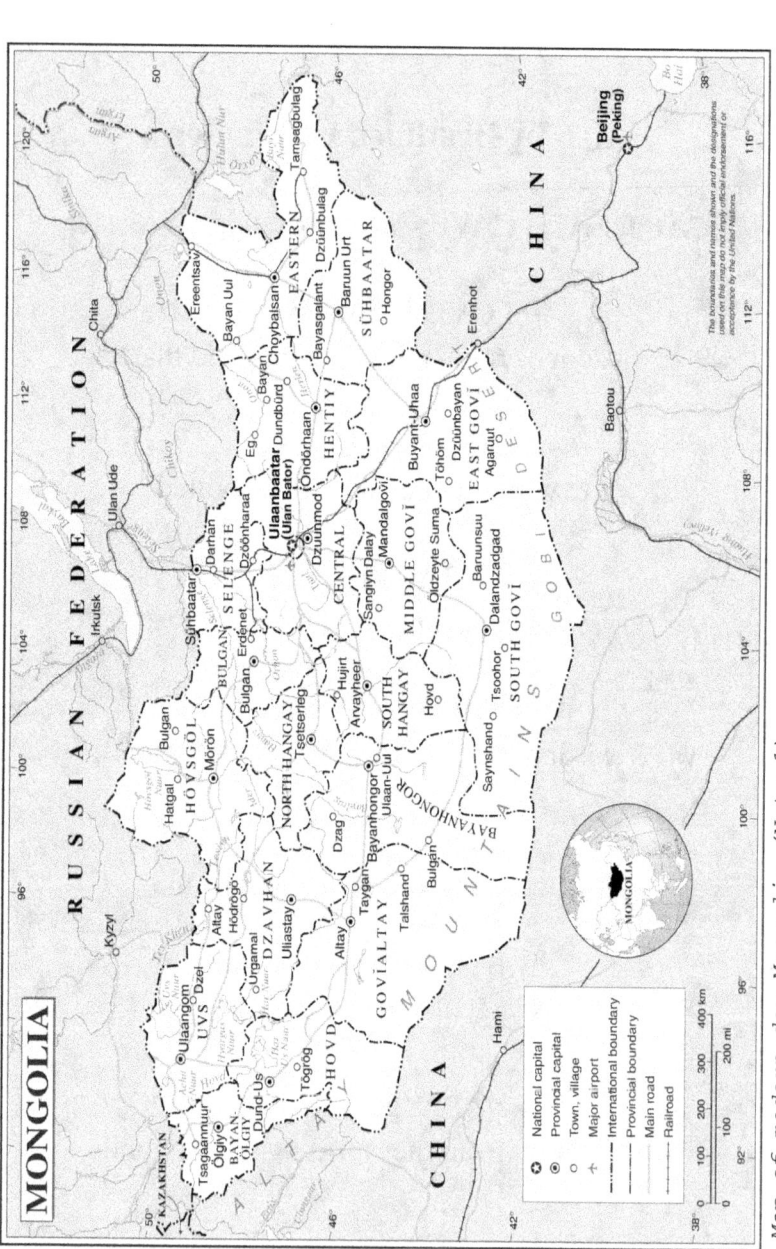

Map of modern-day Mongolia (Note 1)

MONGOLIA AND THE GOLDEN EAGLE

An Archaeological Mystery Thriller

Mongolian eagle hunter on horseback. (Note 3)

Chapter 1

Four horsemen appeared on the ridge above us. Each had a golden eagle perched on his arm. The air was clear and crisp. The horses snorted puffs of steam into the early morning air. The sky seemed very blue.

The lead horseman held up his arm and the eagle stirred. He removed the hood from the eagle's head, whispered something to the bird, and released him. The eagle leaped into the air and spread its eight-foot wings. As it began to circle upward, the other horsemen released their eagles and the wolf hunt began.

I once again wondered how this small nation of herders had built one of the biggest empires known to mankind. It stretched from Korea south to Vietnam, across most of China, northern India, the Middle East, into Eastern Europe and much of Russia. It was far larger and longer lasting than the conquests of Alexander the Great or the Romans. Surpassed in area and population by only the British Empire at its peak.

The Mongols developed a road system across the empire, commonly called the Silk Road. Commerce flourished, science, medicine, and the arts advanced, weights and measures were standardized, paper money was introduced, religious freedom and tolerance expanded.

This Great Empire of the Mongols was weakened by leadership infighting and then destroyed by the Black Death that came out of Asia and traveled over the Silk Road killing over 100 million people.

Cornell bell tower (Note 1)

Chapter 2

[Several months earlier at Cornell University in Ithaca, NY]

"'I was born modest but it didn't last.'" I looked up and saw the Dean standing in front of my desk. I held up the book I was reading and said, "Mark Twain, you know, Samuel Clemens, the American humorist."

"I know who Mark Twain is. I read him as a child."

His derogatory tone seemed rather disapproving of my choice of reading material. The Dean wasn't a bad guy really. A nosy busybody, and a bit of a prig, however these seemed to be the traits the University looked for in their academic Deans.

I said, "Please have a seat, what can I do for you?"

"No, I can't stay long. I just stopped in to say the administration has approved your grant and has asked me to assign your classes to other professors so you can immediately spend full-time on your grant work."

This was interesting since I didn't remember submitting a new grant.

He went on. "The administration didn't seem to care that this would create a great deal of additional work for me and others in the department. Money talks and the rest of us just have to adjust our lives to suit."

I cut him off before he worked himself into a full tirade. "Which grant would this be?"

"Just an eight-figure grant to do Mongolian research. Do you think the University would approve my $50,000 grant?"

He was beginning to work himself up again so again I interrupted him. I figured my best course of action was to get him out of here and find out on my own what was going on.

I said, "Thank you for the good news. Please let me know what I can do to make the transition of my classes to others as smooth as possible."

He looked down at me and said, "May I suggest you would make better use of your time by reading the works of Igor De Rachewiltz and Urgunge Onon."

He turned and walked out. I made a mental note to look up those names.

There was only one person who would involve me in a grant of this size. Especially given that Mongolia had nothing to do with my archaeological area of research. Walter Falone was a tech billionaire, founder and CEO of Falone Advanced Technologies, and a lover of archaeology. His firm did remote sensing, mapping, researching, and more, primarily for the mining and oil industry. It also did a lot more that I didn't really understand. He had hired Abbey and me for a project in Peru. To say it was a success would be an understatement. It fast-tracked Abbey's completion of her PhD and gave me almost rock star status in the small world of archaeology.

I got up and headed to Day Hall to find out what the story really was.

Chapter 3

Leaving Day Hall two hours later I sent a text to Abbey and asked her to meet me at the Sage Hall café.

Sage Hall had been a rundown graduate student dorm when the University decided it was in too central and valuable a location to let students live there. They cut the inside of the building out using massive steel scaffolds to hold the walls up. Then they rebuilt the inside and roof. One of the engineering professors I play squash with tried to explain how they did it. It's now part of the graduate business school. I have no idea what they spent but it looks beautiful and the café is one of my favorites on campus.

I'd finished one cup of coffee and was getting another when I saw Abbey walk in. She waved and mouthed "water." I pointed to where I was sitting and paid for my coffee and her bottle of water.

I first met Abbey as a fifteen-year-old freshman. I was her advisor and it quickly became clear that she was gifted. She stood out even among the many brilliant Cornell students. I was thrilled when she decided to pursue her PhD in archaeology at Cornell. Then during our time in Peru, she completed her PhD, and was now part of the faculty.

Her long red hair was tied back. She wore a sweater, jeans, and running shoes. I realized again just how fit she kept herself now. She had always been a runner but now she was seriously in shape.

I handed her the bottle of water as I sat down.

I said, "Has the Dean been to see you?"

"No, I haven't been in my office since 7:30 this morning. What's up?"

I said, "Our grant has been approved."

She gave me a look that said "What grant?"

"I'm not quite sure, something to do with Mongolia."

Now she looked at me as if I had lost my mind.

"I thought maybe you wrote it. It's fully funded, big time."

She said, "Walter?"

Just then we heard, "Hi folks."

Ned Harris spun a chair around and sat in it backwards facing us.

I said, "Ned, have you bugged my phone?"

"Why would I do that, Professor?"

I thought in his case just for fun. Ned was part of our team in Peru. He never completed college and his mother pleaded with him to go back and get a degree. I helped arrange for him to be enrolled in an accelerated program in the Engineering College for a combined bachelor's and master's degree. From the feedback I received from his professors, they felt a combination of wanting to wring his neck while at the same time liking him and being in awe of his computer skills. Ned viewed himself as a cyber warrior. He actually worked with the security group at Falone Advanced Technologies, where cyber security was a big issue, and for us part-time.

I said, "Just passing through Sage Hall and happened to spot us?"

He said, "Don't you think it is way cool? I mean us all going to Mongolia. You know, they have camels with two humps there. Or at least I think they do."

He obviously knew more about what was going on than we did. Abbey jumped in.

"What is going on? And Ned, no twenty questions." She gave him a hard stare.

Ned had seen Abbey working out with the former military guys and shooting on the range. I guessed he was, if not scared of her, a bit intimidated by her.

"Well, you know, my boss likes things on a need-to-know basis. But he asked me to get my affairs in order a few weeks ago. It seems the administration was a little slower at informing you.

"We go to Mongolia, you two are my independent study professors for the last six credit hours I need, and you oversee the completion of my thesis work. We are all back on full pay and we are out of Ithaca. Sounds good to me."

He leaned back and smiled at us.

Abbey said, "That's it? That is all you know?"

"No, I know we leave a week from Monday. They're sending a jet to pick us up. Call the office, someone must be able to fill you in. I have to run, I've got a lot to do. This is cool. You two don't seem that excited. I've never been to Mongolia. Think two-humped camels."

He gave us two thumbs up. Well, I will say this for Ned, he never lacked for spirit. I looked at Abbey. She just shook her head.

Then she said, "That little shit has one of our phones bugged. He has to. Leave a week from Monday and I was just beginning to have a life here again."

I said, "You can say no or at least finish the semester before joining the project."

She said, "Tell me what you know."

"The grant application was quite general. The project is to do archaeological research in Mongolia in coordination with the Mongolian Interior Ministry. It goes on about the restoration of historically significant documents, site inventories, development of educational resources, and multicultural unity. The provinces of Bayan-Ölgii and Khovd are referenced. Those two provinces cover about 47,000 square miles. That is an area almost the size of New York State. It names me as project director and you as deputy director. The Walter Falone Family Trust funds it, to the tune of ten million dollars. Not much more of use to us in the application."

Abbey sat quietly for a while. I drank my coffee and wondered what was going through her mind.

Finally she said, "I can't let you and Ned have all the fun. I'll go. Someone has to take care of you two."

I didn't realize at the time how prophetic her words would be. My phone vibrated. I took it out and looked at the screen. Then I turned it to show Abbey the screen. It read, "Call me at 19:00 hrs. EST I'll explain. Ian."

Mongolia and The Golden Eagle

Ian was Major Ian Campbell, British Special Air Service retired. He was an executive in the security group at Falone Advanced Technologies and I assumed Ned's boss. Standing six feet five inches tall, the Scotsman cut quite a figure. He was built like Arnold Schwarzenegger, but looked like a young Sean Connery. We worked with him in Peru and both of us had great respect for him.

I said, "I'll talk to him tonight and hopefully we will get a better idea of what's up."

Abbey said, "I'm going to do a workout. Let's meet tomorrow afternoon. How about here at 4:00?"

I nodded yes and as she got up I said, "Do you know the works of Igor De Rachewiltz and Urgunge Onon?"

"Never heard of them. Why?"

"The Dean seemed to think they would be a better use of my reading time than Mark Twain."

She just shook her head and left. I looked at my cold coffee as I thought today is Thursday. That gives me less than ten days to get my life in order to go halfway around the world.

I pulled out my laptop and sent the Dean an email asking who would be taking my courses. I sent the next email to my real estate agent friend asking her to call me in the morning about renting my house. Until I spoke to Ian tonight I didn't even know how long to plan for. I sat a while longer. Abbey at least had a life to be disturbed. My classes would be given to someone, my squash league would find a replacement for me, and my house would be rented. I didn't even have a pet to worry about or miss me. Well, this line of thought wasn't getting me anywhere. I decided to go to the Teagle Hall gym and take a swim.

Chapter 4

The next morning I was in my office at 7:00. I had no classes today so I spent the morning adding notes to each of my lesson plans and made sure they were in order. I organized each of my three courses into a folder to email to whoever the Dean wanted to complete my classes. I had a pretty good idea who would be teaching each course but I would wait to hear from the Dean. It was the first week of April so there wasn't that much left of the semester.

Then I went to visit my favorite research librarian Laura O'Hara. Maybe she could help me. When I explained my situation she burst out laughing.

When she stopped laughing, she said, "Rob, you've spent your entire career studying and researching pre-Columbian cultures in South America. Why would Mr. Falone pick you to head up a major research expedition in Mongolia? Do you even know where Mongolia is?"

I was wondering the same thing. I said, "Perhaps it is my good looks and charming personality? And I know where Mongolia is." I didn't add that I looked it up last night just to make sure.

She patted my cheek and shook her head. "Come back Monday afternoon and I'll have some information for you that might be helpful." Still smiling she walked over to a grad student who had been waiting to talk to her.

I didn't want to run into the Dean so I went to the Straight, the main student union, rather than back to my office. I got coffee and found a quiet spot in the corner. First I sent an email to my real estate agent telling her to try to rent my house for a year. Next I emailed one of my squash league friends who has a big barn and asked if he would store my car. I called my doctor's office, set up an appointment next week, and asked them to check to see if I should have any shots or vaccines to go to Mongolia. Then I went on Amazon and started downloading guidebooks and history books about Mongolia. For the history books I was looking for ones at about the level of *The Complete Idiot's Guide to…*

I bought a turkey sandwich and began making more notes for whoever was stuck with my classes. At about 2:30 I went to the gym to take a swim. I left Teagle at ten to four to meet Abbey. Usually swimming helped me think but not today.

As I walked into the Sage Hall café Abbey got up and stuffed the papers she was reading into her backpack. She walked up to me and said, "Let's get out of here. I need a drink."

We walked across the street to the bar at the Statler Hotel. It wasn't one of our favorite bars but it was the closest. I ordered Abbey a white wine and looked at the beer taps, boutique beers, and hard cider from Critz Farms. I had never heard of it so I ordered a glass of the cider.

I handed Abbey her drink, she took a sip, and said, "I got an earful from the Dean. He went on and on."

She obviously wasn't as comfortable as I was at cutting the Dean off. That was to be expected. Abbey was young, in her first year as a professor, and far more polite than I was.

She continued, "I don't think the others in our department are going to be too happy with us."

I'd been thinking about that too. Last time we left I was overdue for my sabbatical. We had months of notice. Everyone was accustomed to filling in when someone was on sabbatical. This time it was one week's notice, toward the end of the semester, and a mysterious grant that didn't seem to fit our area of study. We would have to do some serious fence mending.

Abbey said, "What did Ian have to say?"

"He cleared up some things but in some ways made it even more confusing. Ian apologized for the short notice. He said this was very important to the company and to Walter. It seems that the company was one of several companies bidding on a major contract with the Mongolian government to do a mineral resource survey of the entire country. Walter went to Mongolia to try to close the deal. He came away with the contract and a separate agreement to do archaeological research. We were specifically named in the contract. Ian said the Mongolian Interior Minister insisted that we lead the research. That made no sense to me.

"What he told me that was somewhat useful was to plan to be gone at least a year. I pressed him on the 'at least' part but he said I would have to talk to Walter about that. He said Walter was sorry he couldn't meet with us himself ahead of time but he is super busy and would see us as soon as he can. Not much else but to be at the airport at 9:00AM Monday."

Taking papers out of my briefcase I said, "These extend the confidentiality agreement we signed before. They want them signed, scanned, and emailed back as soon as you can. I did mine this morning when I was in my office."

She put the papers in her backpack and pulled out a flyer and handed it to me. I looked at it. "Alash master Tuvan throat singers," they were playing tonight. I looked up at Abbey.

She said, "I bought you a ticket. You can join me and my soon to be ex-boyfriend. We can learn something about the culture."

I said, "It says Tuvan not Mongolian."

"Technically it is in Russia but it borders Mongolia and historically was part of a larger Mongolia. People tell me they are amazing. Meet us there at 7:45 and we can have dinner after the show."

I said I would. Not having any more info on what we were going to be doing in Mongolia we finished our drinks and left.

Traditionally dressed Mongolian singer playing an igil. (Note 2)

Chapter 5

The Alash show last night was amazing. How they did that with their voices is a mystery to me. It sounded like a bird singing and a musical instrument playing with both coming out of one person's mouth. They somehow spread out their voice into two, three, or even four pitches. They also played the igil, a traditional two-stringed instrument that is played with a bow, along with more common instruments. Well, I now had one thing to look forward to in Mongolia, more of that amazing singing.

Dinner was a bit subdued with Abbey's boyfriend having just found out she was leaving in a few days. I left as soon as I politely could.

I spent the first part of the morning trying to decide what to take with me. I was piling clothes on the bed in the guest room when my doorbell rang. It was FedEx. I signed for the envelope. It was our employment agreement with Falone Advanced Technologies. It looked like they raised our pay a bit from the very generous level we were paid in Peru. That was good because this time I was on unpaid leave from the University and not on paid sabbatical. It also had other papers having to do with visas, and various permits. Some of them we were to FedEx back and some bring with us.

It was a sunny April day. Funny how in October 50 degrees feel terrible and after a long, cold Ithaca winter a day of 50 degrees seems wonderful. I took a mug of coffee and my iPad out on the back patio.

I started reading a Lonely Planet Guide to Mongolia. The pictures were beautiful. The country was over 600,000 square miles, an area about the size of Alaska. There were just under 3,000,000 people. The country was landlocked, being sandwiched between China and Russia. The terrain seemed quite varied from the Gobi Desert in the south to steppe land and then mountains to the north. All very interesting but I was struck again by how little I knew about this area of the world and I wondered why I would be picked to head up a project of this scope. I closed my iPad.

There was a lot for me to do. My house had a back room that mostly just collected junk. I had used this room to store my personal belongings when I rented my house before. I started moving my stuff into that room and getting my place ready to rent. The real estate lady would stop by this afternoon with the rental paperwork. My cleaning lady said she had time next week to clean the house so it could be shown.

Monday morning I put Abbey's contract paperwork on her desk with a note and then met with the professor who would take over one of my classes. While not thrilled, she didn't seem mad at me, mostly just curious. I politely told her what I knew, thanked her several times, and told her I owed her big time. She said all I needed to do was tell her how to get her research work funded to that level. I hoped my meeting with the other two faculty members went this well.

After my 10:10 class I went to Olin Library to see what Laura O'Hara had for me. She handed me a memory stick.

She said, "I've made two lists. The first is a general listing of useful material to get you familiar with Mongolian culture. The next, more extensive list is quite comprehensive. Homo erectus arrived in Mongolia over 800,000 years ago, however I didn't figure you would want to start that far back. Modern humans arrived about 40,000 years ago. I figured that was a good place to start. I put the reference material in chronological order. I also noted which volumes were available online. We have some of the others here and I could get many others through our lending program. But you can't take them to Mongolia with you. I sent an email to the Mongolian University of Science and Technology and the National University of Mongolia to see how many of these manuscripts and books they have in English. I assume you're not fluent in Mongolian. Although I understand English is replacing Russian as a second language there."

She was enjoying this. I figured there was a lifetime of work on that memory stick.

I said, "Do you know who Igor De Rachewiltz and Urgunge Onon are?"

She thought for a minute and said, "They're in there. I remember seeing their names, some kind of Mongolian scholars. It seems they worked on *The Secret History of the Mongols.*"

I didn't even know what that was. I decided to smile dumbly rather than say something and confirm my ignorance. She had obviously done a lot of work. I thanked her. She had a look on her face that said she knew I was in way over my head.

I had a 1:25 class. So I headed there next. It was interesting to see that most of the students in the two classes I taught today didn't seem to care very much that I was leaving. They knew the replacement professors and it was close to the end of the semester. They just wanted to get done and be off for the summer. I couldn't really blame them.

I sent a text to Abbey to see when she could meet. She said to meet her at 7:00 at Rulloff's for dinner. Rulloff's was on College Avenue in Collegetown. It was a step or two up from a dive bar. I decided I'd better track down the other two professors who would be taking my classes.

I went to Rulloff's about ten minutes early. Being somewhat old-fashioned I didn't think it was polite to leave a woman waiting at a bar. Abbey arrived shortly after 7:00. After handing her a drink, I gave her a copy of the memory stick.

I said, "Laura O'Hara says it's a list of everything we might need to know about Mongolia starting about 40,000 years ago. Most of it isn't online and much of it is written in Mongolian, Chinese, Russian, and several other languages. How about you talk to Elizabeth about getting us some super translator software to at least cover Mongolian, Chinese, and Russian?"

Elizabeth is the new Chief Technology Officer at Falone Advanced Technologies and Abbey worked closely with her when we were in Peru.

I continued, "Perhaps that search software you called 'Bible Analyzer on steroids' would be helpful too. I'm not sure what we'll be doing but it will likely involve reviewing a massive number of documents."

She said, "I hope your day went better than mine. People don't seem that happy about us cutting out like this. I did manage to meet with everyone who will be taking over for me today, so that's done. My lease is up in June so that's not much of a problem. Mom and Dad are coming down Saturday to pick up my personal belongings and help me put the rest in storage."

I said, "I'm sure you can expense the rent for May and June with the short notice we were given."

She smiled and signaled the waitress for two more drinks.

I said, "Did you lookup Igor De Rachewiltz and Urgunge Onon?"

"Yes, Wikipedia is great. The whole world's first reference source. The same facts are in all sorts of places but Wikipedia is free, fast, and about as good as any other general reference source. They are a not-for-profit so I donate each year. Do you?"

I said, "I will tonight. *The Secret History of the Mongols* is what I heard they are or were known for. I don't even know if they are alive or dead and I haven't gotten around to looking up what the book is about."

She said, "Prof, what are we doing? The average tourist going to Mongolia knows more than we do."

"Well, we are fast learners, and Walter must have a plan for us. He doesn't waste money and seems to hire people that fit what is needed. I assume he has a plan in mind and somehow we will fit into it. Plus you are now deputy director of a research project with ten million bucks in funding. That will look good on your résumé." I stopped and took a drink.

She said, "I may have to put my résumé out on the street when we get back unless the Dean cools off a bit. Let's eat and talk about something else."

Chapter
6

The rest of the week went by quickly. I picked Abbey up at a little after 8:00 AM, drove to the general aviation section of the airport, and pulled into the lot of the fixed-base operator Taughannock Aviation. My friend had my other set of keys. He was going to pick up the car, and store it in his barn.

As we parked the car Abbey said, "Looks like you're getting your wish."

I looked at the executive jet on the runway and said, "Wow. Is that a G-4?"

Abbey said, "Better still. It looks like a brand new Gulfstream G650ER. Top of the line."

As before, we were met by the flight crew who took our luggage, checked our passports, and seated us in a friendly, efficient way. Ned was already on board. He was in the cockpit asking questions. The pilots seemed happy enough to answer them. We were seated and the pilots kicked Ned out of the cockpit.

He joined us and said, "Just a short hour flight to Sudbury."

Abbey said, "I thought we were going to Mongolia."

Ned said, "I checked and I was right they do have two-hump camels in Mongolia. We have to pick up Major Campbell and a few others in Canada."

Walter had his initial success in the gold fields of Canada. Falone Advanced Technologies was actually a Canadian company even though there were more employees in Houston than in Sudbury. Being a Canadian company helped when operating in some areas of the world. Abbey and Ned began talking about some software so I took out my iPad and began to read.

Coffee and bagels were served and we started descending before I finished my second cup of coffee. I looked out the window, the Sudbury airport didn't look much bigger than Ithaca's. It had two runways in the shape of a cross and a taxiway to the terminal area.

As we taxied in, one of the attendants told us we could deplane, use the restrooms, and stretch our legs. We would be leaving again in 20 minutes. As I returned from the restroom I saw Major Campbell, Ned, and another man standing by the gate. I walked over and Abbey was a short ways behind me. I said hello to Major Campbell and he introduced me to Hank Nez. He was powerfully built but not that tall, maybe 5 feet 9 inches. He had dark eyes and black hair. As we shook hands I noticed he had on a silver ring with a large carved turquoise stone.

I said, "Is your ring Navajo?"

"Yes. Many of my people try to make a living selling

jewelry and trinkets to the tourists."

I gave him a three-word traditional greeting in Navajo.

He responded in Navajo and then said, "Your pronunciation is quite good."

Abbey said, "Prof knows about six words in a couple dozen languages. He tries to impress people."

He put out his hand and said, "You must be Professor Summers. How is your Navajo?"

She responded in Navajo. I thought what she said was "better than his." Of course that was true of many things.

Ned seemed disturbed by our exchange. He said to Hank, "You told me only full-blooded Navajos could understand your language."

Hank said, "Relax. We teach the tourists a few words. It makes them feel good and they buy more. It's like you saying *bonjour*."

Ned still seemed miffed. At this point they asked us to board the plane. We took our seats. After we took off, one of the attendants handed me a large manila folder. I looked inside, it had six personnel files in it.

I showed it to Abbey and said, "Our team?" I knew we were both thinking the same thing. The nickname our Peru team had given themselves.

Abbey put her hand up. "Don't even say the word."

I smiled and briefly looked at the names on the files. Hank Nez was one of them.

I slid them back in the folder and said, "Since I don't really know what we are going to do, I'm not sure they will mean much to me yet." I gave the folder to Abbey. She reluctantly took it.

I walked back to where Major Campbell was sitting. He was working away on his computer.

I said to him, "All this is a bit too much of a mystery for me. Are you going with us and where exactly are we going?"

He said, "London next. We will meet Walter there and he can do a better job of explaining your role. As with most things Walter does there are lots of moving parts. As for your other question, yes, I'm going to Mongolia. I'm glad Walter chose you and I'm looking forward to working with you again."

I said, "The devil you know?"

"Rob, you get quite cynical." He went back to working on his computer.

I saw Ned was deep in conversation with Hank as I walked back to my seat. In a little while they served lunch. I decided to try and sleep. I was used to long flights north and south, however, going through time zones the other way was harder on my body.

It was the middle of the night when we landed at London City Airport. It is the closest airport to central London and is only a few miles from Canary Wharf. We cleared customs with our overnight bags and were met by a limo. The limo took us to a hotel. Major Campbell was already there and had everyone checked in. He told Abbey and me to meet him in the lobby packed and ready to go at 9:30 in the morning.

The hotel bar was closed. My body wasn't sure what time it was so we just went to our rooms. After a few fitful hours of sleep I got up and ordered room service breakfast. I was having more coffee in the lobby a little after 9:00 when Abbey joined me.

"Sleep well?" I said.

She shook her head and went to get a cup of coffee.

At 9:25 Major Campbell walked in and told a porter to get our bags. "Shall we go? The traffic will be heavy and we don't want to keep Walter waiting."

Perhaps after meeting with Walter I would feel better about things.

I said, "Where are we going?"

Ian said, "We are going to the University of London, the School of Oriental and African Studies. We will meet Walter and Sir Harold Padsworth."

I thought Sir Harold, I wonder what he did to be knighted. Well, the Queen did knight the Beatles and we now have Sir Ringo Starr. I guess you don't have to save King and country these days to be a knight of the realm. Perhaps there were other ways to become a British sir. I could probably find out on Wikipedia.

We pulled up in front of the Brunei Gallery.

Major Campbell said, "They fancy themselves the world's leading institute on Asian studies. Other institutions might dispute that but they no doubt rank high up the list."

We were met at the information desk and walked through a door labeled Employees Only. We went by lab rooms, offices, and what looked like workshops. We took an elevator down, walked through more corridors, and then into a large office decorated with what I assumed were Mongolian artifacts. Walter was deep in conversation with a man who looked to be in his mid-eighties.

The man stood up quite spryly, walked over to us, and said, "Professors Summers and Johnson, Major Campbell, please come in. How very good indeed to meet you."

He politely took Abbey's hand, then he firmly pumped my hand, before grabbing Major Campbell's hand while slapping his back. It was an enthusiastic welcome.

"I'm Harry Padsworth, wonderful to have you here. Walter and I were just discussing your upcoming work. Most exciting. Major, in my youth I served in the regiment founded by one of your ancestors."

Ian said, "I'm not sure how closely related I am to the first Marquess of Argyll."

Sir Harold interrupted. "The same sturdy stock, no doubt. I see it in your eyes."

I must have looked lost.

Ian said, "Sir Harold is referring to Archibald Campbell, 1st Marquess of Argyll, 8th Earl of Argyll, chief of the Campbell Clan, born in 1607. He founded the regiment that is now the Scots Guards. There are lots of Campbells."

Sir Harold went on. "You surely know Torquhil Ian Campbell, the current Earl of Argyll and chief of Clan Campbell. He plays elephant polo. Quite interesting to watch, slower than real polo."

Ian said, "I did have the pleasure of meeting him once."

Walter cleared his throat and said, "Harry has been very helpful sharing his knowledge of Mongolia and introducing me to people there."

I looked around the room and said, "This is quite an impressive collection of artifacts."

He said, "Yes. They all belong to the University's museum. They let me display them as long as I don't break anything. You see the Sultan and I are quite close. That is Sultan Hassanal Bolkiah of Brunei. His full name is Sultan Haji Hassanal Bolkiah Mu'izzaddin Waddaulah ibni Al-Marhum Sultan Haji Omar Ali Saifuddien Sa'adul Khairi Waddien. How would you like to have to write that every time you wrote a check?

"He donated the money for the museum. Let's just say I was helpful in the process. So now the University lets me study what I want and pretty much have the run of the place as long as I don't get in the way. I have the title Emeritus Curator of Asian something."

He stopped and looked at Walter. I thought Sir Harold didn't get many visitors, so when he did, he was a bit overly enthusiastic.

Walter said, "Let's all take a seat. I haven't had a chance to visit with Abbey and Rob. They know almost nothing about our project. I will fill them in on what the company is doing later. Let's focus on the research they will be doing."

Sir Harold jumped in. "Yes. Quite what we need to do. Professor, you are going to help bring the people of Mongolia closer together. Really quite an interesting idea Walter came up with and quite overdue. The western provinces have been neglected too long. Everyone wants to study Genghis Khan and the forbidden land."

I thought "bring the people of Mongolia closer together." You have to be kidding. Almost everything I know about Mongolia is from the guidebooks I've read in the last week.

He went on. "Yes, this Yu-Min Lin chap from the University of California has this Valley of the Khan Project to use non-invasive technology to discover the tomb of Genghis Khan. Some form of international crowdsourcing effort. It won the National Geographic *Adventure* magazine's 2010 Readers Choice Adventurer of the Year. Too many people think Mongolia is all about Genghis Khan.

"However almost everything in Mongolia starts with Genghis Khan. All national people have their historic figures that define them. You Yanks have your founding fathers, Washington, Jefferson, Franklin, and then on to Lincoln, and many others. We Brits have Churchill, Lord Nelson, Wellington, Sir Francis Drake, and the list goes on. The Mongolians have one historic hero who stands far above the rest. Genghis Khan. Mongolians define their beginning as a nation with Genghis Khan.

"It is still hard to fathom what he accomplished. Before Genghis Khan, Mongolia was made up of dozens of nomadic tribes. Within the tribes the clans didn't get along. Let me try to explain it to you this way.

"If over two hundred and fifty years before Columbus sailed for America, a nomadic Plains Indian, son of a dead minor chief, from a weak clan of a small tribe, first went on to unit his tribe. Then he defeated or united all the tribes of the Great Plains into a unified nation. From there he conquered everyone east to the Atlantic Ocean, west to the Pacific Ocean, north to the Arctic Circle and south to about modern-day Brazil. Uniting them into the largest empire the world had ever seen. That would be the equivalent of what Genghis Khan did.

"He then went on to develop trade and commerce, advance science and medicine, standardize weights, measures, and writing. Now he was absolutely brutal to those who resisted him. But on many levels quite amazing even by the standard of other great world leaders.

Re-creation of a Mongol warrior on horseback. (Note 3)

"During the decades the Soviets occupied Mongolia they tried to erase the country's national identity. Thousands and thousands of historians, scholars, and even archaeologists and musicians were put into labor camps or just murdered. After Stalin's death people thought things would be better. A brave government official had a stamp printed with Genghis Khan's image on it. He was first fired, then forced out of his home, and finally hacked to death with an ax. A whole new round of purges of scholars started. The differences between ethnic groups were exploited. One group pitted against another.

"Well, you see how important your work can be."

What I saw was the potential of me making a great fool of myself, and disappointing everyone involved.

Sir Harold said, "Professor, it seems the Mongolian Minister of the Interior was quite impressed with your work in Peru. Once department heads in his Ministry learned he was reading all about your work, well, you know how that goes. They all read about you as well, probably to impress their boss. Gelegdorjiin Damba, the Interior Minister, gets it in his head that this Professor Johnson is just the one who can rediscover the Mongolian history and heritage that was lost during the Soviet occupation and help heal the ethnic divide within the country."

I looked at Walter and said, "Walter, what did you say when the Minster suggested I undertake this, I'm not sure what. Project?"

Walter smiled and said, "I told him you were just the man for the job."

I said, "It's always a good idea to tell the customer what he wants to hear when you are trying to make a sale."

Walter only nodded.

Sir Harold jumped back in. "Quite a strong-willed fellow the Minister is. I understand he is also quite demanding. I'm sure you will get along splendidly.

"I agree with the Minister that your work in Peru was rather remarkable. But I'm not aware of the depth of your knowledge on East Asia and particularly Mongolia."

I resisted the urge to laugh out loud and said, "I saw Alash a week ago Friday and I have this memory stick."

I pulled out the memory stick listing reference material that Laura O'Hara, a research librarian at Cornell, had given me.

Now it seemed that Sir Harold was at a loss for words. He stared at me and said, "Alash?"

"Yes," I said. "Mongolian throat singers. Well, actually they are from Tuva. The memory stick contains a list of over two hundred reference books that should contain everything anyone needs to know about Mongolia. A Cornell reference librarian put it together for me. It starts about 40,000 years ago and ends with this year's Lonely Planet travel guide."

Sir Harold wasn't at a loss for words for long. "Tuvan throat singing is much like Mongolian throat singing. Did you know that genetic evidence suggests that the modern Tuvan people are the closest genetic relatives to the native peoples of North and South America? This adds strength to the theory that the indigenous people migrated to the Americas via a land bridge across what is now the Bering Strait."

Abbey said, "Sir Harold, are you referring to the work of Ilya Zakharov of the Vavilov Institute of General Genetics in Moscow?"

Now both Sir Harold and Walter were impressed. I smiled to myself. This was in our area of study. However we looked at it from the other end. Where did the indigenous people of South America who we spent our careers studying come from? I couldn't have come up with the researchers' names but I wasn't at all that surprised that Abbey did.

"Well yes," Sir Harold said and looked at her with increased respect.

Abbey said, "I think a great research project would be to map all the existing genetic data not just of current population but back through the ages. Then send researchers out in the field to fill in the blanks."

Sir Harold and Abbey went into an animated discussion on the best ways to accomplish this.

Walter while interested looked at his watch and said, "Our time is unfortunately short. Let's focus on the task at hand."

Sir Harold gave a summary of the suffering of the Mongolian people during the Soviet period. He went on to explain that currently Mongolia and the Russian Federation enjoy close and reasonably warm relations.

When he finished he went to his desk, pulled out a packet, and said, "Now I've prepared some letters of introduction for you. I believe these people can be quite helpful. If I were a younger man, even seventy again, I'd love to be there with you."

Sir Harold insisted on walking us out. We thanked him.

Outside two limos were waiting.

Walter said as he headed to one of the limos, "I'll meet you at the airport. We can talk in more detail on our flight to Tel Aviv."

Two men standing next to the limo started talking to Walter as he approached the car. It was clear he was already involved in another issue and for now we were forgotten.

I looked at Abbey. She said, "Tel Aviv?"

I shook my head.

Our limo headed for London City Airport. The traffic was very heavy now. I took in the sights and thought Sir Harold probably had many interesting stories to tell. I would have enjoyed spending an evening with him over dinner and a nice bottle of wine.

Once we arrived a new flight crew took our overnight bags and directed us back on the Gulfstream. Ned and Hank were already on the plane. Then we waited. I read and it was a good hour before I heard them start the engines. Five minutes later Walter climbed on board, the cabin door was closed, and we taxied off.

Walter was seated in the front of the plane in a club seating area. Once we were in the air the flight attendant asked us to join Walter and Major Campbell.

Walter smiled and asked us to please have a seat.

He said, "Abbey, I haven't even had a chance to congratulate you on receiving your PhD and position on Cornell's faculty."

He seemed completely relaxed and as if he had nothing more to do than make small talk.

He continued, "I know all this is on rather short notice and I greatly appreciate you agreeing to help us out with this project. I'm sure you have many questions."

He looked at Abbey.

She didn't know where to start or even if Walter expected her to ask a question. She said, "Tel Aviv?"

Walter laughed. "It does seem a rather indirect way to get to Mongolia. For almost all our projects we contract out for aircraft, drones, and other special equipment. The ones the company owns are used mostly for testing and developing new equipment and software. For this project the drones, pilots, and some other technical support equipment and personnel were contracted with Israel Aerospace Industries. They should be loading that equipment on a larger plane now in Tel Aviv and then we'll proceed to Ulaanbaatar."

From my reading of the last few days I now knew Ulaanbaatar was the capital and largest city in Mongolia. I was almost an expert.

I guess I was shaking my head slightly.

Walter said, "Rob, I know you must be feeling confused. Minerals represent more than 80 percent of Mongolia's export. That percentage is expected to increase. The Mongolian government is negotiating with some of the world's biggest mining companies. They need a much better understanding of what the country's resources are and how to develop these resources without damaging their environment.

"Falone Advanced Technologies and several of our competitors competed for a contract to do a countrywide assessment of the mineral resources. Our proposal included doing a countrywide biological and environmental assessment. Based on our research work in Africa and South America we are far better able to perform this type of wide-scale survey at a cost-effective price.

"In my discussions with the Interior Minister he expressed great interest in and admiration for your work in Peru. He went on about how much historical and archaeological work needed to be done in Mongolia. He lamented the unwillingness of the government to fund much of any work in this area.

"That is when I suggested that perhaps my foundation might be able to fund some meaningful work in this area."

I said, "Walter, ten million dollars seems quite a generous funding level. I don't really understand your business but I would guess that would have to be most if not all of the profit from your government contract. Mongolia is not a wealthy country."

"Quite true, Rob. However performing this contract will be a huge advantage in winning work from the companies that receive the mining concessions in Mongolia. It would also hopefully open the door to work in Kazakhstan, Kyrgyzstan, Uzbekistan, and Turkmenistan. These are all large areas that represent great opportunities for us. Kazakhstan has over a million square miles of territory.

"Minister Gelegdorjiin Damba is a forceful negotiator. He made a compelling case for the work that needs to be done. He also had convinced the competition to fund this work at a similar level. Our negotiation came down to the one thing I could deliver that my competitors couldn't, you and Abbey. I'm hopeful we can make this a positive situation all around."

I wasn't sure if I was flattered or offended to be a bargaining chip in Walter's contract negotiations. I didn't say anything. I just looked past him out the window.

"Rob, had time permitted I would have involved you up-front and given you more input. This is important and I do need your help. You managed the team brilliantly in Peru. Once this project is done we can work on designing a research project that fits your top priorities."

I still wasn't sure how I felt. I said, "We are here and

willing but I not sure we have the skill or knowledge set that is needed. How will the Minister feel when we fail miserably?"

Walter said, "That won't happen, here is the schedule. The day after we land we have a meeting with the Minister and his staff. He outlines his thoughts. Then three weeks later we meet again and you present your plan for the research, he approves it, then you two get to work."

Abbey was looking back and forth at Walter and me like she had just gone down the rabbit hole in *Alice in Wonderland*.

I said, "This ten million dollars of grant funding, how is it to be spent?"

Walter explained. "You, Abbey, and the rest of our team are company employees. You will be paid by the company and are not part of what the grant money is used for. Cornell gets an administrative cut, and the rest is for local hires, equipment, and all the associated expenses. You will need to develop a budget once you develop your work plan. The company accounting department will make sure the funds are available in the proper currencies when and where they are needed. Major Campbell will handle logistics, security, and equipment procurement. Cyber security as always will be a key issue."

Walter went on in detail about what the company's work would entail. It seemed that the drones would be flown out of a former Soviet air base leased by Walter's company near the small city of Choir about 150 miles southeast of the capital. Our team would be based there until we headed to the western provinces of Bayan-Ölgii and Khovd. Officials in Ulaanbaatar were concerned that the drones would be a danger to commercial aviation. That wasn't the case but officials were firm that no drones were to be flown from the commercial airport or in populated areas. The company was also using planes for some of the survey work and they would be flown out of Chinggis Khaan Airport, the only international airport in Mongolia.

I'd learned that there are numerous ways to spell the Great Khan's name: Chinggis Khan, Chinghis Khan, Genghis Khan, and Khan as Khaan. I was becoming more of an expert on Mongolia by the minute.

When Walter finished he told Abbey and Ian that he wanted a word with me. They headed back to their seats.

Once they left he said, "Rob, I know this seems strange to you, however, as I said it is important, I trust you, and have great respect for your abilities. There are no Mongolian experts who I have that level of trust and confidence in that I have with you. It was a stroke of luck that the Minister knew of you and your work in Peru, so it wasn't hard for me to enhance your reputation in his mind."

Not only was I an expert in this area, now Walter has built me up as some kind of superman.

He continued, "When you develop your work plan for the Minister's approval I suggest you leave out Genghis Khan. He is the most studied figure in Mongolia if not all of Asia. It is highly unlikely you will add anything. He is viewed as a saint-like figure by some, and a devil-monster by others. He is an endlessly fascinating historical leader, but not a good fit for us. Our grant territory is to focus on the western provinces Bayan-Ölgii and Khovd. Most of the people in Bayan-Ölgii are Kazakhs not Mongols. In Khovd there are more than 17 nationalities and ethnicities. Each of these groups has its own distinct traditional dwelling and settlement pattern, dress and other cultural distinctions, literary, artistic, and musical traditions. It is important that the central government be seen as directing resources to these areas and being sensitive to their cultures and traditions. That is why I suggest our grant focus on this area of the country. The Minister agreed that it was not only worthwhile work but it would be useful politically."

There was more going on than a simple archaeological project. Being in a remote corner of the country was fine by me. Perhaps I could find an obscure archaeological site and spend my time excavating that. At least I know how to run a proper dig site.

"There is one thing I need you to incorporate into your work plan," Walter said.

He handed me a piece of paper. It said "Bayan-Ölgii Aimag" and had coordinates on it. Quickly judging from the coordinates it looked like an area of about 250 miles by 50 miles.

I waited and then he said, "I know this sounds a bit mysterious but later I will be able to tell you more. Your work plan needs to have a reason for you and a dozen or more people investigating in this area on the Mongolian side of the border. You will need to have a valid archaeological reason to roam over this entire area.

"Rob, please trust me, this is important and at some point I will clear up all your questions."

One of the flight attendants came over and informed Walter the conference call was waiting for him. He politely thanked me again and I went back to my seat next to Abbey.

I sat and handed Abbey the piece of paper. She looked at it and said, "Bayan-Ölgii is the most western province in Mongolia. Aimag is the Mongolian term for province or state. I don't know what the coordinates mean."

I said, "They mean that is where Walter wants us to find something of archaeological importance to research with a dozen or more people."

"Prof, do you think this is an elaborate way to bribe the Interior Minister to give Walter's company the contract?"

"The thought had crossed my mind but, I don't think so the way it is set up. Going through Cornell and having his company's accounting department handle the disbursement of funds has too many eyes on where the money goes."

Abbey said, " 'The Purloined Letter'?"

"No, but something else is going on. Walter said it is important and asked me to trust him. Based on all we have been through with him, I do trust him. How do you feel about all this?"

She smiled and said, "I guess mystified more than anything else. Let's make it an adventure and who knows what we might learn. We may never have another chance to spend time in Mongolia. Plus Ned is all worked up about two-humped camels."

I said, "Yes, there is that to look forward to. Let me have those files on the people that have been assigned to the team."

In addition to Ned and Hank Nez there were four others. Two were national park rangers. Both had military backgrounds, one a former captain and the other a sergeant. I assumed they would act as escorts on our travels. The other two were a young Mongolian male and a female Mongolian of Russian descent. I flipped quickly through them and put them aside again.

I picked up my iPad and went to my Lonely Planet Guide to look up Bayan-Ölgii Aimag.

In a few hours we began our descent into Tel Aviv Ben Gurion Airport. Once we landed we taxied to the section for private aircraft. Again Major Campbell collected our passports and led us to the customs station. It was a bright sunny day and it felt nice to walk a bit.

We didn't actually have to clear customs. We were directed to a lounge and told we would board our other plane in about thirty minutes. I did a double take as I saw three nuns enter the lounge.

I said to Abbey, "Is that the Abbess from the Monastery of Saint Catherine in Arequipa, Peru?"

She said, "It sure looks like her."

We walked over and I said, "Abbess, what a pleasant surprise to see you. What are you doing here?"

She gave a big smile and shook our hands warmly. "His Holiness has asked me to help with an area of growing concern to him. He is quite disturbed by the rise of anti-Semitism in Europe. He felt that the connections I have developed with the European women of the Church would be helpful. We spent this last week here meeting with Jewish religious leaders."

A flight attendant from Falone Advanced Technologies came over and said to the Abbess it was time to board. She said a brief farewell and headed out the door followed by the other two nuns.

Ned came over to us and said, "She likes flying around in Walter's jet. The Pope is all pissed off at the Vatican old guard for not taking the rise in anti-Semitism more seriously so he brought in the Abbess. He is increasingly turning to members of the Church from outside Europe to help institute reforms."

Abbey said, "And how do you know all this?"

Ned said, "It's my job to know stuff." Then he walked off toward the counter with the snacks.

Abbey said, "That little shit probably has the Abbess' phone bugged too."

I went over to the window and watched them loading our plane. It looked like the same plane we took from Houston to Peru. Abbey knew all the detailed specifications. If I remembered correctly it was a Boeing BBJ C featuring quick-change capabilities that allow the aircraft to be used for executive duty during one flight, and to be quickly reconfigured for cargo duty for the next flight. It also has self-contained stairs for disembarking at airports with only limited ground support. It sounded like we would need that feature where we were going.

Our luggage had been loaded. I saw Major Campbell talking to a group of men. They all had a military look. I guess working for Israel Aerospace Industries that was to be expected.

We boarded the Boeing and shortly were airborne.

The pilot said it was 3828 miles to Ulaanbaatar and it would take 7 hours and 57 minutes. We should land about 10:00AM local time. My body didn't know what time it was. We were fed again, I read and tried to sleep.

Genghis Khan Equestrian Statue (Note 3)

Chapter 7

The attendant woke me up and handed me a cup of coffee. She said we would be landing in about an hour and took my breakfast order. I will say flying on Walter's planes was way, way better than commercial airlines.

It was bright and sunny out the window as we began our descent. Chinggis Khaan International Airport didn't look that large from the air. It had two runways. One was asphalt and the other was shorter and looked like grass. I wondered how many countries' national airport still had grass runways.

To the north I could see the city sprawling out. From the guidebooks I'd been reading I knew the city has about 1.4 million people and the elevation is 4,400 feet. It is the financial, industrial, and cultural center of the country.

I was becoming more of an expert on Mongolia by the hour. That black depressing feeling hit me again. What am I doing here? I'm going to make a total fool of myself. To shake off my worsening mood I smiled and said, "Did you sleep well, Abbey?"

She scowled and said no. But then she flashed me her bright smile and poked me playfully in the arm. "Prof, are you ready to rock and roll in Mongolia?"

"You bet, Abbey, you bet." There was no point in spoiling the day for others because of my black mood.

Walter came by our seats and told us Major Campbell would handle our bags and accommodations. He would meet us at the Interior Ministry tomorrow for our meeting. Most of the meeting would concern the company's contract work but the Minister would reserve time to discuss the grant at the end of the meeting.

Walter was first off the plane. He had cleared customs and was driven off before any of us left our seats.

Major Campbell and one of the Israel Aerospace Industries employees got off next. They had all our passports and asked us to stay on the plane. A few minutes later Major Campbell came on board, handed us our passports, and asked us to follow him. From the aircraft door I saw just one van waiting. Major Campbell directed Abbey and me to it. After a few words with the Israelis he got in the front seat. After refueling, the plane would take the rest of the passengers and equipment to the former Soviet air base leased by the company. We would join them after our meeting at the Ministry of the Interior.

The driver spoke excellent English. He said it was about eleven miles from the airport to the city center. As we approached the city, I was struck by the number of modern glass-clad skyscrapers. I hadn't expected so many modern buildings and so many more under construction. There are older Soviet-era buildings as well, but the feel was that of a rapidly growing city. We went past a new Best Western Tuushin Hotel and a resort named Shangri-La under construction. There were high-end stores such as Boss and Louis Vuitton. The center city was much more vibrant and modern than I'd expected.

The driver told us that journalists and diplomats favored the Puma Imperial Hotel, where we were staying, because it was close to the square and the main government offices. We checked in and Major Campbell told us to meet in the morning at 10:00AM in the lobby. Then he was off with the driver.

Abbey said, "Give me forty-five minutes to shower and change, then let's walk around."

"Good, I'll meet you here in forty-five."

We walked around the center city area for a couple of hours. It was great to walk after all those hours on the plane. The sidewalks were wide. There were lots of coffee shops, restaurants, and bars. The feel was young and vibrant, again not what I expected. The mining boom seemed to be fueling growth in all sorts of areas. I had read that the temperature varied from -55 to 102 degrees Fahrenheit. Today was cool and sunny.

As we walked I noticed people staring at Abbey. Not that many tall redheads in Mongolia.

That evening we ate at the Indian restaurant in the hotel. It was quite good. I guess there are good Indian restaurants all over the world. After dinner I decided to go to bed early. I told Abbey I'd meet her for breakfast in the morning.

In the morning Major Campbell escorted us to the Interior Ministry offices. We sat in a waiting room for almost an hour. Finally we were escorted to a large conference room. Most of the people in the room were leaving.

Walter was talking to two men at the head of the table. He said, "Rob, Abbey, I'd like to introduce you to Minister Gelegdorjiin Damba. He has been looking forward to meeting you."

After a warm greeting he asked us to sit and everyone was served tea.

I said, "Minister, I've been most impressed by how modern your capital city is. In our walk yesterday I had the feeling of a place upbeat and on the move."

"Yes, Professor, the growth is quite remarkable. But with rapid growth come many problems: traffic, pollution, economic disparity, and so on. We have many opportunities and many problems.

"I believe your grant work will help address some of the problems. I've decided we should limit the scope of your work."

I saw Major Campbell look at Walter. Walter kept his pleasant look on his face but I saw a tightening around his eyes. This was news to him.

Minister Gelegdorjiin Damba continued, "Mr. Falone pointed out that not much research has been done in the western provinces of Bayan-Ölgii and Khovd. This is very true and our government as a whole has been unable to direct the resources we would like to this region. We have many minority ethnic groups in this area and it would be good policy and politics to devote more attention to them. Therefore I would like you to focus all your work exclusively in these two provinces."

I studied Walter's face. He looked relieved.

I said, "If my memory is correct, Minister, those two provinces cover over 47,000 square miles."

He laughed and said, "No, Professor, I don't expect you to cover every square mile. I just want your work to be within those two provinces. There should be plenty for you to do in such a large area. Perhaps you will make history as you did in Peru."

He was smiling but I again had that sinking feeling. He expected miracles and Walter, well, I'm not sure what he expected. Something else was up with him.

The Minister said, "Sorry, I'm out of time. I look forward to reviewing your work plan in three weeks. Walter, at that time we should also be able to sign the final contract documents."

He got up. Meeting over. There were smiles, and handshakes all around as he walked out.

I started to say something, but Walter held his hand up and said, "Let's walk."

When we reached the street Walter said, "I don't think that the room was bugged but Mongolia did spend decades under Soviet rule so old habits may die hard."

I said, "Walter, is the Minister holding up your company contract signing to see what my research plan will be?"

"It isn't exactly that, Rob. We have already signed several contracts, such as the lease of the former Soviet air base, equipment import permits, work permits, etc. However the Minister is a careful man. Most of the holdup is negotiating the details of how much of the data we generate during this contract can we use with other clients."

I nodded dumbly and said, "Walter, I don't have a work plan."

"No, you don't, Rob, but you have three weeks. I have a meeting in Tokyo. I'll see you in a week or so."

He shook my hand said goodbye to Abbey and Major Campbell, and then got in a waiting car.

Abbey said, "Walter is a busy man. What now, Major?"

"We go to our facility at the old air base and start preparing."

I interrupted, "Preparing for what?"

He answered, "For whatever plan you come up with."

We walked mostly in silence back to the hotel. When we arrived I asked Major Campbell, "I know I won't pronounce his name right but where is Shotenro Enkhbat?"

Major Campbell said, "Not bad on the pronunciation of the name. We use his nickname Sumo. He likes it and it is easy. Anyway he is at the air base. Why?"

I said, "I'd like to stay in Ulaanbaatar a few days and visit with some of the contacts Sir Harold gave me letters of introduction to. I think Shotenro or Sumo if that is what he prefers could be of help to me. He is from Bayan-Ölgii province, speaks several of the local dialects, and is fluent in English. Since my Mongolian covers about a dozen words I could use some help."

"I'll have him flown in today and book him a room at the hotel. What else do you need, Professor?"

I said, "Take Abbey back with you. Show her our work accommodations, introduce her to our team, and she will make a list of equipment that we need to get started."

Abbey was giving me her look. I said, "You know computer

setups, software, standard archaeological field equipment. You can figure it out, you're the assistant project director."

She shook her head and said, "No problem, I'm on it, Prof. By the way I'm starving. Let's get some lunch."

Major Campbell said, "Good idea. You two get lunch. I have some calls to make. There is a good place right down the street and I'll join you shortly."

We walked into the restaurant, it was clean and bright. We stood out as tourists so they sent a waiter who spoke some English. The menu had all sorts of things from burgers to pasta to sushi, to what I assumed were Mongolian dishes. I decided to go with something familiar and start experimenting with Mongolian cuisine later.

Abbey put down her menu and said, "Major Campbell seemed a little worried when the Minister said he was limiting the scope of the work plan. What's up with that?"

I answered, "I'm not sure. Though he hid it well but Walter also looked worried for a moment. When you get to the base, research everything you can find about anything of archaeological interest within or near the area of the coordinates Walter gave me. Something is very important about that area. Ned probably knows a lot of what is going on. See what you can get out of him. Do some detective work but try not to raise people's suspicions."

She said, "Now I'm Mata Hari?"

"No, I'm thinking more like Pippi Longstocking."

Before she could say anything Major Campbell walked up to the table and we let it drop.

He said, "Sumo will be here later this afternoon. Then Abbey and I will take that plane back."

Mata Hari and Pippi Longstocking (Note 2)

He sat down and looked at the menu. I said, "You looked a little worried when the Minister said he was limiting the scope of the work plan. What's going on in Bayan-Ölgii province?"

Major Campbell said, "Let's enjoy lunch. We can't really talk about that here. When we are all back at the base we can discuss it further. Rob, sometimes knowing can be a burden."

I said, "So you don't subscribe to 'The truth will set you free'?"

He said, "Rob, I'll have the Khuushuur with beef rather than mutton. I find the mutton a bit strong."

It was clear that he wasn't going to talk about it anymore so we switched to small talk.

After lunch, Major Campbell gave us both cellphones back at the hotel. He checked to make sure we were using the secure laptops we were issued in Peru. As always cyber security was a very big deal for the company. We knew the drill.

We all headed to our rooms, Major Campbell and Abbey to get their bags and check out and me to think.

I heard a knock on my door. I opened it.

Abbey handed me the files on our team members and said, "About time you read these. I've read them."

I said, "There are only five files now."

She said, "Our girl of Russian descent broke her leg and won't be joining the team. Major Campbell is having HR look for a replacement and wants to know if you had any special skill they should include when looking for a replacement."

I thought a minute, and then said, "Language skills in the various dialects in Bayan-Ölgii province would be helpful, also someone with knowledge of the various religious practices in the area. Strong computer skills are always helpful. It would be nice if they could get along with the rest of the group." I stopped and put up my hands, then added, "You've read the files. What do you think?"

"Well, they are pretty much what we have seen before. Meaning they are all different, but all well-educated over-achievers. The common theme of our Peru group was super strong computer/tech skills. If I had to pick a common strength here it would be language skills. Between them they must cover two dozen languages and dialects."

I said, "I guess that is good given our English and Spanish isn't going to take us very far here."

She smiled at me and said, "Have fun. The Major is waiting in the lobby for me."

Abbey's upbeat attitude made working with her a pleasure.

I sat on the end of the bed and took out the file for Shotenro Enkhbat. It said he likes to be called Sumo. He was or had been a sumo wrestler. I glanced at that part of the file. He won all sorts of matches in Mongolia before going to Japan where he rose to the top of the maegashira ranks. Whatever that was. It said he was six foot three inches tall and weighed 355 pounds. Now retired.

He was 31 years old, educated at the Mongolian University of Science and Technology in the School of Language Education. He spoke numerous dialects of the various peoples of Bayan-Ölgii Aimag as well as English

Mongolia and The Golden Eagle

Sumo wrestling match (Note 2)

and Japanese. He seemed to be somewhat of a local sports hero in his home province.

He started with Falone Advanced Technologies only eight months ago and spent the first six months in Houston training.

I put his file down and picked up the next one. It was Hank's.

I looked at the file cover. It read *Hok'ee (High Backed Wolf) Hank Nez.*

Hok'ee Nez, born in Alamo, New Mexico, to the Navajo Dibélizhiní (Black Sheep Clan) of the Tsénahabiłnii (Sleeping Rock People), nickname Hank. He attended the McKinley County campus of Diné College, a two-year tribally controlled community college serving the Navajo Nation. Hok'ee then transferred to Stanford University where he attended the School of Earth Science, receiving a B.S. in Earth Systems and an M.S. in Computational Geoscience on full scholarship.

Hok'ee then worked for three years for SGS Petroleum Service Corporation before joining Falone Advanced Technologies about two years ago. His educational background and work experience seemed to fit the company.

The phone rang. It was Shotenro or Sumo. I told him I'd meet him in the lobby.

When I walked into the lobby there was no question who Sumo was. To say big didn't seem big enough. As I walked towards where he was sitting, he gracefully stood up and seemed to glide over to meet me. I'm not sure what I expected, perhaps the stamping walk of the Incredible Hulk. But he was light on his feet and seemed as agile as a dancer. I guess being a world-class sumo wrestler takes a lot more than just being big.

He put out his hand and said, "Professor Johnson, how nice to meet you. Welcome to Mongolia."

His handshake was warm and gentle. No need for him to show his manhood with a vise-grip handshake.

"Shotenro, it's a pleasure to meet you as well. I'm looking forward to working with you."

He said, "Call me Sumo. Everybody does."

"OK, if you call me Rob not Professor Johnson. Let's go get a drink someplace where we can visit."

We walked a few blocks to a place that seemed more like a neighborhood bar in the States than in Mongolia. Modern and Western seemed to be in in Ulaanbaatar.

The beer glass looked small in Sumo's hand. He said, "I'm not really sure what my role is on the team. I had a fascinating six months in Houston. I learned a lot about what the company does but not much specifically about what I'm to do."

I said, "Walter has a way of picking the right people. I know I'm going to need your help."

He said, "I'm not sure Mr. Falone picked me. I only met him once and that was after I was hired. He did make me feel welcome in the short time I spent with him. What are we going to do and when do we start?"

I didn't have the heart to say I didn't have a clue so I said, "The detailed plan is still being fleshed out and we will present it to the Minister of the Interior in three weeks. I have four letters of introduction here from Sir Harold Padsworth. He is a British expert on Asian history."

I handed him the four envelopes. "Do you know any of these people?"

He answered. "I know of all of them. They are all well known in their fields. I only know one personally. Galsan Tschinag taught in the School of Language Education at the Mongolian University of Science and Technology where I studied. In addition to teaching he is a novelist, poet, and shaman. He is from my home province of Bayan-Ölgii. He is well respected there as a powerful shaman."

I said, "What I would like you to do is deliver these letters to each person and see if you can arrange for us to get an appointment in the next few days. The letter will do most of the explaining. You need to try to get an appointment of about two hours. The sooner the better, I have a lot to do before we meet the Minister again in three weeks."

He looked at his watch and said, "It's 4:15PM. Do you mind if I go now and see if I can catch any of them before they leave for the day?"

"No. That would be great. Call me when you are done and we'll have dinner." I started to say more and stopped.

He said, "What were you going to say?"

"It isn't really my business but are you really 355 pounds?"

He laughed. "No. Once I retired from wrestling I slimmed way down. I'm 305 or 310 now. A shadow of my former self."

He laughed again and said he would call me later. Again I was struck by how gracefully he moved. I found I liked his upbeat manner.

I ordered another beer or piv in Mongolian. The first letter I'd given Sumo was the one to Galsan Tschinag who he knew personally. The next was to the curator of the ethnographic collection at the Mongolian National Museum. He is in charge of the significant displays of the traditional dress of various Mongolian ethnic groups.

The third letter was to the director of the Mongolian Natural History Museum. This museum is concerned primarily with the flora, fauna, geology, and natural history of the country. Whereas the Mongolian National Museum focuses on the archaeology and history of Mongolia.

The last letter was to the rare manuscripts director of the Mongolian National Library. The library had over three million books and publications, one million of which are rare and valuable books, sutras, and manuscripts, including the world's only surviving copies of many ancient Buddhist texts.

I was hoping that by calling on the assistance of these local experts I might come up with some workable program. I finished my beer and decided I go to my hotel and see what I could find out about the work of each of the men that might prepare me to meet with them.

When I got back to my room I called Abbey. "Hi. How was your flight? What did you find out about archaeologically important things in the area of Bayan-Ölgii province Walter gave me?"

"Prof, I've been here all of three hours. The flight was fine. Thank you for asking. If you need something to work on, check out Altai Tavan Bogd National Park. It sits right in the middle of the area Walter gave you. There is a

World Heritage Site for several thousand petroglyphs and Turkic monoliths. One valley has something like 10,000 petroglyphs. It is a protected area with all sorts of wildlife. There has to be undiscovered stuff there.

"Wait until you see this place. The abandoned air base looks like something out of a doomsday movie. But there is lots of activity now. They are fixing the potholes in the runway and installing all sorts of equipment. Plus mandatory horseback riding lessons."

I said, "What?"

"That is what Major Campbell told me. It is the only way to get around where you plan to take us. I can't wait to see Ned on a horse, or you for that matter. What do you think of Sumo?"

I said, "I like what I've seen so far. He wanted to get right to work when I gave him a job to do. I have work to do. Go be Pippi Longstocking."

"Prof, you are the one that called me. Goodbye."

I thought mandatory horseback riding. My grandfather was a small-town banker and gentleman farmer. I spent many summers with my grandparents when I was young. My grandmother and I would feed, groom, and ride the horses each day. On Sunday Grandpa would plan out a trail ride and Grandma would pack a picnic lunch. We would spend hours riding through the countryside each Sunday. Good memories and I hoped it was like riding a bike. Once you learned you never forgot.

Well, it was time for me to hit the books or in this case the computer. Between the memory stick Laura O'Hara gave me and the internet I had endless material. The fact that I wasn't sure what I was doing wasn't going to stop me. Walter was paying me so I got to work.

At about 8:15PM the phone rang. It was Sumo. He sounded excited and said he was hungry. I realized I was hungry also. I told him I'd meet him in the lobby in ten minutes.

Sumo had a cab waiting. He said, "I feel like Japanese tonight. We are going to Hashi. It is a small Japanese restaurant that has tasty food at a reasonable price. It isn't that far but it is 8:30 already and I'm starving."

I said, "How did your day go?"

The cab was just pulling to the curb. He handed the driver some money and said, "I'll tell you once we have ordered."

He seemed keyed up and I decided it wouldn't be smart to get between Sumo and dinner. He spoke to the woman at the door in Japanese and pointed to a large table. She said something back but Sumo was already leading me to the table.

A waiter came right over and bowed in a formal greeting. Sumo bowed back but remained seated. He started rapidly giving the waiter what I took to be an order. The waiter wrote madly on his small pad.

Sumo stopped, looked at me, and said, "Are you allergic to anything?"

I shook my head no and he went back to ordering in Japanese. The waiter went off at a half run.

The drinks came almost at once, two quart bottles of Japanese beer.

Next the food started arriving, appetizers by the looks of them.

Sumo smiled and pointed to each one. "Beef Tataki; Hot Lady, a raw fish with daikon, scallions, and a special sauce; Spicy Tuna, and Naruto Veggies. They are all good. Dig in."

He was digging in so I did too. After a glass of beer and several bites of the appetizers he said, "I didn't have any lunch today. I got the call from Major Campbell saying to pack a bag and get on the plane to Ulaanbaatar. When the plane landed I got in the car that brought Abbey and the Major to the airport. I met you and you put me to work."

"I like all four of these," I said. "How did you make out this afternoon?"

"Whatever the letters you gave me said, people were impressed. Or at least the two people I was able to get to. I told the secretary at the Mongolian Natural History Museum that I had to place the letter in the director's hand and wait for an answer. That I worked for you and the letter was from Sir Harold Padsworth. If she had been a wrestling fan she would have known me.

"We have an appointment with him at 10:30AM tomorrow. I called about Galsan Tschinag but he wasn't in today so next I went to the Mongolian National Library. There the assistant was rude. He said to give the letter to him or I could mail it. So I left."

I took a card out of my pocket and said, "I think I can help with that." The card was given to me by one of the Minister of the Interior's assistants and he told me to contact him if he could be of help.

I took out my phone and sent him a text briefly outlining the situation. While I was doing this Sumo finished the appetizers and most of the beer.

When I finished Sumo said, "So then I went to the Mongolian National Museum. I was a little worked up after my other experiences. But they couldn't have been nicer. The curator came right out and took me to his office. We have a 2:00PM appointment with him. You will like him."

Sumo sat back, looked around for the waiter, and ordered more beer. Next came tempura rolls, hand rolls, and special rolls, followed by more beer and several of the chef's recommended dishes. I gave up eating and just watched Sumo. He didn't eat particularly fast, just with determined satisfaction.

I asked about his wrestling experience. I knew almost nothing about sumo wrestling so it was interesting and enjoyable. We ended with sake.

Back at the hotel he said he would meet me in the lobby at 10:00AM. He would head out early and see if he could set up the other appointments.

After my dinner experience I was glad I wasn't having breakfast with him in a few hours.

I read some more in my room and went to bed.

Russian-built Sukhoi Su-80 transport aircraft. (Note 2)

Chapter
8

We were in a cab headed to the airport after two produc-
tive days of meetings. The four we met with were very
interested in working with us. As they should be, given we
were providing all the money and doing most of the work.

The cab dropped us at the general aviation area. A
young man came up and introduced himself as the copilot. He took my overnight bag but let Sumo carry his own.
I wondered if it was because I looked old or weak or both.

I said, "I've never seen a plane like that. It has the twin
boom like the Cessna Skymaster but it's much bigger."

The copilot said, "It is a Russian-built Sukhoi Su-80,
modern, rugged, and able to fly in and out of short airfields. It has lots of power with twin 1750hp turboprop
engines. This is the S-80GE model specifically designed
for geological support."

He went on a little longer about rate of climb, cruise
speed, service ceiling, and avionics but I wasn't really listening. We got on board and the pilot said it would only be

about 30 minutes once we were in the air.

We flew out of Ulaanbaatar southeast. I saw a much different view than the city center.

Including whole neighborhoods of gers or yurts, as they are more commonly known in the West, the traditional Mongolian round tent-like domicile.

The old Soviet air base was in Govisümber Province about 15 miles north of the small city of Choir.

Sumo was explaining that there is a depressed area nearby that is called the Choir Depression. It is an area a little over 90 miles long and from six to 12 miles wide. It is 1600 feet below the elevation of the surrounding area. According to Sumo there were millions of pounds of uranium trioxide in the depression and a big Canadian mining company was leading a joint venture that was mining it.

I thought interesting, another Canadian company right next door. I wondered which company it was.

As we descended and approached the air base I saw Abbey was right. It looked like something out of a doomsday film. The runway was longer than the main runway at Ulaanbaatar, made of concrete, and a mess. There were bunkers to protect the jet fighters on each side in one area. There was a row of gutted Soviet-style apartment buildings, old hangar buildings, and various support buildings. They all looked like they had been looted of anything valuable.

However there was also activity. The plane we came in on from Tel Aviv was gone but there were a couple of other planes parked by the runway, along with trucks and trailers.

Bomb-resistant bunker at the former base of the Soviet MiG-21 126th Fighter Aviation Regiment. (Note 2)

Despite looking a mess, one half of the runway had been patched and we made a smooth landing. Once the engines were shut off, they opened the door and let down the stairs. It was sunny with a blue sky and perhaps 55 degrees.

Abbey drove up in a jeep. She said, "Welcome to the home of the 126th Fighter Aviation Regiment and our home now."

I said, "What, and what is this rust bucket you are driving?"

"By your first what, Prof, I assume you mean our new home. It was the base for the Soviet MiG-21 126th Fighter Aviation Regiment. Your second what, I'm driving a Russian UAZ-469 jeep. Its nickname is Kozlik. That is Russian for goat and whoever named it made a good choice. It has a 75hp engine that was designed about 1940 and a top speed of about 55 mph. The transmission is a manual 4-speed piece of junk. On the plus side it is four-wheel-drive and it can burn the cheapest gas made. Also it is able to drive in virtually any terrain and it is very easy to repair. Jump in. I'll give you a tour."

The copilot put our overnight bags in the back. I let Sumo have the front seat. The jeep listed to the right. I slid over to the seat behind Abbey.

Abbey continued, "Lots going on now. They are setting up shop, fixing the runway, assembling living accommodations, and who knows what else."

I didn't respond but said, "What is going on over there?"

She said, "That is what I call 'Ned's cavalry.' But Sumo can tell you about them."

I was looking at about two dozen young boys on horseback charging around the far side of the airfield. Beyond them was a camp with several gers.

Sumo said, "When we first started setting up they wanted to use barbwire to fence off the airfield so none of the grazing animals would wander on the field. I tried to explain that was a bad idea. Herdsmen don't like fences and the Soviets were big fence builders. It still causes bad blood and there is no point in making enemies of our neighbors. So I convinced Major Campbell to let me try another way. I met with local elders and we decided to hire a group of young men to patrol the airfield and keep any herds of animals from wandering onto the field.

"It was quite a scene, a whole group of 15-20 young boys accompanied by what looked like four grandfathers. All on horseback with two trucks following. The grandfathers surveyed the area and then conferred for a few minutes. Once they picked a spot they had the three gers set up in a matter of hours. The trucks left and our little village was all set up. Each day a van or even motorcycle arrived with food and other supplies for them."

I looked and there was Ned, well, I wouldn't exactly say riding, more like bouncing on horseback with all the boys laughing and riding circles around him. The boys looked as young as ten and maybe as old as thirteen or fourteen.

Sumo continued, "Ned used Tootsie Roll diplomacy. When the boys first arrived he marched out with pockets full of Tootsie Rolls, began handing them out to everyone, and helped assemble the gers. I'm not sure he was much help but he has a whole group of new friends. Some of the boys know a little English from school."

Abbey yelled and waved to Ned. He waved back, almost falling off his horse in the process. This produced squeals of laughter from the Mongolian boys who had probably been riding horses since they were three.

She then drove towards the bunkers that were built to house the fighter jets. She pulled up in front of one and said, "Do you like camping, Prof?"

She jumped out and Sumo got out and grabbed both of our overnight bags. I got out and followed them. The door to the bunker looked two feet thick. There was a string of construction lights overhead and two lines of camper vans.

Abbey said, "Welcome to your new home. Not exactly like what we had in Peru."

In Peru we lived in the guesthouse of Walter's ranch with just about any luxury you could want.

Abbey continued, "The third camper is yours. The rest of your bags are in it. All the way in back is the restroom/shower trailer. The dining trailer is in another bunker. They're setting up more stuff each day."

I took my bag from Sumo and said to Abbey, "Give me a few minutes to check out my digs and then let's walk around and get lunch."

My camper looked like the ones you saw being towed behind the family car, not real big but probably OK for one person. I went in. The pop-out sides were out, the bed was made, it had power and a small refrigerator. I opened the fridge door, water, beer, and white wine. Home sweet home.

I came out of my camper and knocked on Abbey's camper. She came out and we walked out of the bunker. The sky was blue but the place had a ghostly feel.

She said, "There is a lot going on. They are setting up facilities and equipment in several places. Several large generators for electricity have been installed, the old wells were rebuilt for water, and the runway is being fixed up. The bunkers on the far side over there are where the drones and other equipment are located."

I asked, "Do we have offices?"

"Yes, if you want to call it offices. It's more like a couple of trailers bolted together. I'll show you. Let's take the jeep."

We drove past several more aircraft bunkers that seemed to be set up for residences like ours. Abbey pulled up to the first of a line of bunkers on the far side of the airfield. There was quite a bit of activity.

Inside were several doublewide construction-site type office trailers. Abbey led me to the first one closest to the big thick blast doors. Inside it was set up with two small private offices at one end, several workstations in the middle, and a conference room at the other end. There were some laptops, printers, and copy machines.

I said, "Do we have any serious computing power here and are we connected to the internet?"

She just shrugged and said, "I'm not sure how that will work. Major Campbell said we would have access to anything we need. I have no idea what that means. One office is yours and I guess the other is mine."

I said, "You take the big one, Abbey." She gave me her look. Both offices were small and identical in size.

We walked out of the trailer and went deeper into the hangar. I heard someone softly whistling and walked toward the sound.

I said, "Peter?"

He looked up and said, "Yup, Peter the fix-it man. Welcome, I've been looking forward to your arrival since Abbey got here a few days ago."

Peter Frank and his wife Dr. Dona Frank were in Peru with us. Both work for Falone Advanced Technologies. They met at Berkeley. After he graduated Peter didn't want to get a real job so he got hired by the University to repair their lab equipment and help build new equipment for various research projects. Dona was getting her PhD and he was asked to help her with problems they were having with some new equipment. They fell in love, got married, and Peter has been fixing complex equipment for Dona ever since. Although what he was working on now looked like it was salvaged from a junkyard.

"That thing looks as bad as the jeep Abbey is driving."

He said, "I'm fixing it just for you. It is a UAZ-452 van, the pride of the Russian automotive industry. Top speed 58 mph."

I said, "Another goat like Abbey's jeep?"

"No, this one's nickname is Bukhanka. That is Russian for bread loaf."

I looked again at the van he was working on. It did look a bit like a loaf of bread. I said, "The Russians have a fatalistic sense of humor at least. But why all this old equipment, when Walter's company usually has the best there is?"

"Rob, this is probably the best there is for where you are going."

I said, "I don't know where I'm going."

He went on. "I do, to the countryside. Once out of the main cities there are almost no paved roads. This van is four-wheel-drive, simple, rugged, and one of the most common vehicles you will find in Mongolia. It runs on 76-octane gas, which is all you can get in most places outside the top few cities. Try running a Range Rover or Toyota Land Cruiser on that junk gas and the engine will knock itself apart.

"I'll have it in great working order for you. I'm adding extra gas tanks. A snorkel exhaust system, power take off for charging your phones and computers, winches front and back, and there will be a chest of spare parts you might need.

"I'm working on some other great stuff for you. Come over here, I'll show you."

We walked deeper into the bunker. I said, "Where is your wife?"

"Oh, Dona is in Tokyo. That is where they are assembling a lot of the remote sensing equipment. I'll be installing that in the drones and aircraft once it arrives. Now look at this beauty.

"It's a Russian IMZ-Ural motorcycle with a sidecar. Fun but it won't go many places you can't get to in the jeep or van. Now this baby is a Tarus-2 all-terrain two-wheel drive motorcycle. The Tarus-2 has a two-cylinder engine and fat low-pressure tires. It has a dry weight of about 100 pounds and can be disassembled in less than five minutes. It will climb stairs, cross streams, and go lots of places most people don't want to go. We have two to put on the roof of the vans.

"Now for your living accommodations I got Walter to spring for a couple of these. An Australian company named Conqueror makes this extreme off-road trailer called the UEV-345. What I really wanted to get you is the UEV-440. That model is arguably the most rugged camper trailer on earth. But it is too heavy for either the Goat or the Bread Loaf to pull it.

"I know you're not really interested in all the details. Major Campbell made a list of what he thought would be needed so I guess you are in good hands. But trust me, this trailer is way better than a tent and cooking over an open fire."

I thanked Peter and said I'd meet him for dinner. Abbey had wandered towards the front of the bunker. When I reached her I said, "What is in the other bunkers on this side?"

She said, "Major Campbell and his security group are in the front of that bunker. The employees of Israel Aerospace Industries have their work area deeper in the same bunker. The next one houses the drones and equipment. The one after that is set up as a range. It seems the Israel Aerospace Industries employees are former military types."

I said, "I think in Israel most able-bodied people are drafted at 18 and serve a few years. After that many of them are in the reserves for decades. It is a small country in a bad part of the world.

"Are you training with them?"

She said, "No, but I hope to train with Major Campbell's men. Get in the jeep. It is time for lunch."

We drove back to the other side of the airfield and up to the next bunker down from the one that housed our camper. Abbey parked and we walked in. There was what looked like a bigger version of the hot trucks that parked near the dorms on Cornell's campus. It was more a trailer than a truck but the same idea.

I said, "Are we going to live on meatball subs here?"

She said, "It does look like the roach coaches we have in Ithaca."

With that appealing thought in mind we walked up to the window serving area. There was a chalkboard with a few choices for lunch. It didn't look like local food, it was soup, tuna salad, and ham, all things that were probably flown in. That seemed safe enough.

We took our trays and walked into another double-wide trailer set up as a dining area with tables and chairs. There were three men at one table and no one else inside. We waved hi and took a table in the corner.

We ate silently for a bit. Then Abbey said, "Have you had any brilliant ideas yet?"

I looked at her and smiled. "I'm hoping for inspiration any moment. Did you find out anything interesting in the last two days?"

"Well, they weren't joking about riding lessons. Major Campbell says it may be the only way to get around in some of the places we want to go. Ned is trying. I think he is afraid he will be left behind if he can't ride a horse. Hank seems quite comfortable on horseback. You and I start today."

I didn't react to that so she went on.

"I tried pumping Ned for info but he wouldn't say much. I'm sure he knows a lot. I might have to try beating him up. Mostly I've been doing research and there is a lot of archaeological interest in the area Walter wants us to explore. Maybe he just knows that's a good place to research."

I shook my head. "No, Abbey, there is more going on and for now they aren't going to tell us. This bread is stale. What time are the riding lessons?"

"They said 4:00PM. We will meet over by the gers."

I said, "OK, drop me off over at Major Campbell's and then go get our secure laptops and meet me at our office trailer. My laptop is in the case next to the table in my camper."

I walked into the bunker where Major Campbell had his offices. I went to the first set of offices, knocked on the door, and said, "Hello Ian," then walked in. There were three men and lots of electronic equipment that they were assembling. I recognized one David Fine from Peru.

"Hi David. Is your boss around?"

"I heard you were coming, Professor, nice to see you. The Major is in the back office."

I looked around. It was a double-wide office trailer much like the one provided for my team. They were assembling cameras and setting up monitors. There was a lot of other equipment that I didn't recognize.

Major Campbell stuck his head out of his office door and said, "Hi Rob. Come back and join me. How do you like our air base?"

I said, "Frankly it gives me the creeps. It feels like one of those movies about life after a nuclear war, living in the ruins of the old civilization."

He said, "We selected it for the airfield. Once we realized that we wouldn't be allowed to fly the drones out of any of the major commercial airfields we had to find someplace. I think it is a fascinating place but I understand how you feel."

I was sure he wasn't going to tell me any more about the area Walter wanted me to work in so I didn't bother asking. I said, "Where is the rest of my team? I like what I've seen so far of Sumo."

He said, "Ned and Hank are here but I'm afraid I'll need a lot of their time for a while. They both have equipment and communications skills I need to set this place up. I'm still looking for the replacement for the woman team member who broke her leg. The two park rangers are on loan to us from the Ministry of the Interior. We can send for them when we need them. I assumed they wouldn't be much help in the planning phase."

I said, "So for now it is just Abbey, Sumo, and I?"

Major Campbell said, "That's it until we have most of the setup work done, then I can give you most of Ned's and Hank's time. Riding lesson are scheduled for 4:00 today."

I think he expected me to object. I said, "I'll be there." Then I said nothing.

He went on. "Abbey wants to work out with my men. Is that OK with you?"

I answered, "Sure. She likes staying in shape and I'll ask her to go easy on your men."

He smiled and I got up to leave, then I thought of one more question. "Do you know when Walter will be here next?"

He said, "Not really but before our meeting with the Minister of the Interior for sure."

We said our goodbyes and I headed over to my office trailer.

Abbey and I worked until about 3:30PM then drove back to our campers to change for riding lessons. I put on blue jeans and work boots. That would have to do.

Sumo and Abbey were waiting in the jeep when I came out. I refrained from making any comment about Sumo on a horse.

I said, "I'm interested in seeing the gers."

Sumo said, "These are relatively simple ones for the boys to stay in while working here. A family ger tends to be well decorated and can be quite elaborate."

There was quite a crowd. The Mongolian boys, their grandfathers, Major Campbell, and a few others who I assumed worked for Major Campbell. There were also horses, lots of horses. I watched the boys. They were holding the reins in their left hand and neck reining the way a cowboy or polo player would, which made sense, leaving the right hand free.

Ned was riding around in circles. He looked anything but graceful but he was staying on the horse.

The young boys were getting horses ready for people, adjusting stirrups, and tightening the saddles. It was clear that most of Major Campbell's men had some riding experience. He undoubtedly picked members of the company's security team who knew how to ride.

No point hanging back. I went up to one boy, pointed to my chest and then to the horse he held. He grinned and nodded his head. I look at the stirrups to see how to adjust them but he reached and did it. I checked the girth and bridle, then grabbed the pommel of the saddle, stuck my left foot in the stirrup, and swung myself into the saddle. Just like riding a bike, once you learn you never forget. The boy held the reins but the horse was calm.

I looked around and saw a whole group of boys who wanted to help Abbey. She was going to get lots of instruction. With her long red hair and green eyes she looked very different from the typical Mongolian woman.

"Are you all set, Professor?"

Sumo rode up next to me. Horse and rider were well matched. While not as big as a Budweiser Clydesdale, the horse was big. It looked like the workhorses you see pulling the hayride wagons and was way bigger than the standard Mongolian horse.

Sumo looked totally at ease on the horse. I realized he had probably been riding horses since about the time he could walk.

I said, "So far so good. What happens now?"

"Those of us who don't need instruction go for a ride to get in shape and the others go with Major Campbell and the instructors he has hired."

I said, "How about I go with you, we stay out of the way, and see the sights around here?"

He looked at the way I was sitting on the horse, nodded his head, and started off at a slow trot. I followed along beside him, my horse taking two strides to each of his. We made a wide circle around the air base. It was basically flat which is what you want for an airfield.

After about 50 minutes we were back where we started.

Sumo said, "Nice job, Professor. You have obviously ridden before."

I said, "It has been years since I was last on a horse and you made it easy for me. Nice flat ground, just walking and trotting."

He said, "You will be stiff tomorrow and we can do more as the days go by."

I was surprised how comfortable I felt sitting in the saddle and realized I'd truly enjoyed the ride. He was right, I'd have some sore muscles. I wondered why I'd stopped riding when I had enjoyed it so much when I was a boy.

The young Mongolian boy came up and held my horse's reins. Sumo said something and the boy laughed. Some joke about me. I dismounted. Yes, I would be a bit sore.

Sumo said he was staying here for a while. I told him

to be in our office at 8:00AM tomorrow. Then I went to look for Abbey. I found her talking with a couple of Major Campbell's men.

She said, "Prof, you didn't break your neck."

"Just lucky, I guess. How did you do? You seemed to have lots of helpers."

She said, "I didn't fall off. You take the jeep back. I'm going to work out with these guys and then go to the range. Keep the jeep. I have the keys to the IMZ-Ural motorcycle."

"OK, I'll see you at our office at 8:00AM." I wasn't sure how much shooting Abbey had done since we returned from Peru. There were several gun clubs and ranges in the Ithaca area.

Mongolia and The Golden Eagle

Traditional Mongolian gers. (Note 2)

Russian UAZ-469 jeep nicknamed Kozlik, Russian for goat. (Note 1)

Russian UAZ-452 van nicknamed Bukhanka, Russian for bread loaf. (Note 3)

Russian IMZ-Ural motorcycle with sidecar. (Note 3)

Australian-made Conqueror UEV-345 extreme off-road trailer. (Note 4)

Bactrian camel (Note 3)

Chapter 9

The next few days fell into a routine. I started out early at the roach coach for coffee and muffins to go, then to the office. We had lunch sent in and worked until 3:30PM. Sumo pushed me a little harder each day during our 4:00PM horseback rides. After that I would shower and work a little longer. Usually I'd have dinner with Peter Frank and sometimes Major Campbell would join us.

After riding Abbey would work out with Major Campbell's men. Judging by the amount of work she was accomplishing she must have been working late into the night after her dinner.

On our tenth day as we started our riding lesson there was a commotion. Several of the boys started racing off to the west. I looked and off in the distance riders were approaching. As they got a little closer I saw that they were mounted on camels. The lead camel was white and the rider was all dressed in white. There were two more riders. Each one also led a second camel.

The boys were now escorting the camel riders in but at a respectful distance to each side.

Beside me I heard Hank Nez say, "She is of a very strong spirit."

I looked at him. He was holding his hands up as you might if you were warming them by a fire. I wasn't sure how Hank knew the rider was female from this distance.

Then he said, "The eyes of a she wolf."

I looked at Hank again and then around. Everyone just sat still on their horses and watched. I looked at Sumo and said, "What?" He just shook his big head.

As the camels approached I saw it did look like a female rider on the white camel. She was wearing what looked like a ceremonial dress. Her hair was white or perhaps platinum in color. The Mongolian grandfathers took off their hats and the boys fell silent. The white camel was headed straight towards me. I noticed the Mongolians slowly moving to the side or back.

I realized later that Abbey was the first to recognize her but she said nothing.

Hank held his position next to me. He looked as if trying to gage the force that approached.

The white camel stopped about fifty feet in front of me. The two other camel riders stopped about fifty feet behind the white camel.

The woman on the white camel said, "What kind of mess has Walt got you in now, Professor?"

I said, "Mitch?" Talk about out of context.

"Looks like I'm back on Walt's payroll too. Major Campbell said you needed help and since I was in the area

I thought OK, why not."

Mitch or Mitchell Baker was on our team in Peru.

Hank nudged his horse forward and said something in Navajo and then in English. "Who are your people?"

Mitch just looked at him. Everyone was quiet. Then Mitch began to tap her camel with the riding stick. The camel made a most unappealing grunting sound and began to kneel.

Mitch stepped off the kneeling camel and walked up to about ten paces in front of Hank's horse. She held her riding stick in the middle parallel to the ground, and said, "You're Navajo, Black Sheep Clan of the Sleeping Rock People." It was a statement, not a question. "My grand-mother was of the Northern Arapaho."

Still holding her riding stick in the same position, she spun in a slow circle. There were hushed murmurs from the Mongolians and one of Major Campbell's men made the sign of the cross.

She dropped her arm to her side, and walked over, smiling, to Abbey's horse. "Abbey, how are you? Great to see you, girl."

Abbey jumped off her horse and gave Mitch a hug. I heard her whisper, "Mitch, nice to see you're as full of shit as ever."

When I met Mitch the first day at Walter's ranch in Peru she had green and orange hair, with many orna-ments hanging from various body piercings. Having been a Cornell professor for years I'd pretty much seen it all before. However Mitch had an attitude and a hard edge to her.

She is a brilliant engineer and computer scientist. She fought against being typed as a nerdy engineer. After working with her I found she was interesting and had a good, if somewhat dark, sense of humor. She would change her hair color and demeanor as often as other women would change their shoes. When we finished our work in Peru she took a leave from Falone Advanced Technologies and went to Princeton University to get a PhD in religion. That was the last I'd heard from her.

One of the two men with Mitch took her camel and Abbey gave her horse to a boy. They walked off side by side towards the motorcycle, deep in conversation. I saw Mitch look at Sumo and say to Abbey, "I bet that big boy can really rock the bed." I tried not to visualize that image. Abbey started the cycle, Mitch jumped into the sidecar, and they roared off.

Ned rode over to where Hank was still sitting on his horse. He looked dazed and said to Ned, "She possesses a powerful spirit. I felt it from way out there."

Ned looked at him and shook his head slightly. He said, "That's just Mitch. You'll get used to her. But we always said, 'You know what Mitch rhymes with, so don't mess with Mitch.' Really she's OK, she works hard, and maybe she'll let me ride her camel."

Hank said, "I'm going to ride for a while."

The Mongolian grandfathers were talking to the two men that rode in with Mitch. The young boys went back to giving riding lessons.

I rode over to Sumo. He said, "Professor, you know her?"

I said, "She was part of our team in Peru. She is a bit melodramatic. But she has skills we need. I'm glad she is here. Although I have no idea why she is in Mongolia."

Sumo and I rode for over an hour. He didn't say much. When we came back I saw our little village had two more gers. The two pack camels must have been carrying the disassembled gers.

I gave my horse to one of the boys. Sumo said he would stay here for a while so I drove the jeep back. After washing up and changing I went over to our office trailer.

Abbey was there. I said, "Mitch made quite an entrance. What was she doing in Mongolia?"

Abbey said, "She said she was here doing field research for her PhD dissertation."

I said, "Funded by Walter, I would guess. Where is she now?"

"She is over in Major Campbell's office complex using the satellite downlink to download software she thinks we'll need. And yes, I'm sure that is who is funding her travels."

I said, "Hard at work already. How does she know what we will need?"

Abbey said, "From the moment we left she started peppering me with questions. We went to my camper, she borrowed a shirt and jeans, and said, 'We got work to do.' You know, Prof, we can really use her help. We know she's good and I can count on her."

"I agree we do need her. Our team is small and who knows how much help we'll get from Ned and Hank. Major Campbell seems to need all their time now.

"What was going on with Hank and Mitch out there?"

Abbey said, "I'm not sure about Hank and the strong spirit and eyes of a she wolf. But you know Mitch, she loves drama."

I said, "Was her grandmother really Northern Arapaho? Plus she knew about Hank's Indian background."

Abbey replied, "I don't know about her grandmother. The part with Hank, Mitch asked the HR department in Houston to brief her on the backgrounds of the team members she didn't know. And the setup was too good for Mitch not to ham it up a bit."

I said, "Well, it sure spooked Hank"

The next morning I got over to our office at 7:50AM. Abbey and Mitch were there hard at work.

Mitch looked up, no hello, she said, "Professor, if you don't mind me saying so, your work plan is shit, it needs a lot of work, and we only have about a week and a half before we have to present it."

I said, "Good morning, Mitch, did you sleep well? Let's just say it's a rough draft."

"I slept better in that camper than I've been sleeping in the ger on dead animal skins. Thank you for caring.

"As for your shitty rough draft, it needs a lot of work. Here is what I've done. I had Houston send me software to analyze the data you want to collect in Altai Tavan Bogd National Park. The company has been improving on what we developed in Peru. It is way better now. Once you collect enough data, I'll set the parameters, and then Ned can run it for you. Ned's OK when it comes to this tech stuff.

"I want to handle the cultural and religious section of

the work plan. I've been studying in this area since I got to Mongolia and it will help with my dissertation. I'll need some help from your boy Sumo, at least until I get rolling. I have my team of locals, the two I rode in with. They are resourceful but let's just say they aren't culturally sensitive.

"Rob, are you with me on this? Does it all sound good to you? I mean it's your show, I'm just here to help."

I had forgotten what it was like working with Mitch. Her in-your-face style took some getting used to.

I said, "It sounds great. The cultural and religious section needs lots of work. I'm not that strong in that area and I need all of Abbey's time to help me with the archaeological aspect of our work. So run with it. However, I also need some of Sumo's time.

"It doesn't seem like we will get much help from Ned or Hank before we present our work plan to the Minister."

I thought Major Campbell must have those two doing more than just setting up security cameras.

Abbey was smiling at me. She gave me a thumbs-up behind Mitch's back. At this point Sumo walked in.

Mitch looked at him and said, "We were wondering if you were going to come to work today."

I looked at the clock. It was two minutes before 8:00.

I said, "Mitch has been pointing out we have a lot of work to do and not that much time. I'd like you to work with Mitch on the cultural and religious aspects of the project. You two figure out your schedules and who does what. We will meet to update each other every other day for the next few days and then do daily updates the last few days before our meeting with the Minister."

Mitch said, "Where is Walt? Won't he want to review our stuff ahead of time?"

I thought now that you're here, why should he worry? But I said, "I'll try and find that out."

I went back to my office and motioned for Abbey to follow. Sumo now had a new wrestling match on his hands.

So we worked. Mitch was in early each morning. This was a change from Peru where she worked all night and reappeared about noon.

I was starting to feel better. We were proposing meaningful work that if properly carried out would advance science and be good for Mongolia. I thought we might just pull this off.

Everyone continued our afternoon riding. Mitch spent time with her two employees that I assumed were now on the company payroll or being paid for out of the grant money. She groomed and rode her white camel each day. Ned was allowed to ride one of the other camels and it bit him. He accused Mitch of telling the camel to do it. The sad part was that no one videoed the entire scene.

I continue to ride with Sumo. He didn't complain about working with Mitch. I didn't push the subject, I just left him plenty of opportunities to bring it up if he wanted to. I was pleased with the quality and quantity of their work. But I knew almost nothing about the cultures and religions of western Mongolia. I hoped it was good enough for the Minister and his staff.

There was still no word on when Walter might arrive. I had no idea what he would think of our work plan for the grant. If he wanted changes there wouldn't be much time before we had to meet with the Minister.

I had Sumo translating our presentation into Mongolian. I would have the written presentation in both English and Mongolian. He was also doing most of the communication with the Mongolian Natural History Museum, the Mongolian National Museum, the Mongolian National Library, and the Mongolian University of Science and Technology. I'd arranged for the Minister's assistant to speak to the appropriate people at each organization on our behalf. Everyone was very cooperative so he seemed to have contacted the right people.

There were only five days left until we were scheduled to present our plan. I was having dinner with Major Campbell when Ned came in and said he needed to talk to the Major.

Ian told Ned to sit down.

Ned said, "It seems we have company. There are three men spying on the facility. They are dressed as locals but our Mongolian grandfathers say they are Chinese. They move in closer to our facility at night. I've intercepted encrypted satellite phone messages from them. They seem to report in only once a day. I haven't been able to break the encryption yet. But the communication is to a Chinese satellite."

Major Campbell said, "OK, don't do anything to alert them we know they are here. Track their exact position and tomorrow night we will set up a little welcome party for them."

He smiled and told Ned to let us finish our dinner.

I said, "Trouble?"

He said, "The Chinese are always trying to steal our trade secrets. They aren't the only ones we have issues with but they are the worst."

The next day a plane arrived with the two Interior Ministry National Park Rangers assigned to be part of our group. There were also six police officers. The plane taxied up to the bunker that housed Major Campbell's office trailer and the men walked off the plane and straight inside.

No one saw these men for the rest of that day. The next morning the plane left at first light.

I went to Major Campbell's office. I wanted to see if he knew when Walter would arrive and I was curious about what happened last night. The two park rangers were in his office. He introduced me to Captain Ganbold and Ranger Batbayar.

After our introductions I said, "What happened last night with the Chinese spies?"

Major Campbell pointed to Captain Ganbold indicating he should answer my question.

His English was fluent. "We arrested the three men for trespassing and for illegally entering Mongolia. They will be deported to China. We will let the Chinese officials know that they are also suspected smugglers and that we expect them to be properly dealt with under Chinese law."

I said, "Not spies then, just common criminals seeing what they might steal?"

"My country of just three million people is sandwiched between the Chinese Dragon and the Russian Bear. We cannot afford to have problems with either. If they are agents of the Chinese government they will be free in a matter of hours when they arrive in China. If they are known criminals the Chinese will deal with them."

I saw his point. Again I asked Major Campbell if he knew when Walter was arriving. He said he would let me know as soon as he knew. So I left, I still had lots to do and only three days left.

Abbey was in our office trailer when I got there. She asked what I knew about last night and I told her I'd just met Captain Ganbold and Ranger Batbayar. Then I told her what the Captain had said.

She said, "Captain Steel-steel and Ranger Firm-happiness."

I said, "What?"

She told me, "That's what their names mean in Mongolian. Anyway Ned was all worked up at breakfast this morning. Major Campbell got one of the Chinese encrypted cellphones and gave it to Ned to try and decipher the encryption software."

I said, "Won't the Chinese just change the software or use a different encryption code once they know the phone is gone?"

She said, "Who knows?"

Finally I heard from Major Campbell that Walter would meet us in Ulaanbaatar the morning of our meeting with the Minister of the Interior. Walter had more faith in me producing a winning work plan for the grant program than I did.

I spent the last day before our meeting worrying and driving the rest of the team nuts.

Mitch said, "Walt can like it or lump it because we have busted our asses and had almost no helpful input."

I thought but didn't say "a budget of ten million was somewhat helpful."

The morning of our meeting we left early for the short flight to Ulaanbaatar. Major Campbell organized the transportation and guided us off the plane and into a waiting car. I knew he was sick of me asking when we would meet Walter so I said nothing.

The car drove to the Interior Ministry headquarters building and let us out. There was still no sign of Walter. I had Abbey, Sumo, and Mitch with me. We would each give part of the presentation. An assistant met Major Campbell and directed us into a conference room. We were the only ones there. He told us to set up in the front of the room.

So we sat, tea was served, and we waited over an hour. Sumo and Abbey read over their presentations. Mitch started to fidget. Finally the conference room door opened and about eight people walked in. The group was led by Walter and the Minister. Everyone was smiling and seemed of good cheer. I hoped that meant the negotiations went well.

Walter shook my hand and said to the Minister, "You remember Professors Johnson and Summers." Then he introduced Mitch and Sumo.

Mitch politely greeted the Minister and then said to Walter, "Great to see you finally."

I thought keep it together, Mitch. The Minister's aides were introduced and everyone sat down.

Everyone seemed to know Sumo at least by reputation and he was warmly received.

I welcomed everyone and told them we would be presenting in English. The written presentation they just received was in English and Mongolian. Sumo would be happy to answer questions or repeat items in Mongolian.

I started by telling them the presentation was in three parts. I would present the first part, Mitch and Sumo the second, and Abbey the third.

I directed them to the first exhibit. It showed:

1. Mongolian University of Science and Technology
2. Mongolian National Museum
3. Mongolian Natural History Museum
4. Mongolian National Library

"We have worked closely with each of these outstanding Mongolian institutions to develop a joint work plan that builds on their unique strengths and fits appropriately with the fieldwork in parts two and three of our work plan. I said we would coordinate our efforts with the Mongol-American Khovd Archaeology Project to assure there was no duplication of effort."

I then went into great detail on what each institution would do and which of their staff members would be involved. There were tables, graphs, flow charts, and references to best practices that would be adopted. I'd learned long ago the less you knew about a topic the more you should pad the report with details and references.

The part that woke them up again was when I finished by saying each institution would receive $1,500,000 to fund their part of the work. Even Walter seemed surprised. Well, I had a $10,000,000 budget and I knew Walter expected me to wow the Minister. Judging from the smiles all around, I had succeeded.

I answered several questions and then asked Sumo and Mitch to present the next part.

Sumo began by saying they would focus their work in Khovd Aimag, or Province. They would document the cultural and religious heritages of the more than 17 nationalities and ethnicities in the province. Documenting these has never been done in a systematic and scientific manner.

He went on to outline the staff from each of our partner institutions that would be involved. He then introduced Mitch who was going to outline all the latest scientific techniques that would be used and the unique research opportunities this presented.

I saw the Minister stir a bit as Mitch stood up. I noticed again that none of his top aides were female.

Mitch thanked Sumo. The two made quite a pair, Sumo six foot three inches tall and three hundred plus pounds. Mitch was about five foot seven inches and maybe one hundred and fifteen pounds. Mitch was dressed conservatively with a white shirt, white slacks and a black jacket. Her only jewelry was the large silver cross I'd seen her wear on special occasions. Her white hair stood out against the black jacket.

When she paused after thanking Sumo, the Minister cleared his throat and said, "Young lady, I understand you have a white camel."

I knew the "young lady" was not going to sit well with Mitch.

She looked straight into the Minister's eyes and said, "Yep, her name is Gertrude."

Some of the Minister's aides stirred. Her tone was not what they expected to be used when addressing their boss.

The Minister said, "White camels are rare and very expensive. Do you know the significance in Mongolian history and culture?"

"Yep," Mitch said, still holding the Minister's gaze.

He continued, "The two men that work for you. These men are known to us, I wouldn't exactly call them criminals, but shall we say they have been known to bend the rules a bit."

They were still staring into each other's eyes. It reminded me of the kids' game of who would blink first. I had a bad feeling about this whole exchange.

Mitch said, "Yep, I often find that helpful when trying to get things done. Don't you, Minister?"

Now I could see that a couple of the Minister's aides were visibly upset.

The Minister broke into a laugh and said, "Yes, I do at times find bending the rules helps get things done. Now tell me where you got your white camel. Gertrude, you said?"

"I got her near Kharkhorin City when I was visiting the Erdene Zuu Monastery and Gertrude became white the same way my hair did."

The Minister shook his head then said, "Please proceed with your presentation."

She started with the radiocarbon dating and explained that until recently the oldest dates that could be reliably measured by radiocarbon dating were around 50,000 years ago. But now with special preparation methods the dating of much older samples is possible.

Next she went through DNA sequencing. She explained that the development of high through-put sequencing and its low cost has allowed far greater use and an exponential increase in the comparative data available.

Then she discussed document preservation, restoration and digitization. It became clear that only a couple of the technical experts on the Minister's staff had any idea what she was talking about. But Mitch wasn't going to dumb it down. She continued on about search software and was going way beyond her allotted time.

Finally Walter interrupted her and said, "I believe you folks see that Mitch has this area well covered. Are there any questions?"

There weren't any.

I introduced Abbey to cover the final section of our work plan.

Abbey stated that this section of the work plan would focus exclusively on the Altai Tavan Bogd National Park in Bayan-Ölgii province. As this group knew, this park is a true treasure of Mongolia. Located at the westernmost point of Mongolia, this park is on the border of both Russia and China. It has views of Kazakhstan from the highest peak of the Tavan Bogd Mountains. The park's over one and a half million acres contains spectacular mountains, lakes, rivers, waterfalls, and glaciers. The park is home to many endangered species including argali sheep, ibex, grey wolves, red deer, black vulture, elk, snow leopards, Altai snowcocks, golden eagles, and many others.

The archaeology in the park includes petroglyphs, standing stones, burial mounds, and Kazakh cemeteries. This is the biggest known concentration of petroglyphs with over 10,000, in the Tsagaan Salaa site. It is situated along a 15-kilometer river valley. This petroglyph complex is a UNESCO World Heritage Site.

So far she was just reviewing what the Minister and his staff knew.

Abbey went on. "We believe that the known archaeological treasures in the park represent as little as one percent of what is there. Our plan is to do a comprehensive remote sensing survey of the site. We will then overlay this with all the characteristics of the known site. We envision the survey will generate over two hundred unique data points covering topography, geographical, hydrological, hydrogeology, geomorphology, bio geomorphology, flora, fauna, atmospherics, bathymetrics, and transportation patterns of both humans and animals.

"We plan to start by ordering high-resolution satellite imagery of the entire park. Ideally I'd like to use GeoEyes. The GeoEye-1 satellite has the highest resolution of any commercial imaging system and is able to collect images with a ground resolution of about half a yard. But we need this work done quickly so I'll also contact DigitalGlobe and Spot Image. Both companies have worked for Falone Advanced Technologies in the past.

"Then we will do an aerial survey using all the various sensing equipment that Falone Advanced Technologies plans to deploy in Mongolia. Most of these are familiar to most of you. However we plan to make extensive use of Lidar, a remote sensing technology that measures distance by illuminating a target with a laser and analyzing the reflected light. It has proven especially helpful to provide archaeologists with the ability to create high-resolution digital elevation models of archaeological sites that can reveal micro-topography that are otherwise hidden by vegetation.

"Some of you may be familiar with the success at Fort Cumberland National Historic Site, in Canada, where previously undiscovered archaeological features below forest canopy have been mapped that are related to the siege of the fort in 1755. Features that could not be distinguished on the ground or through aerial photography were identified by overlaying hill-shades of the digital elevation models created with artificial illumination from various angles. With Lidar the ability to produce high-resolution data sets quickly and relatively cheaply can be an advantage. Beyond efficiency, its ability to penetrate forest canopy has led to the discovery of features that were not distinguishable through traditional geo-spatial methods and are difficult to reach through field surveys.

"In the reference section at the back of my presentation I've included all the parameter and technical standards that we will be employing. It would take far too long to go over all of them now. However I'd be happy to make myself available to answer any question you have in the future.

"There are several other areas of our work I would like to highlight. Mr. Falone's company has adapted what they have developed for the mining and petroleum exploration industry to wildlife management. Large-scale detailed noninvasive tracking of wildlife can be invaluable to saving species while allowing the people in these areas to continue economic development. We will attempt to do this for the major species in the park. We may even find previously unidentified species."

The Minister raised his hand. He looked relaxed and as if he was enjoying himself. I looked at the rest of the people in the room, some looked interested and others seemed bored.

Abbey said, "Yes, sir?"

"Now are we hunting for Almases?"

His staff dutifully laughed.

Abbey flashed her beautiful smile and replied, "We can always hope."

The Minister was referring to the reports of human-like animals, between five and six and a half feet tall, their bodies covered with reddish-brown hair, with anthropomorphic facial features including a pronounced brow ridge, flat nose, and a weak chin. Almases appear in the legends of local people in the Altai mountain region, who tell stories of sightings and human-Almas interactions dating back several hundred years. Much like our Bigfoot legends.

She continued, "Again there is a great deal of additional detail in the reference section. I would like to briefly describe the work we will be doing relating to the lakes in the park. Bathymetry, as you are aware, is the underwater equivalent to topography. To our knowledge almost no work has been done in this area in the park's lakes.

"Dr. Dona Frank, a remote sensing expert with the company, has developed equipment and software to take both Lidar and sonar readings from airborne vehicles. The company has not yet had an opportunity to field test her system so we plan to use it here. We will use more traditional shipboard sonar to verify and calibrate her equipment. If successful we should be able to survey all the lakes in the park. There is more on this in the reference section.

"Finally we will overlay all the data onto one digital map. We will use software developed by Mitch when we worked in Peru to extract the data from the known archaeological sites. This data will feed the probability software Mitch developed and rank the geographic area most likely to contain archaeologically significant sites. At that point we will do on the ground investigations and recalibrate the software as needed. This process was a valuable part of what brought us success in Peru.

"Since much of the data collection we need is the same as the government contract requires, I'm requesting that the government contract work start in the park. The park is in the most south and west part of Mongolia, so I figure you have to start at one end or the other, so why not speed up our work by starting there?"

Abbey entertained a few questions and then I formally thanked the Minister and his staff for their time and attention.

The Minister stood and shook everyone's hand. He said how much he enjoyed the presentation and that he looked forward to outstanding results.

He then turned to Walter and said, "It appears that your Professors Johnson and Summers have lived up to their exceptional reputations in what they have done so far."

I thought but now we actually have to do it.

He continued, "I agree with Professor Summers that your work should start in Altai Tavan Bogd National Park.

Copies of your fully executed contracts will be ready this afternoon. Please arrange for someone to pick them up and then I expect you to expeditiously proceed with the work. Now I'm late for another meeting."

He looked at Mitch and said, "You, young lady, remind me a bit too much of one of my daughters."

Fortunately Mitch said nothing.

As the Minister and his staff left, Walter thanked everyone and told them they had done an outstanding job. He smiled at me and said, "Rob, I think you have successfully spent the whole ten million dollars. How about I buy everyone lunch before we fly back?"

As we walked out, Major Campbell said to Walter, "I need a quick word with you on another subject."

Walter and I stopped. The others walked ahead. Major Campbell looked at me but Walter indicated I should stay. I guess he realized I'd had enough of not knowing what was going on.

Major Campbell said, "We were able to retain one of the Chinese spies' encrypted satellite phones. I have Ned working on deciphering the encryption software. Ned approached me saying he had continued to work on the remote bugging software he developed in Peru while he has been at Cornell. He believes he can use the satellite phone to upload his program into the Chinese satellite. If it works he should be able to harvest all the transmissions to and from the satellite. The software will store the data and then attach it to outbound signals on a randomized basis that he presets. He knows the Israelis have the capability to intercept the satellite's messages and believes they even have the required equipment with them. If we want to do this, the sooner the better, the Chinese may change the encryption code. In fact they may already have done so."

Walter didn't take long to decide. He said, "Have him try it. I'll speak with our Israeli friends when we get back to the air base."

During lunch and during the plane ride back to the air base Walter asked endless questions about our work plan. I had Abbey, Mitch, and Sumo answer most of them. I was impressed by how much he had absorbed during the presentation. He quickly found the weak areas and had a variety of suggestions for improving our plan, ranging from the quite ingenious to simply saying, don't bother with that. As he was asking questions and listening to the answers he was reading the reference material. By the time we landed he had at least skimmed everything we had done.

He went out of his way to apologize for the short amount of time we had to prepare the plan, then praised our effort and work.

I was pleased by what we were able to do in just three weeks. Or more accurately what our plan said we were going to do. Whether we could actually do it was another thing.

I asked for a meeting with Walter and Major Campbell as soon as we could.

Walter looked at his watch and said, "I need to meet with the people from Israel Aerospace Industries for a few hours to get things rolling, then let's meet in Ian's office as soon as I'm done. That should be about 5:00PM. I'm flying out first thing in the morning."

When we landed the plane pulled up in front of the bunker with Major Campbell's and the Israel Aerospace Industries employees' work areas. Walter and Major Campbell deplaned. Then the plane taxied over to the tie-down area.

As we got off one of the Russian UAZ-452 vans pulled up. It did look like its nickname Bread Loaf, or Bukhanka in Russian.

Peter Frank was driving it. He was all hellos, how did it go, and smiles. We piled in and gave him the quick version. His wife, Dona, had arrived that morning with a planeload of equipment. He was happy because his wife was there and because he had lots of new equipment to play with.

He said, "When her plane landed, I met her, she gave me a kiss and then started directing the technicians on where to take the various crates of equipment. I haven't seen her since. But she will be here for a few weeks now.

"Rob, you seem in a rather somber mood. If things went that well you should be celebrating."

I looked around. Everyone else was upbeat. I pasted on a smile. No point in being a downer for everyone else. I said, "I'm just thinking about what we need to do next. I have to meet Walter this afternoon. I want to make sure I cover everything before he leaves so we can keep things rolling. Tonight we celebrate."

When Peter dropped us off I told Abbey, Mitch, and Sumo once again they did a great job. Now go do something fun. Mitch rolled her eyes at the derelict air base around us.

Abbey said, "It is almost time for riding lessons. Come on, Mitch, show us how to ride a camel."

Then she took me aside and said, "You look like you're going to blow a fuse. Take a walk or something, and then talk to Walter. I'll take care of Mitch and Sumo. No point in bringing them down. They've worked really had."

I tried to smile and said, "Thanks."

I changed and walked back to where Peter Frank was working. "Peter, can I try out one of those go anywhere two-wheel-drive motorcycles?"

He showed me how to run it and I was off. No helmet, just my wraparound shades, and the wind blowing through my hair. I didn't go particularly fast and I didn't test the bike's mountain climbing ability, but it gave me a sense of freedom I hadn't experienced in a while. I rode for almost an hour.

Chapter 10

It was almost 6:00PM when I walked into Major Campbell's office. He and Walter were talking to Ned.

Ned looked up and said, "Professor, I hear you knocked them dead at the Ministry. Very cool, but Mitch almost blew it for you."

Ned was enthusiastic but once again I wondered if he had one of our phones bugged. It didn't seem like Ian or Walter would make a comment like that about Mitch.

I just said, "Everyone did a great job."

Ian looked at Ned. He got the hint, said goodbye, and left.

Walter said, "Again I want to thank you for the great job you did. I authorized the satellite survey of the park and we will begin the company's work at the western end of Mongolia in the area of the park."

I sat and said, "Walter, what is going on in the area of Altai Tavan Bogd National Park?"

Major Campbell said, "We are not exactly sure."

I said, "Walter, that's not good enough. Abbey and I were almost killed in Peru. I want to know everything you know or I walk. Abbey can make her own mind up whether to stay."

I was mad and I felt taken advantage of.

Walter said, "I understand how you feel. You have a right to know. It is a rather long story to understand what we know, how we know it, and why we want to be involved.

"Ian, can you have one of your men bring us some wine and something to eat? I believe we will be here a while.

"What do you know about the Uyghur people?"

I said, "Not much but I've seen some things in the news. They are a minority people in western China, who claim to be oppressed by the Chinese government. There was the car that crashed into people in Tiananmen Square. It was said to be driven by Uyghur separatists. Maybe there was a knife attack at a train or subway station. I also remember reading that the Uyghur people were loyal supporters of Genghis Khan once he conquered them."

He said, "That is about all most Westerners know about the Uyghur, an oppressed minority fighting to preserve their identity to some, and labeled terrorists by the Chinese government. As always it's not that simple.

"The Uyghur are a Turkic ethnic group living in eastern and central Asia. They live primarily in the Xinjiang Uyghur Autonomous Region of China. Outside of China most live in Kazakhstan, Kyrgyzstan, and Uzbekistan. However there are Uyghur in Mongolia, Russia, and small communities in about a dozen other countries including the US and Canada.

"Turkic ethnic groups cover the alphabet of over twenty existing societies from Azerbaijanis to Yakuts that live in northern, eastern, central, and western Asia, northwestern China, and parts of eastern Europe.

"Uyghur are the second largest Muslim ethnic group in China after the Hui. The majority of modern Uyghur are Sunnis.

"Their history goes back many thousands of year in this region. The part relevant to us started in about 1920. Pan-Turkic jihadist Islamists began to challenge the Chinese warlord Yang Zengxin who controlled Xinjiang. Uyghur staged several uprisings against Chinese rule. Twice, in 1933 and 1944, the Uyghur successfully gained their independence backed by the Soviets. Both times their independence was short-lived. The First East Turkestan Republic only lasted about two years and the Second East Turkestan Republic from 1944 to 1949 was a Soviet puppet Communist state.

"The Soviet Union continued to support Uyghur nationalist propaganda and Uyghur separatist movements against China. The Soviet historians claimed that the Uyghur native land was Xinjiang.

"The Soviet Union was involved in funding and supporting the East Turkestan People's Revolutionary Party, the largest militant Uyghur separatist organization in its time, to start a violent uprising against China in 1968. In the 1970s, the Soviets also supported the United Revolutionary Front of East Turkestan to fight against the Chinese.

"In 1979 Soviet KGB agent Victor Louis wrote a thesis claiming that the Soviets should support a 'war of liberation' against imperial China to support Uyghur, Tibetan, Mongol, and Manchu independence. The Soviet KGB itself supported Uyghur separatists against China.

"Xinjiang's importance to China increased after the Soviet invasion of Afghanistan in 1979 because they felt they were being encircled by the Soviets. The Chinese supported the Afghan mujahedeen during the Soviet invasion, and broadcast reports of Soviet atrocities on Afghan Muslims to Uyghur in order to counter Soviet propaganda broadcasts into Xinjiang, which boasted that Soviet minorities lived better and incited Muslims to revolt against the Chinese.

"With the fall of the Soviet Union and the declarations of independence of Kazakhstan, Kyrgyzstan, Tajikistan, Turkmenistan, and Uzbekistan there were renewed calls for the liberation of East Turkestan from China. The East Turkestan independence movement is the term for a variety of groups that are pushing for independence. Some advocate peaceful means and some violent revolution.

"Bear with me, Rob. To understand the situations and the decisions we are making, you need to know the background.

"Let's jump up to the last few years. East Turkestan Islamic Movement, which is also known by other names, is an Islamic terrorist and separatist organization of Uyghur militants in western China. It is fighting for the independence of East Turkestan from China. According to the Chinese government, it is a violent separatist movement, and is often responsible for terrorist attacks in Xinjiang. They claim that from 1990 to 2001 the East Turkestan

Islamic Movement committed over 200 acts of terrorism, resulting in at least 162 deaths and over 440 injuries. After the 9/11 attacks, the US and several other countries designated the group as a terrorist organization.

"Al Qaeda appointed two members of the group to important positions. Abdul Haq al-Turkistani was appointed to Al Qaeda's Shura Majlis, or executive leadership council. They appointed Abdul Shakoor al-Turkistani as military commander of their forces in the FATA, or Federally Administered Tribal Areas of Pakistan.

"The East Turkestan Islamic Movement sent the Turkistan Brigade to fight in the Syrian civil war where they played a prominent role in the 2015 Jisr al-Shughur offensive. In Syria they fight alongside the Al Qaeda branch Al Nusrah Front. As you probably know from news reports, Rob, Al Nusrah Front's stronghold was one of the first places bombed when the US first struck inside Syria."

Walter refilled my wine glass. Before I said anything he went on.

"That is some of the background to one part of what is going on.

"From our discussion when you were in Peru you understand the lengths to which some of our competitors and foreign countries will go to steal our company's sophisticated sensing systems and the data they generate. We have sensitive data and information of our clients that we must protect. If our clients don't believe their data is safe with us they won't hire us.

"The biggest problem is China. We have all heard of the scandal at the US Office of Personnel Management

involving stolen records of millions of government employees. Earlier there was the reporting on Ghost Net. It was
widely reported back in 2009 as a major Chinese government cyber spying operation. Things are only getting worse.
In May 2014 the US Justice Department announced that
a federal grand jury had returned an indictment of five
Chinese People's Liberation Army Unit 61398 officers on
charges of theft of confidential business information and
intellectual property from US commercial firms and of
planting malware on their computers. Forensic evidence
traces the base of operations to a 12-story building in
Pudong in Shanghai.

"Working with our cyber experts we have found that
another People's Liberation Army Unit, this one 61486, is
also deeply involved in computer hacking attacks to steal
trade and military secrets from foreign targets. According
to Western intelligence experts, the Chinese cyber spying
operation is estimated to have 100,000-plus hackers, lin-
guists and other experts.

"Some cyber experts are saying that essentially all of
the Fortune 500 companies have been hacked and are
being hacked now.

"The businesses that have their plans, trade secrets,
product designs, and so on stolen lose future potential
economic growth derived from that secret in addition to
forfeited development investment. When this happens to
many companies you can ultimately have a hollowing-out
effect on an entire economy. The loss from one cyber
attack is too small to be fatal on its own, but their accumu-
lation might prove crippling, 'death by a thousand cuts.'

Mongolia and The Golden Eagle

As China tries to become the world's largest economy, experts argue that the Chinese government is increasingly using cyber espionage to maintain its expansion.

"Falone Advanced Technologies spends tens of millions of dollars to defend itself from cyber attacks. Now we have the opportunity to go on the offensive."

I held up my hand and said, "Walter, up to now you haven't told me anything I couldn't find in the press if I looked. Whatever you tell me I will keep in confidence, except from Abbey, she deserves to know."

He said, "I'm fine with that. You can fill her in and tell her if she has questions to just ask me. If I'm not available she can talk to Major Campbell."

I looked at Ian. It seemed his military background had him conflicted. On the one hand he wanted everyone on a need-to-know basis while on the other he needed to follow his commanding officer's orders. He said nothing.

Walter continued, "As you know I've an excellent working relationship with Israel Aerospace Industries. They have been victims of the Chinese cyber attacks. When we were discussing this contract they brought up an intriguing idea. They felt that from locations in Mongolia, Chinese government communication might be susceptible to passive interception. The former Soviet air base, in addition to having a long runway, was in an area the Israelis believed might work well to passively intercept Chinese communications."

I said, "A natural Sugar Grove Radio Quiet Zone."

Walter said, "Exactly right."

Ian looked puzzled and Walter said, "You explain it to him, Rob."

I said, "Sugar Grove in is Pendleton County, West Virginia. In 1958 Congress established a 13,000-square-mile National Radio Quiet Zone. The Sugar Grove station site was first developed by the Naval Research Laboratory in the early 1960s to gather radio astronomical data on outer space. However the *New York Times* revealed in about 2005 that the site is really part of the communications network operated by the United States and its allies to intercept and process electronic telecommunications. I guess you can do your best spying when you're not near other radio waves to interfere with your intercept work. I think I read they are now closing it."

Walter said, "Yes, there isn't much in the way of commercial radio waves here as there are in most developed parts of the world. The Israelis have the equipment so we will see if we can learn anything that helps improve our cyber security.

"Ned's experiment with the Chinese cellphone just makes the whole thing more interesting."

He stopped and I said, "Now, Walter, I have two questions. Does the fact that we caught those Chinese spies here mean they are onto your plan already? Plus back to my original question. What is so important about Altai Tavan Bogd National Park? You didn't need Abbey and me or the research grant to do what you've explained so far."

He said, "To your first question, we don't know. The Chinese are spying on both our company and Israel Aerospace Industries all the time. Perhaps just us being here was enough to make them want a look. It isn't as if the Chinese Ministry of State Security is short on manpower.

"Your second question goes back to my long-winded account of the Uyghur people in western China. Israeli intelligence keeps track of all the Islamic terrorist groups in the Middle East. They came across some interesting information. Two members of East Turkestan Islamic Movement traveled from Kazakhstan to Syria to consult with one of the commanders of the Turkistan Brigade fighting with the Al Qaeda branch Al Nusrah Front. According to Israeli intelligence the men claim that a member of their part of the Turkestan Islamic Movement has recovered the head of a Chinese rocket. It is now being hidden by a small group of fighters in the mountain area where the borders of China, Mongolia, Kazakhstan, and Russia all come together.

"These two men apparently were sent to find out what it is and what value this object has. They also want help in finding a buyer."

I said, "Given what you have said, I would think they would take it to the Russians."

Walter said, "I'm sure the Russians are one potential buyer. However it seems that the Uyghur militants are less sure of the Russians now. With Russia's activity in the Ukraine and Western economic sanctions, Putin is moving closer to China. The Chinese are financing the new 'Power of Siberia' gas pipeline. In September 2014 President Putin and Chinese Deputy Premier Minister Zhang Gaoli attended the construction groundbreaking ceremony in Yakutsk after Russia signed a 30-year gas deal with the Chinese earlier that year.

"Also they have their own problems with Islamic terrorist groups in the Russian republics of Chechnya and

Dagestan. So they are much less interested in helping the Uyghur militants.

"Israeli intelligence isn't sure what it is that the Uyghur militants have. It appears they moved it with a horse or camel to a remote mountain hiding place, so it can't be too big. It could be a satellite of some type or the head of a test rocket. It may well be a burned-up piece of space junk. The China National Space Administration didn't have any manned space launches scheduled during the time period and Israeli intelligence couldn't find that any of the Chinese commercial launches went down. That means it is most likely a military rocket. The Chinese have been developing and testing several anti-missile missile systems. If it is related to this and isn't just fried metal it could be an intelligence coup."

I said, "Israel wants it and they are paying you to help find it? All this archaeological work is just a cover? I'm the pawn in an international spy drama?"

He said, "They have asked for my help and I feel it is worthwhile. If we are successful and it is valuable, the Israelis have agreed to provide my company with sophisticated cyber defense equipment that is not available commercially. This would be extremely helpful in protecting the company from ongoing cyber attacks from the Chinese and others.

"The Mongolian Minister of the Interior is a big fan of what you did in Peru. That and the grant offer helped the company secure the contract. Think of the rest as a positive by-product and I prefer to think of you as the king of the archaeological grant, not a pawn."

My head was spinning. I said, "So what do I do?"

Walter said, "Implement that work plan for the grant you gave the wonderful presentation on today. If we need to be in the Altai Tavan Bogd National Park area to examine what the Uyghur found then we will let you know. Perhaps nothing will happen. But I agree you need to know what could go on and to know you have my complete trust."

I thought of what Abbey said about how Walter works. "Wheels within wheels."

I said, "So I'm authorized to proceed with the plan? I will incorporate the suggestions you made today."

He said, "Please proceed with all speed and those were only suggestions I made. Use them only if you believe they will help. I'm flying out first thing in the morning and I need to talk to several other people tonight. Thank you again for the great presentation and for being part of the team."

He shook my hand warmly. I looked at my watch. It was after 8:00PM.

I went to the bunker that had the dining area in it. I hadn't really gotten used to everything being inside one of the bunkers. I understood now that putting everything in the bunkers helped keep down the background electromagnetic noise from all our electronic devices.

I grabbed a beer and went into the dining trailer. Abbey was with one of several groups at various tables. I asked if I could interrupt her for a little bit. We went to a quiet spot in a corner. I filled her in on what Walter had told me.

When I finished all she said was, "Let's do our job and see what happens."

I looked at her. It was hard to tell what she was thinking. She didn't seem her usual upbeat self. I said, "Mad, sad, confused, how are you feeling?"

"Prof, I don't know how I feel. I thought our team did a good job with the presentation today. Given the short amount of time and guidance we had, we developed a comprehensive program that should advance science and help Mongolia. Now we need to do it.

"This place still gives me the creeps. I feel like a rat scurrying from bunker to bunker. The sooner we get into the field the better as far as I'm concerned."

I said, "Shall we have everyone take a few days off? Maybe go somewhere?"

She shook her head and said, "Let's get things rolling. There is a lot to do and the faster we get it done the sooner we get out of here."

I wasn't sure if she meant the air base or Mongolia. I said, "Let the team know we will have a 9:00AM meeting. I think I'll head to my trailer and turn in early."

Abbey decided to walk back with me.

Chapter 11

The next morning I grabbed coffee and a roll and headed to the office early. It was 7:15AM when I entered the office trailer. Mitch had three laptops going and was pounding away on her keyboard. She glanced up, waved hello, and went back to work.

At my desk I started thinking about how to group our team members to get the most done. We had to work with the Mongolian University of Science and Technology, Mongolian National Museum, Mongolian Natural History Museum, and Mongolian National Library. I wanted a detailed written description of how each institution would spend the grant money.

I was more than a little worried that a major scandal could result if the funds were misused or wasted. We also needed to coordinate between the institutions so there wasn't any duplication of effort.

I reread the files on the team members I hadn't worked with in the past.

At 9:00AM the team was in the conference area. Someone had set up a whiteboard. Everyone was sitting as if they were students again and I was going to deliver a lecture. The irony was I didn't really have a lesson plan. Today I would discuss step one. By tomorrow I hoped I'd know what step two was. One step at a time as my grandmother was fond of telling me.

I asked, "Ned, has Major Campbell told you your schedule over the next few weeks?"

"The Major said I could attend the meeting so I know what is going on but he has me pretty much booked for at least two weeks."

I asked, "How about you, Hank?"

"The Major told me he needed me about half time."

I said, "OK, I'll put you down for twelve hours a day."

The new folks laughed politely, Abbey shook her head slightly, Mitch put her finger in her mouth as if she was going to puke.

It was a pretty pathetic attempt at humor. I went to the whiteboard and said as I wrote:

"We need to work jointly with our four institutions to develop a detailed plan of how their grant money will be used. Develop a list of the equipment that is needed. For anything technical or expensive we will give the specifications to Major Campbell and he will arrange procurement and training if training is needed. Then next develop milestones with budgets and a time line.

"Abbey, Mitch, and Captain Ganbold will work with the Mongolian Natural History Museum and Mongolian National Library. Captain Ganbold, I'd appreciate your help with our limited grasp of the Mongolian language and in reducing the bureaucratic friction encountered along the way."

Captain Ganbold smiled and nodded. He knew what I was worried about, that men in those institutions might not like taking advice from two young women.

"Sumo and I will work with the Mongolian University of Science and Technology, and Mongolian National Museum.

"Ranger Batbayar, I would like you to stay on base and complete the work on the vehicle and equipment we will be taking to the park. Peter Frank has been helping with this but now he has to spend full time setting up the company equipment. Peter will show you what he has done. Make a list of what you think we still need."

He said, "Yes, Professor." He looked relieved and happy.

From reading the file on him I judged if he couldn't be on horseback he was happiest taking apart engines, transmissions, and other vehicle components and then putting them back together again.

Captain Ganbold was looking at me appraisingly.

"Hank, in the time you have, I would like you to research how best to quantify the 200 or so data points we outlined in the work plan. We will use the company's pattern recognition software to analyze the data but it would be nice to see what others have done in this area.

"Ned, in any free time you have, familiarize yourself with the latest version of that software. Mitch can set that up for you."

We spent another hour discussing details. We decided on three days of work here before heading to Ulaanbaatar to meet with the representatives of the four institutions.

In Ulaanbaatar we again stayed at the Puma Imperial Hotel. In the morning we met in the hotel for a breakfast meeting before heading out. In the evening Sumo would pick a place for dinner. The rule was, no real business was discussed in the evening outside of funny things that might have happened during the day.

I did have to make a couple of calls to the Minister's assistant to keep things moving and make sure we received full cooperation. This assistant must have been one of the Minister's heavies because he was very effective at knocking heads together. One call from him was all it took.

After five days I decided to go back to the air base. I wanted to meet with Major Campbell about the equipment we needed. Mitch said she would go with me. She missed Gertrude. Abbey, Captain Ganbold, and Sumo would keep working in Ulaanbaatar.

When we landed I noticed two police cars, jeeps actually, out in front of the bunker where Major Campbell had his office.

Ned met the plane as it parked. He said, "Welcome back, you missed the action. Two more Chinese spies showed up. This time things didn't go so smoothly, one policeman was wounded, one spy is dead, and the other is critically wounded. They sent him to a hospital in Ulaanbaatar.

"But on the plus side I got another satellite phone and we now have six policemen stationed here full-time with two jeeps and two motorcycles."

Mitch said, "How is Gertrude?"

Ned replied, "She is fine. But your men wouldn't let

me ride her."

Mitch said, "Good."

Ned dropped us off in front of the bunker that had our campers. Mitch said she was going to exercise Gertrude. I decided to walk over to Major Campbell's office after I dumped my bag.

There was another trailer connected to Major Campbell's office trailers now. Space for the police, I assumed. I texted ahead that I was coming, so Ian was waiting for me in his office.

I said, "I hear you had more visitors."

He didn't look happy and said, "Bad business, one dead, the other near dead, and a policeman wounded. We don't need this. It isn't as simple as last time when the Mongolian police could just deport them back to China. There will be a full investigation. It is bound to be a big distraction from our work."

I said, "Are you sure they were Chinese spies?"

He replied, "They didn't have any ID that showed them as Chinese. They didn't have any ID for that matter. But they had satellite phones, which we monitored communicating with a Chinese satellite, and they were armed. The Mongolians will probably treat them as criminals and not even notify the Chinese authorities. It will be interesting to see if the Chinese make any effort on behalf of the seriously wounded man."

I said, "Ned told me he now has another Chinese satellite phone."

Ian said, "We will check to see if the encryption software is the same as the first one."

"Was he able to upload his software to the Chinese satellite?"

"We think so, the question is will it work."

I went over the equipment that was needed and outlined what training I thought would be required so the people at our four institutions could properly operate it. Everything was written out in great detail so I was comfortable we would receive what was needed.

Major Campbell told me the satellite images of the park had been downloaded onto the server in my office trailer. That would be my next stop.

When I got to our trailer Hank was there.

I said, "You are just the one I need to help me. The satellite images of the park are here. I believe you know more about handling them than I do."

Hank said, "I've worked extensively with satellite imaging data in the oil and gas exploration field. I can download and display the data for you but if we aren't looking for oil I don't have a clue what to look for in the data."

I told him to go ahead and he started reviewing the list of images on the computer and preparing to display the ones I wanted to see on our large-screen TV.

I said, "Abbey is the expert on this but I'll give you some examples of where satellite imagery has been successfully applied to archaeology.

"Tom Sever, a NASA archaeologist, used satellite remote sensing to study the ancient Mayan remains in Guatemala. The Petén is a hilly, thickly forested landscape that is very difficult for field archaeologists to penetrate. He was able to identify previously undiscovered roads and causeways the ancient Maya built to connect cities and settlements that are not visible from the ground.

"In another case using terrain analysis, largely from satellite imagery, scholars have tried to determine the route Moses took in the biblical exodus from Egypt.

"Probably the most popular example is the work of Dr. Sarah Parcak using satellite imagery to aide her in her hunt for lost settlements, tombs, and pyramids in the sands of Egypt's northern delta. Dr. Parcak is probably the world's expert in this field.

"She is using the most advanced tools available to map, and quantify hundreds of previously unidentified structures. The human eye can see only part of the light spectrum. With help from infrared satellite imagery, reflected light from different parts of the spectrum becomes visible. The mud brick that the ancient Egyptians used retains water and is denser than the surrounding soil. Satellites can detect those differences and help archaeologists reveal outlines of buried settlements, temples, tombs, and roads.

"Now none of this is as easy as looking at satellite images and just seeing ancient ruins. Dr. Parcak has spent thousands of hours studying satellite images. She has done extensive fieldwork on the ground in Egypt. She has developed sophisticated software to help analyze the data. She also has a much better idea of the characteristics of what she is looking for than we do."

I pointed to the book on the table.

"Her book *Satellite Remote Sensing for Archaeology* is the first book dedicated to the use of satellite-based remote sensing techniques in archaeological research.

It has a companion website with all sorts of additional information and images. She is doing a real service to the whole field of archaeology with her work. I'll get you the eBook edition. I plan to continue reading it tonight and you should read it.

"Fortunately Abbey is really into this. She has gotten the best commercially available software for archaeological analysis of satellite data and sent it to Elizabeth Walters, the company's Chief Technology Officer. The company may have far more sophisticated software that we can recalibrate or maybe she can improve on the commercial software."

He said, "Since we don't know what parameters are helpful, where do we start?"

"Good point," I said. "First download the images in the visible light spectrum and let's just look at them for fun and to get a feel for the park.

"Then let's focus on the five or six square miles that contains the rock paintings of Tsagaan Salaa on the southern side of the White River Valley. There are about 10,000 petroglyphs dating from the Neolithic to the Bronze Age. Also let's examine the Upper Tsagaan Gol petroglyph site. We will pull off as many of the 200 data points we want to collect as the satellite image provides. We could see how the data compares to other places we know have no petroglyphs. Not very scientific but we can do it right now and you never know. Plus I need to understand how to display the images. You tell me what you see and maybe we'll find a gold mine or strike oil."

Hank smiled politely at me and loaded the high-definition stereoscopic photo images of the park. The detail was quite stunning. He started with the whole park and then began to zoom in on the coordinates of the rock paintings of Tsagaan Salaa. He kept zooming in until he reached the individual pixel level and then backed off to a point of clear resolution.

We worked our way around the area of the petroglyphs. It was interesting, fun, and maybe worthwhile in that we were becoming more familiar with the terrain.

Hank said, "In Houston the company has a video wall in its Electronic Visualization Laboratory. It must be ten feet by ten feet. That is just what we need. I've been there when they have done some amazing work detecting large-scale features of the sub-surface geology in the search for oil and gas. Some of the 3D images are, well, as I said, amazing."

I said, "I'm not sure one of those is in our budget but we could probably arrange to use the one in Houston if it has downtime."

We kept zooming around the area. We were totally engrossed in what we were doing when I heard a book drop on the desk behind us. Hank jumped and we both turned around.

It was Mitch, she had her hand resting on Dr. Parcak's book. She said, "Maybe Walt should have hired Dr. Parcak, she really knows this stuff. I read her book when it was first published in April of 2009. Have you two read it?"

Hank was visibly startled.

I said, "Hi Mitch, nice of you to stop by. How is Gertrude? I'm enjoying reading Dr. Parcak's book."

She said, "It's funny. Gertrude knows she is special now and that she is being treated differently."

I said, "So it's true blondes do have more fun." I looked at my watch. "Let's go get a drink."

We shut down the computers and went out. Mitch had driven over on the motorcycle with the sidecar.

Mitch said, "Jump in. This baby will take three."

Hank looked pale. Mitch looked at him. "Hok'ee." She used his Navajo name. "I'm not going to put a curse on you or turn you into a toad, at least not today. Get on behind me and Rob, get in the sidecar."

Hank jumped on, making a brave show of nonchalance.

I expected her to roar off or pop a wheelie for effect but she slowly and smoothly drove away. She probably did it because she knew I'd expected her to roar off.

Chapter 12

We spent the next two weeks organizing. Mitch wanted to go to Khovd Aimag to start the field documentation work. There wasn't much rigorous documentation of the traditional dwellings and settlement patterns, dress and other cultural distinctions, literary, artistic, and musical traditions of the dozen nationalities and ethnicities we decided to focus on. She was also interested in the religious practices and in particular the extent to which shamanism was still practiced.

She had arranged for the National Museum of Mongolian History to do the literature search and a comprehensive review of everything in their collection relating to Khovd Aimag.

I wanted to take the road trip to Khovd but I couldn't justify taking the week or so it would require our caravan of three UAZ-452 vans to make the over one thousand mile trip. The jeep and motorcycle with sidecar would remain at the base. Khovd is considered remote even by

Mongolian standards and the roads are far from highway quality. I would fly in later and meet the group.

The plan was to send Mitch, Sumo, Captain Ganbold, Ranger Batbayar, and Mitch's two Mongolian retainers with our vans, campers, and equipment. I'd arranged for Peter Frank to get another of the Tarus-2 all-terrain two-wheel-drive motorcycles. Each van would then have a motorcycle on the roof in case of breakdown or other trouble.

As they drove away, I again wished I were going with them. This air base was giving me the creeps.

The rest of us stuck to our routine. Work until 4:00PM horseback riding. These rides were now over two hours and for me a high point of the day. Evening dinners were quiet and the food was dull at best.

Abbey and Hank worked with me on the satellite mapping of the Altai Tavan Bogd National Park. We were starting to get data from the company's work for the Mongolian government that we incorporated. Ned was still working full-time for Major Campbell.

After a few breakdowns and minor mishaps our little caravan made it to Khovd City, the capital of Khovd Aimag. I decided to fly out the next day. Abbey wasn't happy about being stuck at the air base but she knew there was still a lot to be done before our fieldwork started in the Altai Tavan Bogd National Park.

I spoke to Ian about transportation at dinner. He said there was a supply truck leaving at 7:00AM for the airport in Ulaanbaatar and I could catch a ride on that, then take a commercial flight to Khovd City. No company jet for this trip.

I changed the topic. "Have we had any more Chinese agents sneaking around?"

He said, "We haven't spotted any. So they are being much more careful or they aren't here. However, our computer systems have been under almost constant cyber attack. So far as best we know, none of the hacks have been successful. With each attack we learn something about their techniques. There is some benefit to that.

"How is your work progressing?"

I filled him in and said goodnight right after dinner so I could pack.

Early the next morning I rode in one of the company's supply trucks to Ulaanbaatar airport and then took a Fokker 50 operated by Aero Mongolia to Khovd City.

I sat on a left side window seat of the airplane. I'd made a mental list of what I wanted to try and see from the air during the flight starting with the Manjusri Monastery. It is located about ten miles south of Ulaanbaatar. The monastery at its height was one of the country's largest and most important monastic centers with 20 temples and more than 300 monks. Unfortunately Mongolian Communists destroyed it in 1937. In February 1937, the monastery's last remaining 53 monks were arrested and many were later shot. All 20 temples of the monastery were then destroyed. Fortunately the valuable Buddhist scriptures were moved to the Mongolian National Library and not destroyed. In the cliff above the monastery are several eighteenth century Buddhist cave paintings and reliefs that escaped destruction in 1937.

From the air I could see the restored temple and the

remains of walls and buildings. I'd have to make time to visit when I was in Ulaanbaatar.

Next about 60 miles west of Ulaanbaatar I looked down at Khustain Nuruu National Park, which is also called Hustai National Park. It seemed every place had several names and several ways to spell the name. As if I wasn't confused enough.

The park is about 125,000 acres. It is home to 44 species of mammals, over 200 species of birds, and many hundreds of species of plants. In 1993 it was designated a Specially Protected Area after the reintroduction of the Przewalski's horse of Mongolia, a rare and endangered subspecies of wild horse.

I could see the Tuul River running through the park and not much else at the altitude we were flying. As I flew west the empty vastness of the country was obvious.

About halfway through the three-hour flight I could see the eastern edge of the Great Lakes Depression. It is a large semi-arid depression that covers parts of the five western aimags of Uvs, Khovd, Bayan-Ölgii, Zavkhan, and Govi-Altai. It covers over 245,000 acres and the northern end extends into Russia.

It contains six major lakes. Three are saline: Uvs Nuur, Khyargas Nuur, Dörgön Nuur. The other three, Khar-Us Nuur, Khar Nuur, and Airag Nuur, are freshwater lakes. The land around the lakes is made up in large part by three and a half million acres of salt marshes and large sandy areas. Northern parts are dominated by arid steppes, and surrounded by semi-deserts or deserts.

Mongolia and The Golden Eagle

Przewalski's Mongolian wild horses in Hustai National Park. (Note 3)

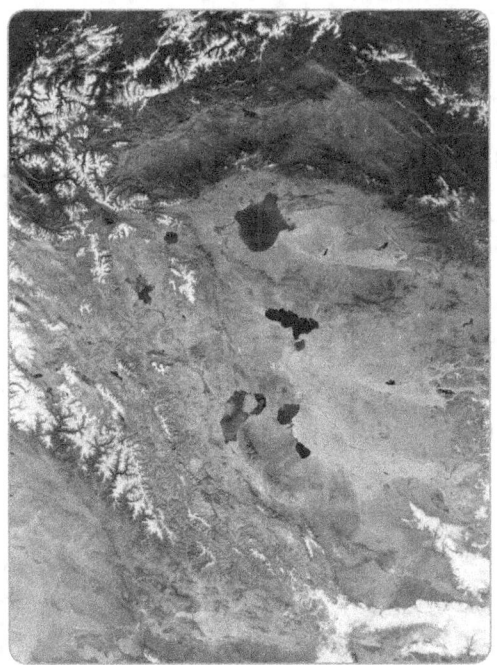

Great Lakes Depression (Note 1)

The plane started to descend as we were passing over Khar-Us Nuur. Khovd City is about 15 miles west of the lake. It looked flat, dusty and most of the roads were dirt. The city is situated at the foot of the Altai Mountains on the Buyant River. To the north of the city I could see the ruins of the Manchu fort called Sangiin Kherem. The fort was built in the eighteenth century, and later became the seat of the Manchu amban, or high official. In addition to the Manchu amban's offices the fort contained the treasury, military barracks, commercial firms, a Chinese Buddhist temple, and a mosque. In 1912 Mongol troops captured the city of Khovd and destroyed all the Manchu garrisons. After that the fort fell into disrepair.

The city was small. There were a few four-story buildings but most were one and two stories. About half the residences were gers. The rest looked like mud block or brick.

We circled for our landing at the airport that was a few miles south of the city. Not much to the airport, two runways, one paved and one grass.

I walked down the airplane stairs. It was sunny and almost 70 degrees. Sumo was waiting for me.

"How was your flight, Professor?"

"Nice to see you, Sumo. My flight was quick, comfortable, and interesting. I got a feel for the vastness of your country. How was your trip?"

We collected my bag and he directed me to a waiting taxi.

He said, "Well, mine wasn't quick or comfortable but it was interesting.

"We are staying at the Royal Hotel. It is the newest hotel in the city. It isn't very royal but it is clean, has indoor bathrooms, and hot water. None of the other hotels have all three."

Khovd City had none of the modern feel of Ulaanbaatar. It was dusty with a rundown look. I had been told that Khovd Aimag was remote even by Mongolian standards. If this was the busy capital of the province then I believed them.

When we pulled up in front of the hotel Sumo said, "Go check in and get settled. I need to go back to the Mongolian State University of Agriculture's local branch and take care of a few things. We will meet in the lobby at 6:30PM. I've made dinner plans for all of us."

I got out, grabbed my bag, and as I shut the door I said, "Dare I ask what Mitch is doing?"

The cab started to pull away and Sumo said out the window, "She's after the Mongolian Death Worm. Ask her tonight."

I looked at my watch, it was after 4:00PM. I checked in and went to my room. It was small but clean and modern. The hot water worked so I took a shower and organized my thoughts on what I wanted to accomplish over the next few days.

I went to the lobby at 6:30PM and Sumo was waiting for me. I said, "Any sign of Mitch?"

Before he could answer the lobby door opened and Mitch walked in.

"Hi Sumo. Rob, you finally decided to show up and do some real work? Where are we going for dinner?"

I smiled and waved hello.

Sumo said, "Altai."

"OK, I'll meet you two there after I take a shower and change."

We decided to walk. I said, "How is it going working with Mitch?"

He said, "She isn't bad to work with. We've split up and I've been working with the University. We don't actually work that closely. Mitch has her two men and Captain Ganbold. So she doesn't need me to translate or help her get around. It took me a while to get used to her style."

I thought or lack of style. I said, "Well, I'm going to need your help with both the language and getting around. What is Ranger Batbayar doing?"

"He is mostly tending to the three vans and making sure none of our equipment disappears."

We walked into the small restaurant. Sumo said something and we were directed to a corner table. He ordered beer and something else as we went to the table. Sumo didn't waste time when it came to getting served. The staff seemed to know him. Not that you would forget Sumo.

We sat and he said, "The chef trained in Russia. The place doesn't look like much but it is by far the best food in the city. As you have seen the city is not prosperous, it survives on an agricultural economy, food processing, and some light manufacturing of textiles and building materials. This area is known for its watermelons and tomatoes."

The beer arrived followed by two large plates.

Sumo said, "Salami with Russian bread and butter and pickled tomatoes. Both are traditional Russian appetizers. Russians usually have them with vodka but I prefer beer."

I told him I also preferred beer. Then I asked him how

his work with the local University was going. He gave me a rundown and then asked what I planned.

"I'd like to visit the University officials with you and then go to meet with the officials at the museum. After that I want to go to the cave paintings at Tsenkheriin Agui in Mankhan district."

He said, "The cave paintings at Tsenkheriin Agui are over 60 miles away and because of the poor roads it is best to plan at least two days depending on how much time you want to spend examining the caves.

"Tsenkheriin Agui is in Khar Us Nuur National Park and the rangers run a ger camp. There are showers and a bar-restaurant in the camp. We can take one of our vans with a camper and set up at the ranger camp. The caves are only a mile away and the burial mounds and petroglyphs aren't far away. The mosquitoes are bad this time of year."

I found the pickled tomatoes went well with beer and we ordered another two beers.

I said, "Let's start with the University and then go to the museum. After that we will decide when to leave for the park."

Mitch walked in. She wore blue jeans, and a black flannel shirt that set off her platinum hair. Around her neck was the large ornate silver cross that she said was given to her by her grandmother. I wondered again if one of her grandmothers was really of the Northern Arapaho.

I said, "Beer and pickled tomatoes. Join us." I stood and pulled out a chair for her. Sumo also stood. As I did it I had the thought, will she take this as a patronizing sexist gesture?

But she just smiled, sat, and said, "After a week of beer and pickled tomatoes we'll see what you think. Every other place in the city only has mutton pancakes and goulash so plan on being back here often."

Sumo said, "Do you trust me to order for everyone?"

Mitch said, "Go to it, big boy."

I nodded yes.

Sumo went on. "As I told you the chef is Russian trained but he is somewhat limited by what ingredients he can buy locally. So it ends up being sort of a Russian/Mongolian hybrid."

When the food arrived Sumo pointed to the family-style plates heaped with food and said, "The Russian name of that dish is Miasnaia Solianka, meat soup with tomatoes, onions, and cucumbers. This one is Pelmeni Siberian, it is meat dumplings. The dumplings aren't much different than Mongolian dumplings. The last dish is Kurnik. The true Russian dish is a chicken and rice pie. Here he uses lamb in place of the chicken."

They were all flavorful and a bit spicy.

I said to Mitch, "I don't know much about the Mongolian Death Worm."

Mitch said, "Now you will. The Mongolian name is Olgoi-Khorkhoi. It is bright red with a wide body between two and five feet long. It spits acid that turns anything it touches yellow and corroded. This acid is said to kill people. It can also kill at a distance by means of electric discharge.

"The Czech cryptozoologist Ivan Mackerle described the animal from second-hand reports as a 'sausage-like worm over 20 inches long, and thick as a man's arm, resembling the intestine of cattle. Its skin serves as an exoskeleton, molting whenever hurt. Its tail is short, as if it were cut off, but not tapered. It is difficult to tell its head from its tail because it has no visible eyes, nostrils or mouth. Its color is dark red, like blood.'

"They say that the worm lives underground. Its movement can be detected from above via the waves of sand that it displaces. It hibernates most of the year underground except for when it becomes active in June and July. It is reported that it is mostly seen on the surface when it rains and the ground is wet.

"British zoologist Karl Shuker hypothesized that the death worm was an amphisbaena or lizard worm. There are over 120 documented species of lizard worms. They are limbless, burrowing lizards that have a carnivorous diet. The eyes are highly reduced, while the ear bone is large. Together with another bone, the extracollumella, the ear bone is used to detect vibrations of prey items, allowing the lizard worm to be able to hunt for invertebrates underground.

"Now there is one species of lizard worm that is red, Amphisbaena Alba. But it is only found in South America. Most of the species are found in Central and South America. Plus most are only six inches long with a few up to 18 inches. No species of worm lizard has been found in Mongolia.

"In 2005 a group of cryptozoologists investigated new reports and sighting of the creature. They found no evidence of its existence, but could not rule out that it might live deep in the Gobi Desert along the prohibited areas of the Mongolian-Chinese border. As you both know, cryptozoology is not a recognized branch of zoology or a discipline of science.

"Also in 2005 zoological journalist Richard Freeman mounted an expedition to hunt for the Death Worm but he found nothing. Freeman's conclusion was that the tales of the worm had to be apocryphal, and that reported sightings likely involved non-poisonous burrowing reptiles.

"So I've spent the last few days traveling around to see people who had seen the Death Worm. When I get to the person they say they never actually saw the creature, but knew of someone else who did. That sent me on to the next person who had a similar tale. The one thing they all have in common is that they all firmly believe in its existence and can describe it minutely.

"Interesting folk tale like Bigfoot and Chupacabra but I'm not spending any more time on it, other than to write it up and document it for the National Museum and Library.

Mongolian Death Worm (Note 2)

"Now I'm on to Mongolian shamanism, both yellow shamanism and black shamanism. I'll be traveling around the region for a week or so."

Sumo said, "I've heard stories of the Mongolian Death Worm all my life. Some Mongolian people will always believe in it just as other cultures believe in voodoo and ghosts."

I said, "It is no stranger than many beliefs. Who knows, there may be a Mongolian Death Worm and there may have been a virgin birth. What do they have for dessert?"

The next morning Sumo and I headed over to the University. Its main building was a four-story structure that looked modern by Khovd City standards. The Chancellor met us when we arrived. She was professionally dressed in a pinstriped pantsuit.

We started with a tour of the facility. The building was neat and well maintained. She showed us each lab, classroom, library, and office with great pride. To me the labs looked like something you might see in a good US high school in about 1985.

Each department head gave us a brief overview of what their department was doing. I was impressed with how much they did on a very limited budget. There was no archaeology department to support, but the library and labs could use all the help they could get.

I thanked the Chancellor and told her we would be back in contact with her. I was determined to help as much as we could. We had set aside funds for Khovd State University in the one and a half million we allocated to the Mongolian University system.

When we left I said to Sumo, "Go through the budget

and see what we allocated for Khovd State University. Then identify other budget line items we may be able to use to help the University. Look at what we allocated to the National Library and see what can be used for the University's library. Be creative. Then go back to the Chancellor and develop a priority listing of what is most needed in the area of science and technology. When you have both lists we will sit down and get things going as fast as we can."

Sumo said, "You want this when?"

I said, "You tell me. Say two weeks since you have to help me with some other things for the next several days."

If he was going to be successful at Falone Advanced Technologies he had to learn to move fast. If it were back at Cornell they would take two months just to decide who should be on the committee to make up the lists.

Next we went to the museum. It is housed in a yellow two-story building across from the police station. We started with a tour of the collection of archaeological artifacts of nomadic life in Mongolia containing bowls, tools, and traditional style thermoses. Next we toured the traditional costumes of the ten ethnic groups of Khovd. The ethnic groups are all ones we included in our work plan to research. This would fall in Mitch's area of responsibility.

We saw several displays of Buddhist relics and statuettes, and old documents and hangings in ancient Mongolian script. There was also a collection of stuffed animals.

I spent considerable time examining the photographic depiction of the cave paintings we planned to visit in Khar Us Nuur National Park.

The museum operated on even more of a limited budget than the University. I could see lots of meaningful ways to help here. I asked the director of the museum to make a list of the most urgently needed equipment and supplies required to maintain the existing collection. My hope was to make something useful happen right away. I had the feeling these institutions heard lots of promises and received little in actual help. If we could deliver needed equipment fast I believed we would get good cooperation going forward.

Sumo wanted to get to work over at the University. We decided to leave for the Khar Us Nuur National Park the day after tomorrow. I went back to the hotel to call Abbey and get some other work done.

She answered the phone by saying. "Prof, get me out of here."

I knew how she felt. I was happy to get away from the air base. I said, "Soon. How is the work going?"

"We have loaded all the satellite data and all the other available relevant data we could find. The company's data from the government survey still hasn't arrived."

I said, "I'll be back there in a few days. See if you can use what you have to identify potential cave locations. Run it through the probability software we used in Peru. There have to be hundreds of caves in the park that haven't been explored. Let's explore a few and see if one is worth excavating. Given that the Tsagaan Salaa Rock Paintings have over 10,000 petroglyphs there must be other undiscovered archaeological treasures.

"I say we find one and begin working it. We will be in the area where Walter wants us. The rest of his plan is his problem. We will be doing the work we know and perhaps will advance science a bit."

Abbey said, "The sooner the better. How are Mitch and Sumo doing?"

I gave her a quick rundown on what they were doing and said goodbye.

The next day I visited Sangiin Kherem, the Manchu fort ruins.

The following morning I met Sumo in the lobby of our small hotel at 7:30AM. He had thermoses of tea and a bag of Mongolian pancakes called gambir. They are slightly sweet pan-fried dough.

The van was parked in front of the hotel. It was towing one of our Australian off-road camper trailers. I put my overnight bag in the back and climbed in. Sumo drove a few blocks to a cinderblock house and blew the horn. Three men came out.

Sumo said, "They work in the park and needed a ride. More people to push if we get stuck."

It was all smiles and handshakes as the men loaded their bags of supplies and got in the van. From Sumo's translation I gathered one was a park ranger and the other two worked at the park.

Sumo gave everyone large paper cups of tea and then we drove off. I had the honor of having the first fried pancake from the bag.

It would take almost three hours to cover the sixty miles to the park because of the bad roads.

When we arrived we dropped our riders off at the ranger station. The rangers had several gers set up to rent to visitors. I was happy to see there was a bar-restaurant and showers with hot water. A hot shower for 2000 tögrög or about $1.15 seemed like a good deal to me.

Sumo began to look around for a good place to set up our camper. He wanted to avoid the worst of the mosquitoes, which can be incredibly bad during the summer. After that we went to view the burial mounds. The tourists were not very impressed by these as they basically looked like a pile of rocks. Just beyond the burial mounds there are a series of petroglyphs. The figures of antelopes, tigers, and some undistinguished forms were etched into the rocks. We would examine the Tsenkheriin Agui cave paintings in the morning.

The evening scenery was beautiful but the mosquitoes were out in force. We went to the bar-restaurant had a leisurely dinner and then back to our camper. It was tight but comfortable and no bugs. Much, much better than sleeping on the ground in a tent and I made a mental note to thank Peter Frank.

In the morning we walked up the slope over a mile to the cave entrance. The main chamber is at least eighty-five feet high. There are several smaller galleries leading off from the main chamber but one long chamber was blocked by a rock fall in 1995. The first thing that jumped out at me was how much damage has been caused by recent graffiti. I read about the graffiti but seeing the damage done to priceless artwork from many thousands of years ago made me wonder again about man's desire to destroy things.

The paintings were done with light pink and red-brown ochre pigments. There was a debate over their age but most experts date them from 17,000 to 22,000 years ago. Some of the paintings depict Paleolithic animals such as mammoths and ostriches. Other paintings depict more common animals like camels, sheep, bulls, and ibex.

Stone Age people inhabited the cave during the Upper Paleolithic perhaps as far back as 40,000 years ago. Mongolian and American scientists discovered stone weapons in the cave that were used by ancient peoples about 7000 years ago.

I explored the cave for several hours. Sumo said he would go back and disassemble our camper. We planned to head back to Khovd City today.

As I went back down the hill I decided that the latest photographic equipment for documenting the cave paintings and petroglyphs would be the first items we should deliver to the University and museum. I wanted to see this UNESCO World Cultural Heritage Site thoroughly documented before more damage was done. I hoped the Tsagaan Salaa Rock Paintings in Altai Tavan Bogd National Park with its over 10,000 images was being better protected.

Mongolia and The Golden Eagle

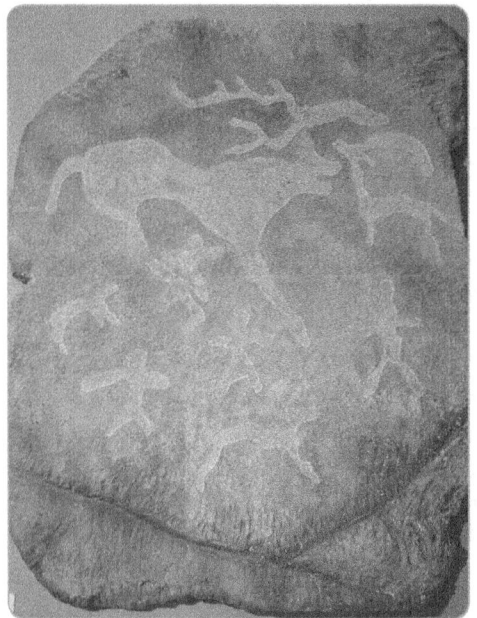

Petroglyph or cave painting
exhibited in the National Museum
of Mongolia. (Note 1)

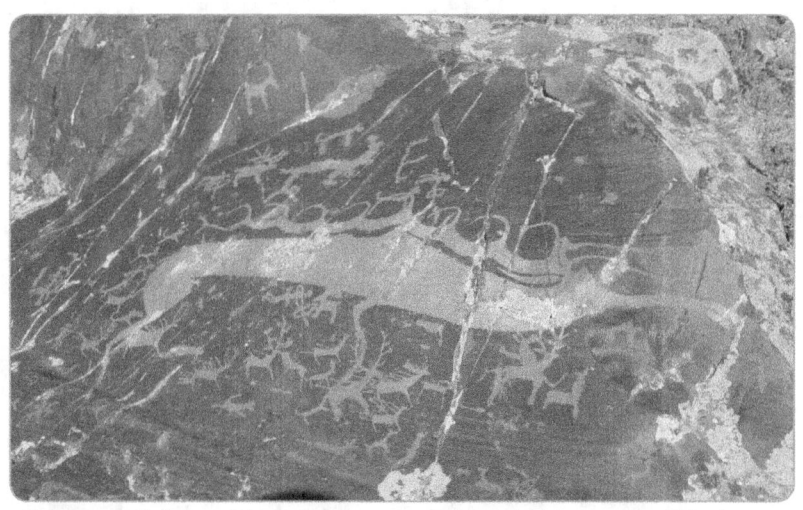

Tsagaan Salaa petroglyph or rock paintings in Altai
Tavan Bogd National Park. (Note 3)

Chapter 13

The next morning we flew out of Khovd City back to Ulaanbaatar. Captain Ganbold decided to return as well. Both Sumo and I had a couple days' worth of work to do with our partner institutes in Ulaanbaatar before we returned to the air base. Captain Ganbold would take a supply truck back to the base right away.

After dropping our bags at the Puma Imperial Hotel, I headed to the Mongolian National Museum and Sumo to the Mongolian University of Science and Technology. I wanted to check on the progress they were making and make sure they were following through with helping the University and museum in Khovd. It was clear that the people in the institutes in the remote provinces of Khovd and Bayan-Ölgii no longer had much faith in the promises of help from far-away officials in Ulaanbaatar. I wanted to adopt Winston Churchill's wartime note to his memos of "Action this day!" but it seemed a bit pushy.

Back at the hotel I emailed Major Campbell a list of

equipment I wanted to deliver to the museum in Khovd when I returned in a few weeks. I would not go back empty-handed. I told him we would be ready to return to the air base in another day. He said he would meet us at the airport and fly us back.

I decided to take a walk. I walked for over an hour and sent Sumo a text saying I'd meet him in the bar at the hotel's Indian restaurant.

I was drinking my second beer and nibbling on an appetizer of Chat Papdi when a fit, casually dressed man walked up to my table.

He said, "You look like an American." He put out his hand. "I'm Chad Dillon."

I stood and said, "Rob Johnson," and I shook his hand.

He said, "May I join you for a drink?"

I said yes. We both sat down and he ordered a beer.

He asked me, "Are you vacationing in Mongolia?"

"No, I'm here on a research grant."

"How interesting. What type of research?" he replied.

"We're doing archaeological work in conjunction with museums and universities. What about you, are you on vacation here?"

This all seemed simple enough. An American in a faraway country spots another American in a bar and they have a beer together.

His answer made the back of my neck tingle a little.

"No, I'm with the economic development group at the US Embassy here. Tell me, where in Mongolia is your grant work taking you?"

Now none of this would have seemed odd if it weren't

for what happened earlier today. At the National Museum a fit, well-dressed man in his late thirties had asked in excellent English if I was an American. He asked what I was doing and I politely asked the same question of him.

He was with the cultural exchange department at the Russian Embassy. He was also interested in where in Mongolia my work would take me. At the time it just seemed like general conversation. When we parted he handed me his card and said to call him if he could be of help. He then added, "You never know when you may need a little help in a foreign country."

I said to Chad Dillon, "Our grant work is primarily focused on the aimags of Bayan-Ölgii and Khovd. However we are partnering with several institutions in Ulaanbaatar. How long have you been in Mongolia and does your work take you around the country?"

He said, "I've been here four years and I get to travel a bit for work. I also use my vacation time to explore the country."

We continued with small talk and it didn't seem he was pumping me for information. A few minutes later Sumo came in. I introduced Sumo and we visited a few minutes longer.

Chad stood and said, "It is a pleasure to meet you two. Best of luck with your research."

He then handed me his card and said, "Call me if I can be of help. As a fellow American I'm happy to be available because you never know when you may need a little help in a foreign country."

I smiled and thanked him. Then I put his card in my shirt pocket next to the Russian's card.

Sumo called the waiter over and ordered more beer and then several dishes. I guess I wasn't to be consulted on what was for dinner tonight. OK by me, he always ordered plenty and I'd find some things I'd like.

The dishes of food came out slowly and the beer came out steadily. We discussed our day and our plans for tomorrow. Sumo had a gentle, warm manner. The contrast between his bulk and graceful movement still seemed odd to me. He couldn't have accomplished all he had as a sumo wrestler if he wasn't fiercely competitive but it didn't show. I found I enjoyed his company.

It was almost 10:00 when we finally finished. We would go our separate ways tomorrow and meet Major Campbell at the airport at 4:00PM.

I got to the airport at about twenty minutes to four. I went into the small waiting area of the cargo hangar. Major Campbell was there chatting with a pilot of one of the cargo planes. We exchanged greetings and the pilot wandered off.

I handed Major Campbell the two cards I received yesterday.

He looked at the top one and said, "CIA." He handed it back to me and looked at the other card. "FSB or Federal Security Service of the Russian Federation." Then he handed that one back.

He didn't seem the least bit concerned. He said, "Go ahead."

I said, "What?"

"You're dying to tell me all about your meeting with them."

I was a little miffed that it seemed no big deal to him so I gave him a matter-of-fact short version of the encounters.

When I was done I said, "Well, what do you think?"

He said, "I think they are doing their job." I let it drop and headed to the men's room.

When I returned Sumo was there. Major Campbell said, "Let's go pre-flight the plane and get back to base."

Sumo grabbed my bag along with his and we headed out to the tarmac. I followed Major Campbell. He was walking towards a plane that looked as if it was made by a ninth-grade shop class. In Peru Walter's company had the latest and highest tech everything. Here we had a Russian jeep called the Goat, and for good reason, vans called Bread Loafs and this.

I used the Russian and said, "Is this the result of breeding the Kozlik and the Bukhanka?"

Gavilán 358, a Colombian light utility transport aircraft. (Note 3)

Major Campbell looked amused, not offended. "No, this is Gavilán. That is Spanish for sparrow hawk. The Colombians don't have the same sense of irony that the Russians do. More precisely the airframe is Gavilán 358 which is a Colombian light utility transport aircraft produced in the 1990s.

"I was hoping for the airframe of a Kodiak made by Quest Aircraft Company, a Japanese-owned company located in Sandpoint, Idaho. Very modern, rugged, but they cost over a million dollars without engines.

"Walter gave the specification for the airframe to purchasing, they put out the word, and one of the company's engineers in Colombia bought this surplus from the Colombian air force. It probably cost more to ship it to Houston than it did to buy it."

I said, "It says 'EXPERIMENTAL' on the side of it."

"Technically it is experimental. That way we aren't required to go through the FAA certification process. We did some modifications," he said.

I had heard that before. It seemed that everything in Peru had been high-tech customized. Major Campbell loved all things that flew and the fancier and more unique the better. I knew I was in for an earful. I winked at Sumo and decided to listen patiently.

He continued, "I've renamed it the 'Shadow Hawk.' It is a gas electric series-hybrid powered, ultra-quiet, STOL airplane specifically built to do remote sensing of wild animal herds."

I said to Sumo, "STOL is short takeoff and landing." Then I said to Major Campbell, "Gas electric series-hybrid like a Toyota Prius?"

"Exactly, Rob. The series-hybrids use an electric motor powered by batteries that are continually recharged by a generator that is powered by a gas-driven engine. For the engine we use a Wankel rotary engine. The advantages of a rotary engine are it is approximately one third of the weight of a piston engine of equivalent power plus it is only one third of the size of a piston engine. We use an Austro Engine AE50R to power the generator. It is a light aircraft rotary engine used in several home-built models. It's 55hp and only weighs 61 pounds.

"We were able to position the engine, generator, and batteries to optimize the overall weight within the aircraft. Not only did we improve its STOL characteristic, we greatly improved its glide ratio."

I said, "Why? Why build a plane like this?"

He looked at me with almost pity in his eyes or as if he was looking at a dimwitted child.

He said, "Because it is quiet. If you fly an airplane or drone close enough to a herd of wild animals to get the biometric reading we need, you will scare them half to death. It would be bad for the animals, you wouldn't get any meaningful data, and can you imagine if the Humane Society or some other animal rights group heard about it.

"First, this aircraft is much quieter than a normal plane. Then turn off the engine and run on the batteries only and it is even quieter. Finally turn off the electric motor, feather the prop, and fly it like a glider. Now it is very, very quiet, as quiet as the shadow of a hawk."

I looked at the airplane again. OK, it looked sturdy enough. It was boxy and had fixed landing gear.

I said, "How fast is it?"

"Not very, about 130kn or 150mph," he replied.

"Can it land on a tennis court without hitting the net?" I added.

He didn't answer me and said to Sumo, "Put the bags in here and let's go. Sumo, take the copilot's seat and Rob, get in back."

It was roomy inside. I buckled myself in. Ian talked to the tower. Then he flipped a switch and the engine started. He flipped another switch and the electric motor started turning the propeller. It was much quieter than any small plane I'd been in.

After doing a run-up and checking his control surfaces he taxied onto the grass runway. Next Ian lowered the flaps, stood on the brakes, and pushed the speed lever for the electric motor to maximum. He released the brakes, the plane rolled forward and seemed to leap into the air at a slower speed than I'd ever seen a small plane take off. It took off in only a few hundred feet of the 6500 feet of the grass airstrip. Ian flew straight down the runway gaining altitude.

He smiled at both of us and said, "Well, chaps, how cool is this?"

He looked like a little boy at Christmas. He climbed the plane to about 2000 feet. It was a clear day. I thought again how much more fun flying in a small plane was. It is a totally different experience than flying on an airliner, the smaller the plane the freer the feeling.

At 150 mph it would take about an hour to get to the air base. We were flying over relatively flat steppe land.

The quiet plane became even quieter. Major Campbell had just switched off the engine and the batteries were powering the electric motor.

I said, "How long can you run on just the batteries?"

Major Campbell said, "It depends on how many batteries we have on board. Currently we can go about an hour and still have a half-hour reserve. Depending on what remote sensing equipment we are using we can add or take out batteries."

Next he turned off the electric motor and feathered the prop. It was now very quiet with just the wind noise around the cockpit and the wings. He glided until he was down to about 1500 feet and then turned on the motor and the engine.

As we came in for a landing I noticed more satellite dishes and antennas next to the bunkers. The general activity level seemed higher.

Abbey pulled up to the plane in the jeep as we parked. Two of Major Campbell's men also met the plane.

He said, "Let's talk tomorrow. I need to get some things done now."

I said, "Thanks for the ride. I like your new toy."

He squeezed my shoulder and said, "Don't call it a toy when Walter is around. He thinks we should do everything with unmanned drones."

I realized there was no reason you couldn't make a gas electric series-hybrid drone. But then Ian couldn't go flying.

Sumo put the bags in the jeep. I gave Abbey a hug.

She said, "Get in. I want to show you what we have done."

She asked us about our trip as she drove to the bunker that housed our office complex. The base seemed less ghostly with the increased activity.

We walked into the trailer. Hank was there and there was a new large-screen TV taking up most of one wall.

"Hi Hank," I said. "I like your new TV."

"Welcome back, Professor. It's a Sharp LC-90LE657U 90-inch Aquos HD 1080p 120Hz 3D Smart LED TV. It cost almost seven grand but it is way better than the small screen we were using before you left. Peter Frank had it flown in from Tokyo when they were bringing in drone equipment."

Abbey said, "Show them what we found."

Hank brought up satellite images of the Altai Tavan Bogd National Park.

He said, "Actually Abbey found these areas, I just did what she told me to do. You wanted us to identify several areas where there were potentially large caves. Especially in areas that are less likely to have been disturbed by recent hikers and fossil hunters. We started in the area of the coordinates you gave us in the most southwestern part of the park that borders China and the west end bordering Russia."

Hank put up a map on another smaller screen.

He continued, "We worked our way along the north shore of Lake Khurgan and then continued west along the north shore of Lake Khoton. In this area of the park there are thousands of petroglyphs plus numerous Turkic Stone Men and stone burial mounds. People have been living here for thousands of years.

"But you know all this. What Abbey has us doing is looking for areas that are not currently visited by locals or tourists that might contain cave formations that would have been attractive places for ancient peoples to live."

Hank wasn't an archaeologist. This was all new to him. I was glad to see he was interested and excited about what we were doing.

He went on. "We want to find an archaeologically significant cave that no one has found and disturbed. Then we can do a first-rate exploration of it using the latest equipment and methods."

He stopped and put up his hands. "You know all this."

"Hank, I couldn't have said it any better. Show me what you found."

Hank said, "We loaded all the data we had and then we ran it through the probability software. It identified all the known sites that fit our criteria. That made me think that maybe this software actually worked.

"Within our target coordinates, the best fit for major caves was around Mount Dongoroh. There are streams on both the east and west sides of the mountain that flow into Lake Khoton. Smaller streams as you move up the mountain feed these streams. On the east side there are small lakes or ponds.

"We asked the company to do a low-flying drone survey in these areas of Mount Dongoroh. The satellite photos don't give us the detail we need. Plus the drones have magnetometers. An aeromagnetic survey is part of the company's contract anyway so we just requested they do this area first and in a little greater detail than they might have. They tell me the data will be ready any day now.

"I'm looking forward to getting this data. I've spent a lot of time analyzing magnetometer readings both for the company and in my previous job. Albeit, mostly looking for oil.

"Then we go out in the field and take a look."

Then Hank went back to the big screen and began to scroll the satellite images up the north shore of Lake Khoton. About three miles up the shore a small river ran up the east side of Mount Dongoroh. As it twisted up the mountainside it split into several smaller streams. The streams' headwaters were at various elevations below the mountain's peak of over 10,000 feet.

After following each stream to its headwater he scrolled back to the north shore of the lake and then to the west end where several rivers enter the lake. He then followed the Rashaan River to tributary streams that ran up the west side of the mountain. The terrain seemed as if it could contain sizable caves.

Hank said, "Once we get the magnetometer reading we can decide on areas to go and examine."

Abbey said, "I've talked Major Campbell into letting me take his quadcopter with us."

This type of drone was a novelty a few years ago when we were in Peru. Now it seems at least one kid on every block has one. Major Campbell's is a bit more sophisticated.

I said, "Ask Captain Ganbold what he knows about these areas. He probably knows or the local rangers know which areas are untraveled. He may have some other helpful insights."

I looked at my watch, it was after 7:00PM. I said, "Let's go get a drink."

Hank began shutting down the equipment.

Abbey said, "How soon can we get out of here and to the park? This place is really getting on my nerves."

I said, "I'll talk to Major Campbell tomorrow. I don't see any reason we can't leave in a few days."

I'd only been back a few hours and I was ready to leave again. I understood how Abbey must feel.

The next morning I stopped by our office trailer at 8:00AM. Abbey already had Captain Ganbold reviewing the satellite images of the park. They were deep in conversation and looked like they had been at it for a while. I didn't disturb them and went out again to find Major Campbell.

I headed to his trailer. One nice thing, there was always good coffee in the security office. In Mongolia it is mostly tea.

"Good morning, Ian. I want to head to Altai Tavan Bogd National Park in a couple of days. Abbey and Hank have identified several areas we would like to research."

I walked over to the large wall map of Mongolia and pointed to the area of the park we were interested in.

After looking at the location he said, "Perfect."

I said, "I'd like to take Hank along with Abbey, Sumo, and Captain Ganbold. We would fly to Khovd City, meet up with Ranger Batbayar, and then drive to Ölgii City in two of the vans. We would resupply there and then head to the park. Mitch will continue her work in Khovd."

He said, "It is fine to take Hank. However I still need Ned here."

"That's OK, I don't need Ned in the field and I may need him to do computer analysis work here. But I don't think he will like being left behind."

Ian said, "I'll keep him busy here."

I went on. "Any word on the mysterious rocket part?"

"We are working on that. You go set up in the park and I will hope to join you before too long. Things seem to be running smoothly here. The Interior Ministry seems to be happy with the company's progress on the resource assessment and the money you allocated to the institutions has made a lot of politicians happy. There are no major equipment problems, everything seems to be running on track."

I said, "Almost too good to be true." Then I left.

We spent three more days working at the base then I sent Abbey and Sumo to Ulaanbaatar. Abbey needed a break and I want them to visit each of our four partner institutions there. They would make sure everything was progressing smoothly.

Hank and I would continue working at the base for a couple more days then join them. Captain Ganbold went to Ulaanbaatar. Then he would fly to Khovd City ahead of us and prepare for our drive to Ölgii City.

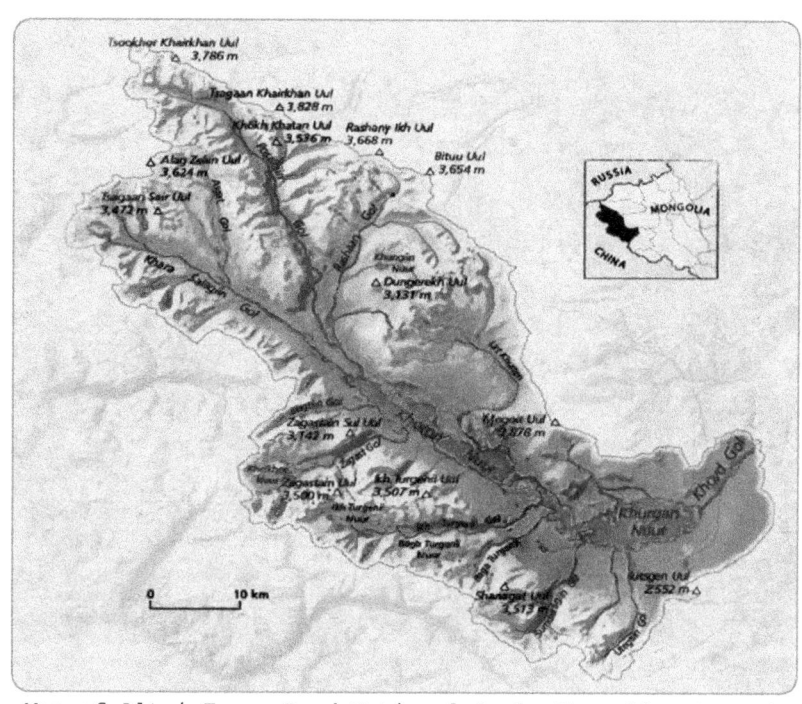

Map of Altai Tavan Bogd National Park, Mongolia. (Note 2)

Chapter 14

Hank and I were driven to Ulaanbaatar airport where we met Abbey and Sumo. The flight was uneventful to Khovd City. Captain Ganbold met our flight and drove us to the hotel. I wanted to spend the rest of today and tomorrow meeting with the people at Khovd State University and the museum.

Then we left for Ölgii City. Ranger Batbayar drove one van and Captain Ganbold drove the other. We headed west on the route that was called A0305 on one of my maps and highway AH4 on another. It was marked on the map as the major road between the cities of Khovd and Ölgii. It isn't much more than a well-worn dirt track. It was about 135 miles but it would be slow going.

The scenery varied from barren plains to picturesque snow-capped mountains. We traveled along the rough dirt road through streams and over rickety wooden bridges. We came across several stuck or broken-down vehicles. Each one was a mini celebration with everyone piling out of the vans. There were hands waving, heads shaking, and voices cursing at the condition of the road.

We used our van's winches to pull out the stuck cars, helped change tires, and Captain Ganbold radioed to Ölgii City for help for the drivers we couldn't help. The 135-mile journey took all day. I looked at my team, they were all happy and smiling. It was an adventure and a nice change for them. We reached Ölgii City, all of us muddy and tired, in the late afternoon.

Wooden bridge on the road from Khovd City to Ölgii City. (Note 2)

Ölgii City is more like a dusty, windblown frontier town than a city. Its mostly concrete buildings straddle both sides of the Khovd River. It is surrounded by gers or as the Kazakhs call them yurts. The population is mostly

Kazakh so the feel is more Muslim-influenced Central Asia than Buddhist Mongolia. What stood out most was the radio tower that is over 1000 feet tall. Everywhere you look you see rugged mountains rising up in the distance. The clothes, customs, and low, mud-brick houses of the Kazakh locals make you feel like you've left Mongolia and entered Kyrgyzstan.

We checked into the Tavan Bogd Hotel. It is located across from the Kazakh Theater in the center of town. It features bathrooms with hot water showers, a restaurant, and WiFi, by far the nicest place in town.

The next morning I took Abbey, Sumo, and Hank to the museum. Captain Ganbold and Ranger Batbayar went to stock up on provisions for our trip to Altai Tavan Bogd National Park.

The museum has three floors. One entire floor is dedicated to various tribes living in Bayan-Ölgii Province including the majority Kazakhs, Uriankhai, Dörvöd, Tuva, and Khoshuud. There is a full-size Kazakh yurt that is much larger and more colorful than the typical Mongolian gers. There are costumes and ancient artifacts from each tribe. The second floor has local history from the Communist era. The ground floor covers local wildlife of the province. Outside is a small display of ancient Turkic Stone Men. The museum was quite dated. After meeting with the officials I decided to leave Sumo and Hank for a few days to flush out the details of the assistance the museum would receive under the grant. Abbey and I would head to the National Park with Captain Ganbold. Ranger Batbayar would bring Sumo and Hank when they finished their work with the museum.

The park is about twice the size of the state of Rhode Island. It has three large freshwater lakes, several waterfalls, and 34 glaciers. The largest, Pontuninii Glacier covers about nine square miles. The Tavan Bogd Mountains are considered sacred to local Kazakhs, Tuvans, and Mongolians. The work Abbey and Hank had done narrowed our primary search area to two sides of Mount Dongoroh. That was a manageable search area. If we didn't find a suitable research site there, well, I wasn't going to worry about that now.

I was anxious to get to the park and visit its full spectrum of archaeological sites with petroglyphs, standing stones, burial mounds, and Kazakh cemeteries. I particularly wanted to see petroglyph complexes that make up the UNESCO World Heritage Site.

The Altai Mountains within the park are thought to have been inhabited for around 12,000 years. The oldest images in the park are from 11,000 to 6,000 BC depicting the hunting of large mammals and ancient culture scenes. Thousands of years of petroglyphs show the transition from hunter-gatherer to pastoralism and later to the current semi-nomadic cultures that developed over the last 3,000 to 4,000 years. Around 4,000 years ago, the use of horses and domestication of animals led to the rise of the Blue Turks. These warriors left upright carved stone statues known as Turkic Stone Men spread over the Altai Mountains.

Later, in 700 BC, a group of horse-riding warrior nomads known as the Scythians started from the Altai Mountains and conquered a region stretching to the

Black Sea. They faded after being defeated by Alexander the Great in modern-day Turkmenistan in 329 BC, but not before leaving many stone burial mounds in the park. These mounds, or khirigsuur, were designed to preserve bodies in frozen ground with horses, weapons, armor, and food for the afterlife.

The next morning we headed out. It is about 110 miles to the park. Given the rough, non-existent roads, high mountain passes, and lack of bridges it would take most of the day.

As I got into the van Abbey handed me a big mug.

She said, "Coffee. I made it in the restaurant kitchen a few minutes ago. I can only take so much tea." She look excited, and happy, even radiant.

"Thanks, it smells great. The real fun begins today."

I got in the back seat, Captain Ganbold put the van in gear, and we were off, towing our camper. It was a very scenic six-hour drive. When we arrived Captain Ganbold drove to the Syrgal park ranger station between Lake Khurgan and Lake Khoton. At this ranger station there is a shop with limited stock and a gas station. We set up camp here.

For the next two days Captain Ganbold drove us to various archaeological sites in the park. The park was the most stunning scenery I'd seen in Mongolia with towering snow-capped mountains, glaciers, deep lush valleys, and large lakes.

At the end of the second day Captain Ganbold said, "Tomorrow we will see the true wonders of the park. Far better that the thousands of years old rock piles you have been visiting. The wildlife of the park is what I find endlessly fascinating.

"While the mammoth, ostriches, and rhinoceros pictured on the older petroglyphs have long since gone extinct at least locally, many rare and endangered species still live inside the park, including the largest wild sheep, fastest falcon, and largest eagle in the wild. The argali sheep, the largest wild sheep in the world, with curled horns of a male weighing over 40 pounds, and the ibex, with large backward curved horns, both live in these mountains. Hunting is banned in the park but poachers are a big problem. Some Chinese believe the horns of the argali sheep and ibex have medicinal properties, much the same as rhino horn. They pay thousands of dollars a pound for their horns.

"There are also gray wolves, brown bears, beech marten, marmots, red deer, and corsac fox.

"I've arranged for horses tomorrow and we will head up into the mountains for a few days."

That night we ate a simple dinner prepared on our cookstove. Someone had been smart enough to stock the camper with boxes of mosquito coils and all forms of bug spray. Without it Abbey and I would have been miserable.

In the morning we saddled up the horses and packed our supplies. Then we closed up the camper and locked the van next to the ranger station. The morning air was cool and crisp. It was another one of those very blue-sky days.

As we rode I noticed Abbey looked totally at ease on horseback.

I said, "Abbey, how much did you ride before arriving in Mongolia?"

"I took introduction to riding for my PE requirements one semester and road a pony at the county fair when I was little."

I smiled and nodded my head.

She went on. "You ride well and you aren't exactly the athletic type."

"Ouch," I said.

"Prof, I know you swim and play a little squash but..." She stopped, sensing she was only making it worse.

"I guess I'm just a natural horseman." I wasn't going to tell her about all the summers I rode with my grandmother.

Two rangers from the local station were with us. The local rangers each led a packhorse.

We passed Kazakh nomads living on the shores of the lake. I thought about how their lives were so much the same as they were a thousand years ago and how different my life was from my grandparents' just a few decades back.

We followed the trail along the north shore of Lake Khoton to a small river that ran between Mount Asgat and Mount Dongoroh. Then we followed the river as it led up the east side of Mount Dongoroh.

After several hours of riding we stopped for a lunch of cold mutton and fried dough washed down with tea.

When we rode on I wondered where the wonderful wildlife was. I saw what I thought were eagles or hawks flying off in the distance but not much else. Perhaps we were making too much noise.

Just then Captain Ganbold stopped his horse and pointed to the north.

He said, "Look, a cinereous or black vulture."

I looked where he was pointing, the bird was huge.

He went on. "It is the largest true bird of prey in the world. The condor may be marginally larger, but I don't consider it a true raptor. The females can be as tall as a man and have a wingspan over ten feet. They feed on carrion of almost any type, from the largest mammals, to fish, and reptiles. Locals have even reported seeing them grab turtles and then drop them from above a hundred feet on the rocks to kill them and break open their shells.

"The park has several species of falcon including the highly prized saker, peregrine, gyrfalcon, and Altai falcons. Another impressive bird, the Eurasian eagle owl with its six-foot wingspan, is a year-round resident along with the snowcock. Many migratory birds pass through each spring and fall in transit between Siberia and Southeast Asia. They include the Eurasian spoonbill, Relict gull, Black Kite hawk, and six of the fifteen species of crane in the world."

Cinereous or black vulture with wingspans as large as ten feet. (Note 3)

Who knew Captain Ganbold was a bird lover? We rode on up the mountainside and he pointed out tracks he said were from ibex and argali sheep. But I still saw no large mammals.

As we rode Abbey checked the GPS coordinates on her phone and inspected the mountainside with binoculars. This was more a sightseeing and orientation trip than a systematic search of the areas we identified from the satellite survey.

As evening approached Captain Ganbold picked out a campsite. It was in a little fold in the mountainside with a stream that formed a pond. The outlet to the pond cascaded over a small waterfall and down the mountain. It was still a crystal-clear day.

The two rangers unpacked and attended to the horses. Captain Ganbold and I began setting up camp. Abbey was putting out mosquito coils. We had one large tent and individual pup tents for sleeping. With the clear sky we decided we didn't need the big tent.

The cookstove was lit and water for tea was put on to boil. No campfires are allowed in the park. It looked like dinner would be a mutton stew with a few veggies in it and rice. A vodka bottle appeared. Abbey pulled out a bottle of Chardonnay. I decided to drink her wine.

I stretched out my legs and said to Abbey, "Are you stiff?"

"My butt is a bit sore but my legs feel great. How about you?"

I said, "I'm stiff now and expect to be stiffer in the morning. But a half hour on the horse in the morning will fix that."

She said, "So tell me, when did you learn to ride? And no BS about being a natural."

As we ate, I told her about my summers with my grandparents. The rangers passed the vodka bottle around between them. They were laughing and enjoying their own stories.

The sun set, the stars were bright, and it seemed the world was at peace. Tired, we crawled into our tents early.

I woke to the hushed but urgent voices of the rangers. I slid out of my tent and put my boots on.

I quietly said to Captain Ganbold, "What is going on?"

"Poachers or at least one poacher," he replied as he pointed down the hillside. "Stay out of sight below the ridge, be quiet, and don't light the stove. We are going to go down and arrest them."

Abbey stuck her head out of her tent. I explained the situation to her. She ducked back into her tent to dress.

The two rangers had their rifles. Captain Ganbold just had his sidearm in a holster. They worked their way around the side of the mountain before heading down.

I moved to the edge of the ridge and peered down. I saw that the rangers were swinging southwest down and around the trail we came up. I squatted behind a boulder and looked over the valley below. I didn't see any sign of the poachers.

Abbey came up beside me. I said, "I don't see anything."

She shook her head and studied the valley below. After a few minutes she pointed to a spot a few hundred yards down the valley overlooking the stream.

At first I didn't see him. He was lying behind a small group of boulders with his rifle resting on one boulder pointed towards the stream. I looked up and down the stream and didn't see anything. The rangers were still circling to come in behind him.

The minutes dragged on, the rangers slowly advanced, then Abbey touched my arm, and pointed down the valley to a bend in the stream. Coming up the path was an absolutely magnificent male ibex. His horns were bigger than the stuffed one I had seen in the museum in Ulaanbaatar.

The beautiful creature was slowly working his way along the stream. I looked at the poacher. He saw the goat. I looked back and forth between them. Then it hit me, when the goat advanced another few dozen yards, the poacher would have a clear shot. I looked for the rangers. They wouldn't be there in time and they couldn't see the goat from where they were. I felt a chill run down my spine. I knew what I would soon witness.

I was beginning to stand up and to shout a warning. Perhaps it would scare off the goat. Then a shot rang out, my heart jumped. The poor magnificent ibex, I thought. But the poacher's gun flew into the air and the poacher summersaulted backwards.

My ears were ringing. I looked over. Abbey had Captain Ganbold's rifle. She calmly ejected the spent cartridge. She chambered another round and bent down, picked up the brass cartridge, and put it in her pocket.

I started to say something stupid like "You shot him." But then I looked to where Abbey was pointing. The rangers were closing in at a run. The poacher was starting to stand up. He looked dazed. But I didn't see any blood.

He didn't try to run. The rifles of the two rangers soon

covered him while Captain Ganbold tied his hands and hobbled his ankles.

Abbey said, "Let's make some tea and get breakfast started. I'm starving and I'm sure they will be hungry when they get back here."

I looked at her for a second and then said, "Nice shot." Not much else I could say. I would feel foolish telling her how relieved I was that I didn't have to see the ibex shot and that she hadn't killed anyone.

Ibex, a species of wild goat. (Note 3)

I started the camp stove. Abbey began to disassemble and clean Captain Ganbold's rifle. The adrenaline was still making my heart race. Not able to think of anything better to say I said, "What type of rifle is that?"

She smiled at me knowingly. "It is a Russian Mosin-Nagant five-shot, bolt-action, internal magazine-fed military rifle. The Imperial Russian Army developed it in about 1890. Something like 37 million were produced. It was used by the Russian Empire and then by the Soviet Union, plus lots of other nations. It is still used in lots of places today because it is plentiful, cheap, rugged, and effective. In 1916 the Russian government contracted with Remington Arms for 1.5 million rifles and with New England Westinghouse for 1.8 million because they couldn't produce enough domestically.

"When the Bolsheviks took over the Russian government, they defaulted on the Imperial Russian contracts with the American arsenals, with the result that New England Westinghouse and Remington were stuck with hundreds of thousands of Mosin-Nagant rifles. The US government bought up the remaining stock, saving Remington and Westinghouse from bankruptcy."

Still not knowing what to say I said, "Like bailing out GM and Chrysler."

It was strange, she had done the shooting but I was the one who was still a bundle of nerves.

She went on. "Many were sent to the British in World War I. The rifles still in the US ended up being primarily used as training firearms for the US Army. Some were used to equip National Guard, SATC, and ROTC units. Between the World Wars the rifles which had been taken over by the US military were sold to private citizens in the United States for $3.00 each."

I knew how she knew all of this. Her grandfather who she adored had been a career Marine gunnery sergeant. The Captain's rifle was now reassembled and probably cleaner than it had been in decades.

I handed her a cup of tea and said, "I thought that was what it was but I wanted to be sure."

Captain Ganbold arrived first, followed by one ranger leading the poacher, who was looking most unhappy. I noticed his face was swollen on one side and starting to bruise. The other ranger was leading the poacher's horse. There were ibex horns tied to the back of the saddle. So he had already killed more than one ibex.

Captain Ganbold looked back and forth between Abbey and me. Abbey was holding his now gleaming rifle comfortably cradled in one arm. That answered his question.

He said, "Quit a shot. I'd say 250 yards."

Abbey didn't answer. She handed him his rifle, reached into her pocket, and gave him the spent shell casing.

He signaled for the ranger leading the horse to come up. Then he pulled the poacher's rifle from a strap on the saddle and gave it to me.

I took it reluctantly. Abbey's shot had struck the front end of the rifle's barrel.

I said, "It's a Russian Mosin-Nagant like yours but not as clean. Would you like some tea?"

Abbey rolled her eyes. I was starting to feel better. I gave the rifle back to Captain Ganbold.

This had effectively ended our trip. We ate, packed up, and headed down to turn the poacher over to other rangers for transport to jail in Ölgii City.

I was over my adrenaline rush but I was keyed up in a way that made it feel great to be alive. The colors seemed brighter and the scenery even more beautiful.

Chapter 15

Ranger Batbayar, Sumo, Hank, and a group of rangers were there to meet us when we rode in. Word of Abbey's shooting the barrel of the poacher's rifle was all abuzz. Captain Ganbold must have mentioned when he radioed in that he had arrested a poacher.

Several of the rangers went straight to the poacher's horse and started passing his rifle around. Some stared at Abbey. Not only was she tall with green eyes and red hair, she was now some kind of Annie Oakley. The two rangers who were with us appeared to be telling the story over and over as the rifle went from hand to hand. Tonight after much vodka the distance of the shot would probably be over a mile.

Captain Ganbold turned the poacher over to two other rangers who loaded him into a van and drove off. No one seemed to think his bruised and swollen face needed medical attention.

We dismounted and a ranger took our horses. Abbey and I walked over to where Sumo and Hank were standing.

I could see Sumo translating the rangers' story for Hank. Hank said, "It sounds like you two had an exciting time. Sorry we missed the fun."

Both were looking at Abbey. They knew she worked out with Major Campbell's security men but this was new.

I said, "Quick thinking on Abbey's part saved a magnificent male ibex."

Sumo said, "Also some amazing shooting according to the rangers' account."

Abbey frowned slightly and said, "It wouldn't have mattered if I'd missed. The bullet would have hit the rocks in front of the poacher and disrupted his shot."

"But you didn't miss," Sumo replied.

"I'm going to take a shower before you men use up all the hot water." With that she walked off.

Hank said, "Your Professor Summers is quite a talented girl."

I smiled and nodded yes. They didn't even know the half of it when it came to Abbey.

I guess the rule on no campfires in the park didn't apply to the rangers when they wanted to celebrate. Earlier we had set up our camp for the night. Sumo took over the cooking. He didn't like the quality or quantity of food prepared by Ranger Batbayar.

People kept arriving at the rangers' fire. More bottles of vodka were passed around along with the poacher's rifle. The voices got louder as the night went on. We watched from our camp area. Abbey sipped some wine and looked content.

I said, "A penny for your thoughts."

She smiled. "It's way better here than at the air base. That place gave me the creeps. The scenery, the people, the whole way of life is so different.

"But I keep wondering, are we doing our job? Does any of what we are doing really mean anything? Does it matter?"

I said, "I don't know. Perhaps time will tell, there must be a cave up there that hasn't been explored with something interesting in it. That would be interesting work even if it were only a marginal addition to archaeology and science.

"One more beer and then I'm going to bed. We might need earplugs to sleep with all the partying."

She handed me her glass. I went for a beer and refilled her glass.

In the morning it was quiet. Several people were passed out by the now burned-out fire. I lit the camp stove and made coffee. The Australian off-road campers Peter Frank got for us are a big step above living in a tent.

I decided today would be a day off. Judging by the quantity of vodka consumed, the rangers had to be hurting. We would get organized today and head back up the mountain tomorrow.

I sat in a camp chair, sipping a mug of coffee. Captain Ganbold walked over.

I said, "You look like you got a better night's sleep than those folks." I pointed to the bodies still passed out around last night's campfire.

He said, "I find I enjoy drinking more when I drink less."

"I know what you mean. But sometimes it is a slippery slope. You need to know where the edge is."

He put on water for his tea and replied, "Knowing where the edge is, is important in many things."

Something in his tone made me feel he meant it as more than an idle reply to my comment, a warning perhaps?

He made his tea and we sat quietly enjoying the still of the early morning.

I jumped a little when I felt a wet nose touch my arm. I looked over to see a dog, a very big dog sniffing me over. His tail was wagging and he seemed to have a grin on his big face.

I said to Captain Ganbold, "He is more the size of a pony than a dog."

"He is a Bankhar, an ancient breed of working dogs used to protect livestock all through the Mongolian steppe. They are big enough to fight off wolves and even leopards. They say some have grown to over 300 pounds. But most are around 160 pounds. I think they call them Tibetan mastiff in the West."

I said, "He looks young but he is a beast already. Does he have a name?"

The dog had finished sniffing his way around us and flopped down next to my chair.

"He is about a year and a half old. The rangers tell me he showed up about a week ago. He was probably separated from his nomad family when they passed through. If he has a name we don't know it."

I rubbed his head and said, "I'll call you Beast, because you are. Who is taking care of him?"

Beast tilted his head so I could rub behind his ear.

"The rangers are feeding him. They figure that his nomadic family may pass this way again. But if he is from a big litter they may not care much if he returns. They only need a few dogs to guard their flocks and more are just an extra cost."

I got up to get more coffee and Beast followed me with his eyes until I returned to my chair. I patted his head again. He was a furry beast.

Mongolian Bankhar, similar breed to Tibetan mastiff.
(Note 2)

Abbey stepped out of her camper and looked over at the campfire site. "Quite a party last night. It doesn't look like your rangers will get much done this morning."

She helped herself to coffee and pulled up a chair on the other side of Captain Ganbold.

"Prof, who is your friend there?"

I was still petting his head. "I'm calling him Beast."

She said, "He could use a bath."

She was right about that.

Next to appear was Sumo. He looked like he had partied hard last night.

He grunted a good morning, went to the kitchen area of my camper, and began pulling out various things to cook.

I said to him, "Is Hank still sleeping off the party?"

"No, he didn't party much. I heard him head out early this morning. He said yesterday he wanted to hike along the lakeshore."

Shortly, Sumo started handing out plates of food. Hash brown style potatoes, eggs, and fried dough. The eggs must have been powdered or from a can. I took a bite and much to my surprise the eggs were good.

I said, "Great eggs, Sumo. Thanks."

Sumo said, "I fired Ranger Batbayar as cook."

Abbey looked at her untouched eggs again and tried a bite. She smiled and took another bigger bite.

She said, "So, Prof, what is the game plan?"

I answered, "If it works for Captain Ganbold we will get organized today and head out first thing tomorrow. Let's plan to check out the top dozen or so locations you and Hank identified."

Looking at the still passed-out bodies, Captain Ganbold said, "I assume my men will be recovered enough to ride by then." He was shaking his head. "How long of a trip are you thinking of?"

"I guess four or five days up the east side of Mount Dongoroh. Then back here to resupply and analyze what we found for few days, then go up the west side of the mountain to check out those places we've identified.

"After that we will decide where to sample and examine in greater detail."

Abbey said, "Good breakfast, Sumo. I'm going for a run, do you want to come?"

He shook his big head. The tea and breakfast might have helped but he still looked hung over.

I put my plate down for Beast to finish the little bit left on it.

Ranger Batbayar wandered over looking worse than Sumo. He got a mug of tea and came over to Abbey and said, "Ms. Summers, I mean Dr. Summers, I got drunk last night." He hesitated and Abbey didn't say anything. "Well, I bet Ranger Yisu you could outshoot him."

He looked over at Captain Ganbold, who didn't say anything but didn't look pleased.

"I bet him a week's wages."

Captain Ganbold said, "Professor Summers, don't feel obligated to do anything. Losing a week's pay may teach him to keep his mouth shut."

Abbey said to Ranger Batbayar, "Give me the details."

He said, "I don't remember agreeing to details. Just you could outshoot him."

"Captain Ganbold, may I borrow your rifle?"

He nodded yes.

Abbey turned to Ranger Batbayar. "He uses the same type rifle. I assume that's what his rifle is. Let's say five shots at targets from 200 yards and average the score of the five shots. Plus I want to meet him in one hour."

"Yes, Professor. I'll go wake him and we will set it up. Thank you."

I smiled. Ranger Batbayar wouldn't mind if Ranger Yisu was still hung over. He had a week's wages riding on the contest.

Captain Ganbold said, "I believe I will act as judge for this contest. Batbayar, you go get Yisu. I'll set up the target and we start in one hour."

I thought it is probably better that Ranger Yisu has the excuse of being hung over when Abbey beats him.

Captain Ganbold went to set things up. The word spread fast. People were moving around. Some kicked the sleeping bodies awake.

I looked at Abbey. She said, "Ranger Batbayar is a good guy, plus this will provide a little excitement for the day. Let's have another cup of coffee and then go see what the Captain has set up for targets."

We lingered for another thirty minutes or so then I said, "I'm going to use the restroom."

Abbey said, "Good idea."

Beast got up and followed me.

Captain Ganbold had his men setting up two wooden crates. They were about five feet high and two feet wide. A circular bull's-eye target was drawn on the upper end of the crate. The men were staking the crates to the ground so they wouldn't tip over when shot.

Captain Ganbold had paced off two hundred yards. A small crowd was forming. Many of the men looked very hung over.

Abbey went over to Captain Ganbold, got his rifle and a box of cartridges. She inspected the rifle. Then she looked at the cartridges individually and selected five.

After inserting the cartridges she seemed to test the balance of the gun and then set it down.

Ranger Yisu came over with a show of bravado followed by several other rangers all talking at once.

Captain Ganbold made a show of looking at his watch and then said in Mongolian and then English, "Five shots each from a standing position. The target has a bull's-eye and four rings. The bull's-eye is 50, the first ring 40 then 30, 20, and 10 points. The highest total points win. You will alternate shots. Professor Summers, you were challenged so you may choose to go first or second. Any questions?"

Abbey said, "I'll go second."

Ranger Yisu steadied his rifle and fired. Captain Ganbold looked through his binoculars and said, "30 points."

Abbey stepped up, slowly took aim, and squeezed off her shot.

Captain Ganbold looked again through his binoculars. "50 points."

Ranger Yisu stared at Abbey for a second and then stepped to the firing line.

Captain Ganbold announced. "10 points."

Abbey looked at me and gave me a wink.

She stepped forward to the firing line, pointed the rifle straight up in the air, and fired.

The crowd gasped. Captain Ganbold looked at her and after a few seconds said, "Zero points."

I looked at Ranger Batbayar. He looked stunned.

Abbey's next three shots were all bull's-eyes and she won.

Ranger Batbayar was jumping up and down and thanking Abbey over and over again.

Abbey thanked Captain Ganbold for the use of his rifle, then told him she would clean it, and return it later today.

We walked back to our campers in silence. Beast followed along with us.

When we got to the campers she said, "Maybe I was rude."

I said, "They wanted a show and you gave it to them. I loved it."

She said, "I'm going to take a run and then I'll help you give your dog a bath."

I looked at Beast and I wasn't sure how that was going to go.

When I came out of my camper the next morning Beast was asleep by the door. He looked at me and slowly got up. I scratched his head. He again turned it so I could get behind his ears. His tail was wagging.

I said, "Beast, let's make some coffee and get this day going."

I refilled his water bowl from yesterday and then starting making the coffee. He took a drink then seemed to study me. After a second he trotted a few dozen feet out of the camp and took a big tinkle on a rock. He watched me the whole time, then trotted back and took another drink.

I smiled and said, "I'm not going to run away on you." Again I scratched his ears.

He looked better after the bath Abbey and I gave him in the stream yesterday. It was all play for Beast and we ended up wetter than the dog. Clean he looked even furrier.

I took a cup of coffee, sat, and said, "I'll enjoy my coffee and when Sumo gets up he can make us some breakfast."

"Who are you talking to?"

I looked around to see Abbey standing there.

"He listens to me more attentively than half the undergrads I teach."

She said, "Better-looking than some too."

She grabbed a cup of coffee and sat in a camp chair next to me. "The sky is so blue again today. Sometimes we would get a few cool, clear, blue-sky days at home like this."

I said, "Feeling homesick?" Abbey had grown up in Plattsburgh, New York, not too far from the Canadian border in the northeast of the state.

"Probably. My parents would always find an excuse to come to Ithaca every month or two. You know for a football game, my birthday, or just to visit. We Skype. They know I'm fine and they seem OK, just so far away.

"In Peru we had such a driving sense of purpose and the team was so energized and motivated."

I said, "At Walter's ranch in Peru it was like living in a five-star resort with a state-of-the-art research facility. Here a hot water shower is rare."

"Prof, I like the outdoors part now that we are away from the air base. But I don't have a sense of mission or purpose."

I said, "Walter is doing something he believes is important. But I know how you feel. I keep telling myself, work the plan, try to enjoy Mongolia, and probably something good will result."

Abbey said, "I guess. Walter plays his super spy game and we wander around the mountains looking for caves that might or might not contain something of archaeological interest."

"Abbey, now you're sounding cynical like me. A bad sign." She took my coffee cup to refill it. "No way I'm that bad."

Within a few minutes things began to get busy. Sumo was cooking. Hank was helping the rangers with the horses. I went to pack my things.

Everyone dove into Sumo's breakfast. Then we folded up the campers and stowed gear in the vans. Again we would leave them at the Syrgal ranger station.

Captain Ganbold took the lead when we rode off. Abbey, Hank, and I were next. Sumo, Ranger Batbayar, and another ranger brought up the rear, each leading a packhorse.

Beast was stride for stride by my horse, with his nose sniffing, and his tail wagging. I looked at Captain Ganbold to see what he thought.

He said, "For thousands of years this is what the Bankhar dog was bred to do. He can keep the wolves away from the horses. Plus it seems he has adopted you."

I said, "Right, wolves."

The Captain laughed. "Wolves can find plenty to eat this time of year. Just the smell of man and dog should keep them away. In the winter when they are hungry they become much more aggressive."

Ten horses, seven people, and a dog heading towards Mount Dongoroh under the Mongolian eternal blue sky. I had a sense of adventure but also I felt at peace. No black mood for me today. I looked around, everyone seemed upbeat.

We rode over two hours before Captain Ganbold stopped us by the small river we were following. He told us to dismount, stretch our legs, and water our horses. With the other two rangers he checked the loads on each pack-horse to make sure there were no sores developing on the horses. Then they checked the hooves of each horse. Sumo poured us tea he made this morning. The whole stop was less than fifteen minutes and then back in the saddle.

Abbey had picked a spot for our first camp beyond where we had camped before when we encountered the poacher. Captain Ganbold wanted to get there in time to set up camp before dark.

We rode on with only two more short stops. The pace wasn't rushed, just a steady full-stride walk for the horses. Probably the pace the ancient Mongol armies used to conquer the world.

When we reached the area Abbey picked, Captain Ganbold was impressed. He looked at her and shook his head slightly. It was a fairly level area close to a stream with grass nearby for the horses. He didn't realize she had access to ultra high-resolution satellite images of the whole park.

The horses were unloaded. Hank, one of the rangers, and I led the horses to the stream for water.

"Hank, what do you think?"

He said, "Mr. Falone is spending a lot of money for us to find some more rock paintings."

I said, "With Walter it always leads to something. Wheels within wheels as Abbey puts it."

"Well, Professor, I'm not complaining, I never even dreamed of visiting Mongolia. The nomadic way of life here is similar to my people's before the white man subjugated us. A fascinating experience and it seems like a paid vacation to me."

"Yes, it seems like a paid vacation to me too."

As we watered and then tethered the horses, Beast went around the edge of the area lifting his leg and marking rocks. I guess he was telling wolves and any other predators that these were his horses and they would have him to deal with.

Everyone was busy setting up camp. We each had a one-man sleeping tent and there was one large tent. If the weather were bad we would all cram in for meals and social time. Fortunately it was another clear summer day.

Sumo had the cookstove going. Ranger Batbayar brought out a bottle of vodka. Fortunately Abbey had them pack a supply of wine. No beer, I guess it was too bulky for the punch it packed. I would make do on wine.

We sat around and toasted the day. My legs were sore from the long ride and I hoped the wine would help. If anyone else was sore they didn't admit it.

The rangers fell into their own conversation. Abbey was unpacking the quadcopter.

Hank said, "So tomorrow we ride around and look for caves?"

Sumo brought over a plate of something to pass around. He said, "This is probably a dumb question but why are archaeologists always looking for caves?"

I wasn't sure who he addressed the question to but I nodded to Abbey.

Abbey said, "No, that's a fair question especially if you're not in our field. Ancient man lived all over in all sorts of shelters. However most of those shelters, along with what was in them, decayed and rotted away after at most a few hundred years. The ancient Egyptians, Incas, Aztecs, and some other peoples built extensively with stone. Some of these structures lasted for thousands of years and we have been able to rediscover them and study what remains.

"If we want to find what remains from very ancient humans or even Neanderthals we are looking at a time as far back as 30,000 to 60,000 years ago. Caves made a good natural shelter for man. The best ones had a small entrance that is easy to protect and even a stream in them. Whenever they could find a good cave they moved into it. The same cave could have been occupied by different peoples over tens of thousands of years.

"Like the stone temples of the ancient Egyptians, caves, under the right conditions, protected the remains of these ancient people. Perhaps there was a rock slide that sealed off part of the cave and protected what it contained, or dirt and bird droppings covered items up. Just as we see in ancient cities where the new was built on top of the old, some cave excavations reveal thousands of years of different peoples living in the same cave."

Sumo said, "So what kind of cave goes back to Neanderthal man?"

"An old one." Abbey smiled. "The maps that show where it is believed Neanderthals lived extend east to these Altai Mountains. Most show the area ending just west of here but no one knows, it is all guesswork based on the fossil remains that have been found. Neanderthal man may have camped right here some 50,000 years ago."

Sumo looked intrigued and puzzled. He took a sip from his mug and said, "Then man came, Neanderthal was too dumb to compete, and man drove him to extinction as he has done with many other species."

Abbey continued, "Until recently that was the most accepted theory. Neanderthals were brutes, bigger and stronger than man but without the social and language skills of man. The first true Neanderthals appeared in Eurasia between 200,000 and 250,000 years ago. But proto-Neanderthal traits are believed to have existed in Eurasia as early as 350,000 to 600,000 years ago.

"Recently, evidence has emerged that Neanderthals painted pictures, adorned themselves with shells and feathers, created ochre and other pigments, buried their dead, and had the capacity for speech. They also seem to have built boats and sailed around the Mediterranean for 50,000 years before modern humans took to the sea. Their brains were bigger and their eyesight was better than ours. They were better able to tolerate cold temperatures and were far stronger than modern man. So why about 42,000 years ago, did they enter a steep decline and eventually go extinct, along with many of the large animals they had shared Eurasia with for some 200,000 years?"

The rangers were enjoying their vodka and their own stories. Sumo handed us more plates of food that we passed around.

I said as I stroked Beast's head, "The whites of their eyes."

Hank and Sumo looked at me. Abbey laughed and said, "Perhaps, Prof is referring to a theory anthropologist

Pat Shipman put forth in her new book *The Invaders: How Humans and Their Dogs Drove Neanderthals to Extinction.* She argues that dogs may have been pivotal in humans outlasting Neanderthals.

"Up until the last few years, paleoanthropologists mostly assumed that by 40,000 years ago Neanderthals and modern humans were coexisting in parts of Eurasia and continued to do so until as late as 24,000 years ago. This is a remarkably long period for such similar predators to coexist.

"The earlier theories had two main points. The first point was that the greater intelligence and resourcefulness of modern humans simply outsmarted Neanderthals in the competition for habitat and food. The second was the Campanian Ignimbrite, a massive volcano eruption that occurred between 40,000 and 39,000 BC, near modern-day Naples, and brought on a period of volcanic winter, which forced the Neanderthals into tiny isolated refuges on the Iberian Peninsula, where ultimately they died out.

"Another explanation began to emerge early in 2013, when a newly refined radiocarbon-dating technique reexamined the evidence at eleven Neanderthal sites on the Iberian Peninsula. The new dating technique pushed the date back from about 24,000 years ago to 41,000, quite possibly before the Campanian Ignimbrite and just a few thousand years after the arrival of modern human beings. These sites, incorrectly dated to roughly 24,000 years ago, were the sole basis for the theory that Neanderthals had coexisted in Europe for millennia with human beings. This made it seem more likely that people, not climate change, triggered the demise of the Neanderthals.

"If Neanderthals were smart, plus bigger and stronger than man, with better eyesight, how did we drive them to extinction in just a few thousand years? The answer Shipman suggests in her book would have been laughable until recently. Her theory is that dogs were our secret weapons. The domestication of wolves and their breeding into dogs was generally thought to have been 18,000 to 14,000 years ago, long after the demise of the Neanderthals.

"However in 2009 researchers developed a technique for distinguishing the craniums of wolves and dogs, which they then used to date an early dog skull to roughly when humans entered Eurasia. Other similar early dog craniums have since been identified, but only at human, not Neanderthal, sites.

"Shipman doesn't claim the alliance of humans and dogs alone led to the extinction of the Neanderthals. Other factors such as climate change and infectious diseases brought by humans from Africa were likely at work.

"She puts forth a fascinating range of evidence, genetic, archaeological, and anthropological, that provides support for the theory that the unprecedented alliance of humans with another top predator, dog, may have been the final stress that pushed Neanderthals and many other species down the slippery slope toward extinction."

Sumo poured more vodka and lime soda into his mug and said, "Professor, you said, 'The whites of their eyes.' I've never seen dog's eyes like that."

"You're right," I said. "But people do. Shipman comes up with some imaginative ideas in her couple hundred-page book.

"Modern humans are the only extant primates whose irises are surrounded by white sclera, the whites of our eyes. We're also the only primates to have eyelids that expose much of our sclera. What evolutionary advantage could this have possibly given us? Her theory is, the white sclera and open eyelids make the direction of a person's gaze highly visible from a distance. Having white sclera allowed us to communicate subtly at a distance among ourselves and with our dogs, a biological advantage that may have made all the difference as we competed for prey with Neanderthals."

Hank said, "I saw a PBS series that had a whole different take on modern humans and Neanderthals. If I remember correctly, DNA sequencing of Neanderthals by the Max Planck Institute in Germany was compared to modern human DNA. They found about five percent Neanderthal DNA in today's Eurasian peoples' DNA. The percentage was higher in Europe and lower in Asia. There was no Neanderthal DNA found in modern man in Africa. So they made the case for interbreeding which until now experts thought was impossible."

I said, "That is a pretty good summary of what paleoanthropologists and others in the field are suggesting. Not that many experts agree with Shipman's dog theory at this point."

Hank said, "The part of that program that I thought was total BS was the way they implied that the interbreeding took place. They made it sound like man came out of Africa into Neanderthal territory, met, traded, and interbred. All happy, everybody gets along. Over time the much less numerous Neanderthals were just absorbed into the population of modern man and no longer existed as a separate species.

"I think it was more like what happened to the Native American peoples when the Europeans came to the Americas. They brought smallpox and other infectious diseases that the Native Americans had little or no resistance to. Weakened by disease and outnumbered, the Neanderthals lost battles with modern man from Africa. The Neanderthal men and boys were killed, the girls and women were taken, and the old were left to starve. The interbreeding came from the Neanderthal women and girls taken as slaves.

"Given what we see throughout history that different tribes and cultures can't get along and massacre each other, the idea of peaceful interbreeding between modern man and Neanderthal seems like total BS."

Abbey said, "I watched that program *First People* as well. I agree that the scenes of modern man and Neanderthal meeting were a little far-fetched."

Sumo, who had now consumed several mugs of his vodka-lime soda mix, spoke up. "I don't see why anyone would be surprised that man drove Neanderthal extinct. Look at all the other species man has driven extinct. The mammoths, woolly rhinos, and ostriches depicted in the cave painting, they are extinct. Now here in the park the ibex, argali sheep, and snow leopard are endangered species. All over the world species from tigers to sea turtles to toads are dying out. Man is the ultimate killing machine. Not only other species but millions and millions of other men. The Neanderthal never stood a chance."

Sumo stood. "I'll make dinner and you didn't even mention Denisovan man who was found in these Altai Mountains not far from here over the border in Russia. Maybe we'll find Denisovans."

Abbey said, "What were those half dozen plates we just ate?"

He said, "Starters to go with our drinks. Tell me about Denisovan man."

Abbey refilled her wine glass and handed me the bottle.

"OK, in the remote Denisova Cave in Siberia scientists found a finger bone fragment of a juvenile female who lived about 41,000 years ago. The Denisova Cave is known to have been inhabited by both Neanderthals and modern humans. Analysis of the mitochondrial DNA of the finger bone showed it to be genetically distinct from that of Neanderthals and modern humans. Another extinct species of human had been discovered.

"Subsequent study of the DNA from this specimen suggests that this group shares a common origin with Neanderthals, and that they ranged from Siberia to Southeast Asia. It also suggests that they lived among and interbred with the ancestors of some present-day modern humans. Melanesians and Aboriginal Australians have three to five percent of their DNA from Denisovans.

"Now here it gets really interesting. A detailed comparison of the Denisovan, Neanderthal, and human genomes has revealed evidence for a complex web of interbreeding among the lineages. There was also evidence of a contribution to the nuclear genome from an ancient human lineage yet to be identified. The Denisova Cave is the one place where we are sure all three human forms have lived at one time or another."

Hank said, "So are we looking for a cave that Neanderthals, Denisovans, or modern humans lived in? Not that I'm an expert on this but our work plan doesn't seem to have the focus or rigor of other major grants I've read about. Ride into this section of mountains, find a cave, and examine it. When you boil it down that is what this part of our work plan says. I didn't even see any reason why this mountain area was selected."

Hank was right, of course it didn't make any sense. He has a strong science background and knows research projects usually have much greater structure and focus than what he was seeing.

Abbey jumped in. "There are two things. One is that much of what Walter is doing with this grant is trying to progress Mongolian science and education in a general way. That is the work we are doing with the universities and museums. They are getting funding, equipment, and lots of raw data to work with. This should benefit them for years to come.

"The second area that I'm particularly interested in is using the newly refined radiocarbon-dating techniques and DNA sequencing to analyze what we do find. I outlined the technical advances in both these areas in the appendix to my part of the presentation to the Interior Minister.

"We could just analyze the existing areas that have been researched, but why not find something new? Plus the level of detail and sophistication of the archaeological research that has been done to date in Mongolia does not compare to that done in say, Europe or the Middle East. We have the knowhow and budget to do it. Walter has given us a unique opportunity. A big part of his motivation may have been to win the government contract but we should take full advantage of the opportunity."

Wow. Quick thinking, Abbey, and all true more or less.

Hank seemed satisfied. Sumo handed everyone a plate with some kind of stew over rice.

The conversation turned to general chat. Beast much to my surprise sat quietly by as we ate. Once we were done Sumo put together a big bowl of scraps for him.

I stood to refill his water bowl. My legs and butt were sore. I tried not to show it.

That night Beast slept in front of my pup tent. When one of the horses whinnied he got up and made a circuit around the horses. Satisfied that everything was all right he flopped back down by my tent.

I was fascinated by the way the horses all got along with Beast. I wasn't sure if they knew him individually from the time he was at the ranger station. Probably not, it was more likely the horses were all brought up with dogs like Beast who were bred to guard livestock.

After a quick breakfast in the morning we saddled the horses. The two rangers were going to stay in camp with the packhorses. We would return to this campsite for another night.

Captain Ganbold and Abbey took the lead. They had mapped out the day's route. Hank and I followed with Sumo bringing up the rear.

We rode about an hour to the first outcropping to be explored and dismounted. Abbey took out the quadcopter and programed in a route that ended back here where it started. I was using my binoculars to study the hillside.

This is not the way archaeologists normally do things. Usually some hiker or caver finds something unusual and then the scientists come in to examine it.

Captain Ganbold was asking Abbey about the quadcopter, Sumo held the horses, and Hank looked mildly amused.

We didn't have cell or internet service here so there was no real-time video. The quadcopter could be programmed to fly a course or be radio controlled. It would video during its flight and we would watch the video on an iPad when it landed.

The flight was about twenty minutes. We huddled around Abbey's iPad to watch the video. Lots of rocks and shadows, were the shadows the mouth of a cave? You couldn't really tell.

I had Abbey stop the video at one of the large shadows, then calculate where it was in its flight when that was taken. Next I looked up to the spot with my binoculars, nothing. This didn't seem to be working the way we hoped. We watched the rest of the video.

I looked at Abbey. She said, "We could hike up and take a look."

That idea didn't appeal to me.

Hank was shaking his head. He said in an accent that mimicked the Indians in the old Western movies, "White Man with all his tools not too bright."

"I'm open to suggestions," I said.

He said, "What lives in caves? Bats and birds, so look for birds flying in and out of a place. Then wait until dusk and see where the bats fly out of."

I said, "I'll stay here and look for birds. Abbey, you can go climb around if you like. But if we wait until dusk to try and see bats we'll never get back to camp before dark.

"Let's call this a level-one survey or reconnaissance mission." I knew this was a copout but... "We will ride the planned route, look for birds, and use our binoculars. When we stop to rest the horses we can video with the quadcopter and watch it back at camp. I like the idea of looking for bats but we aren't prepared to stay overnight or travel back in the dark."

Abbey seemed as though she was going to disagree but then said, "OK, other places we identified are more promising than here anyway."

We rode and found a few overhangs that looked promising but when we hiked up they weren't really caves. They ended just a few feet in. We ate lunch and decided to head back to camp.

That night Abbey and Captain Ganbold worked out the location for our next camp. We would go farther up the east side of the mountain closer to the areas we wanted to examine. From our new camp we would form two groups. Abbey would go with Sumo and Ranger Batbayar. I would go with Hank and Captain Ganbold. The other ranger would stay at the base camp. In theory we should cover be able to twice as much territory.

We spent two more days in the mountains. We found several small caves. Hank found a couple by going out at dusk with Ranger Batbayar and spotting bats leaving the caves.

We measured and photographed the caves. We took duplicate core samples. One set would be sent to Houston for analysis and the other given to the Mongolian Natural History Museum in Ulaanbaatar. We didn't see anything special, no cave paintings, no woolly mammoth tusks, and no Neanderthal skulls waiting for us to pick them up.

I was sore, dirty, and tired after four days of riding and climbing around the mountains. I wanted to get back to base camp, take a shower, and sleep in the relative comfort of the camper trailer.

I said, "Captain, let's head back to the base camp."

I looked around. Everyone looked pleased. It seemed everyone was ready to go back but no one wanted to admit it or seem weak.

I said, "What do you think, Abbey?"

"It's the best decision you've made in days, Prof."

Chapter 16

After a hot shower, big meal, and a good night's sleep in my camper I was up early, stiff but ready to go back to work. I thought again about my grandmother teaching me to ride all those years ago. Who knew that in Mongolia, decades later, how much help it would turn out to be?

Beast sat next to my camp chair as I enjoyed a mug of coffee and listed what I wanted to get done today.

Abbey flopped into a chair next to me. She said, "I see the mad scientist is at work this morning."

"Yes, thank you, I did have a good night's sleep. How about you?" I said.

She smiled. "After those nights on the ground in a tent the camper feels like the Ritz. Have you heard from Walter or Major Campbell?"

"No. I'll email Ian later and let him know the samples we took are coming. I'd like to have someone meet the flight in Ulaanbaatar to forward one set to Houston and get the other over to the museum.

"Would you email the test protocols you want run to Houston? What is the internet connection like?"

"It's slow but it works well enough over by the ranger station. I'll send the test info out this morning. What else?"

I said, "I'm going to send Sumo with one of the rangers to take the samples to the Ölgii City airport. They can get additional supplies we need, stay overnight, and come back tomorrow. Do you want to go along?"

She shook her head no. "Just tell Sumo to get a case of decent white wine."

I made a note and said, "One case of China Great Wall Wine Co., Ltd., white wine is on the list. They produce over 50,000 tons of wine a year and are the biggest wine producer in China."

"You know this how?"

"It was in one of the guidebooks. You never know when facts like this will come in handy."

She took my mug and went to refill it.

I took the now full mug from her and said, "Let's go pack the samples. Sumo will probably want to get on the road."

Sumo wanted to get going but not before he made a big breakfast. Hank decided he would go too. Once they were off, I took my laptop over to the ranger station and sat on a bench outside. I had my email set on the "Out of Office" automatic response. Now that I wasn't getting all the University announcements and related BS, the number of emails I had to deal with dropped way off.

Abbey joined me on the bench. We worked away in silence.

I got to an email from Walter. I read it and said, "It looks like we are going to get company."

Abbey stopped typing and looked up.

"Walter says his dear friend, distinguished professor, and lover of archaeology will be joining us in about ten days. Major Campbell will be accompanying him and will confirm the exact timing. He is Professor Uri Cohen. I don't recognize the name, not that I know everybody in our field."

Abbey was typing away and then said, "Professor Cohen is distinguished all right, just not in archaeology. He has a BS in aerospace engineering from Kingston University in Kingston upon Thames just southwest of London and a PhD also in aerospace engineering from MIT. He is a fellow at the Norman and Helen Asher Space Research Institute at Technion – Israel Institute of Technology in Haifa and a consultant to Israel Aerospace Industries. He is said to be a leading expert in electric propulsion systems for small satellites that are the most efficient and effective rocket propulsion engines for spacecraft and satellites. He is pioneering the next generation of small thrusters."

"It doesn't mention his love of archaeology?" I said.

"Nope. He probably keeps a low profile in our field. I wonder if he can ride a horse."

I said, "Wheels within wheels. Let's watch the quad-copter videos and then plan where we go next. Unless we see something very promising on the video, I say we start exploring this west side of Mount Dongoroh. We can move our base camp to the north end of Lake Khoton so we are closer to the streams running up the west side of the mountain. Captain Ganbold says there is a small military base there. He will arrange for us to camp near it and they will watch our vans and campers when we head up the mountains."

Nothing striking was on the video so we planned to move the base camp to the other end of Lake Khoton. We spent most of the rest of the day planning our routes to explore the west side of Mount Dongoroh.

That night we made dinner from some canned goods in our supplies. Not very exciting but we washed it down with one of Abbey's last bottles of wine. The next day I decided to hike along the lake. Beast followed me as I wandered along the lakeshore. I was happy not to be on horseback for a couple of days.

As I walked I felt mildly depressed. I realized I was just going through the motions. I wasn't engaged and engrossed in my work like I usually was when I had a chance to do fieldwork. It was more about Walter's government contract and Israeli spying than archaeology. I was a pawn in the Cornell University machine. Why should it bother me to be a pawn in Walter's corporate machine? Walter paid me better and treated me with greater respect than Cornell did.

I walked for several hours with Beast happily running back and forth but always keeping an eye on me. I returned to our base camp about 4:00PM. Sumo and the others were back.

Sumo reached into an ice chest and handed me a beer. He said, "Ice-cold beer while the ice lasts. One of Mongolia's finest."

I thanked him and looked at the label, Jalam Khar Gold pale lager. I took a big swig and said, "Tastes great. I'm glad you're back. My cooking stinks. Give me a rundown on your trip."

He did and it sounded like everything went smoothly.

In the morning we packed up the campers and hitched them to the vans. I got in the back of one of the vans and Beast looked at me. There was no room in the van for him. I said I'd be back. It wasn't far but given the rutty track we would go slowly. The military base was small and there was no gas station or supply shop. Not that the shop at the Syrgal ranger station had much in it, just vodka, water, and a few other things. Captain Ganbold was warmly received. I'd read that the military personnel at the base were not particularly friendly to tourists, however that wasn't the case with us. Several soldiers came out to meet Sumo. They also wanted to see Abbey. The stories of her shooting expertise had quickly spread up the lake.

We picked a spot a few hundred yards away and began setting up camp. Abbey put out the mosquito coils. I saw Sumo take fishing gear from one of the vans. He and Hank headed towards the lake. We set up tents and the campers. It was now early August and the weather was still clear, cool at night but into the seventies most days.

I set up camp chairs around the cooking stove. No email or cellphones here. We did have secure satellite phones issued to us by Major Campbell but I didn't think I'd be getting any cold callers selling junk on it. It was midafternoon. I dug out a book and got a beer from the cooler. Happy hour would start early today.

It was beautiful here. I looked over at the river flowing from the mountain passes south of Tavan Bogd Mountains into Lake Khoton. In the distance were the snow-covered peaks. I was half reading and half enjoying the scenery when I noticed horsemen coming up the track in the distance. As they came closer I saw it was two men each leading a string of horses.

Once they were closer I stood for a better look. Two rangers were leading our horses from the Syrgal ranger station and running alongside the horses was Beast. I walked out to greet them. Well, mostly to greet Beast. He spotted me but held his position beside the horse until the rangers stopped and dismounted. It was as if he was showing me he knew not to leave his job until the horses safely arrived. Once he felt he safely delivered the horses he came bounding over to me. Not just his tail, but his whole rear end was wagging, and he almost knocked me over with his enthusiastic greeting. I realized I was just as happy to see him. I got him a bowl of water and another beer for me. He drank and then sat by my chair.

Abbey joined me with a glass of wine. "I see your friend caught up with you."

"He's a good boy," I said. I sounded a little sappy. "How is that wine Sumo got you?" I was trying to change the subject.

She looked at Beast and me. "Beast thinks you're a good boy too. Sumo's wine is excellent, not only can he cook but he knows wine."

Hank and Sumo came walking into camp. Hank was carrying the fishing gear and Sumo had one fish. But it was over three feet long and must have been six inches across. By the way he held it, it looked heavy.

Abbey said, "A baby whale?"

Sumo replied, "It's a taimen or River Wolf. It is also known as Siberian salmon. Very good eating."

He held it up. I looked more closely. It was olive green on the head, blending to reddish brown in the tail with fins that were dark red. It looked a bit like the salmon of northern New York.

He went on. "They can be over four feet long and weigh more than sixty-five pounds. There are stories of a large taimen crawling onto land, eating livestock and people. There is even an old legend of a giant taimen trapped in river ice. Starving herders were able to survive the winter by hacking off pieces of its flesh. In the spring, the ice melted and the giant taimen climbed onto the land, tracked down the herders, and ate them all.

"The Chinese claim there are giant taimens that weigh over four tons. This one is about thirty pounds and will provide us with an excellent dinner."

Between the taimen and the fresh supplies Sumo brought from Ölgii City it was an excellent meal. We made a mini celebration of it. Everyone knew we wouldn't eat like this once we started up the mountain. Sumo even made a jumbo dinner bowl for Beast out of all the parts of the fish we wouldn't eat.

The next morning I was up early. Beast again slept at the door to my camper. I made and enjoyed coffee knowing I would get only tea during our ride up the mountain.

As Sumo made breakfast we packed. The camper and

vans were moved next to the military barracks. Then we loaded the packhorses and headed out.

From the end of the lake we followed the river for just over a mile to where it meets the Rashaan River that branches to the northwest. We rode to the point where a small river came in running steeply down the west side of Mount Dongoroh. We rode up the south side looking for caves until we were close to the snow line and then worked our way down the north side of the stream.

That was pretty much what we did for the next four days. We rode north along the Rashaan River. When a minor river or stream flowed into the Rashaan River we would follow up the mountainside looking for caves. There were several petroglyphs and burial mounds, all of which had been discovered long before we were there. We found a few unremarkable caves. They were photographed, samples were taken, and again we would have analysis done.

Before dawn on the fifth day Captain Ganbold was getting everyone up. I opened the flap to my pup tent. Lying on the ground Beast looked in at me. He didn't want to get up yet either. It would be a long ride back to base camp and Captain Ganbold wanted us safely there before dark.

After long hours of riding we arrived back at the head of Lake Khoton. Without all the zigzagging up and down each tributary of the river we weren't really that far away.

I was tired, and sore. I also had a nagging feeling we really hadn't accomplished much.

The rangers took the horses and we moved the vans and campers back to our camping spot. First I found the cooler. Having not been opened the beer was still cold.

After a big sip of my beer I opened a bottle of wine and poured a glass for Abbey.

I handed her the glass. She said, "Thanks. You're walking bowlegged like a cowboy."

"I feel 'rode hard and put away wet' as they say. I need Advil. Do you want some?"

"No. I'll let the wine do its work."

We opened up the campers. I set up the cookstove and the camp chairs. Abbey and I each had a camper, Sumo and Hank used a van each, and the rangers used their tents.

I took another beer and sat in a camp chair. Everyone seemed to hold up better on the long rides than I did. They were all younger, Sumo had been a professional athlete, Hank looked fit enough, and Abbey was in serious shape. At least I'd been successful in not holding the others up and I tried not to complain.

The Advil and beer were beginning to work. Abbey came back over and sat. She had the bottle of wine with her.

She said, "Candy is dandy but liquor is quicker. Cheers." She tapped her glass to my beer can. "What do we do next?"

I said, "We need to send these samples back for analysis. We can spend a couple of days here while someone takes them Ölgii City. How is that for an elaborate plan?"

She reached for the wine bottle. "It is beautiful here."

"Yes, Abbey, it is that."

She said, "Do you think we will find anything important? Is there anything out there?"

I said, "That is the great thing about archaeology, we have only found a small fraction of what is out there to be discovered. The question is, will we find anything and are we even going about it in a rational way?"

She said, "It is so different than Peru. The team was so motivated. They all wanted to repay Walter for believing in them and the opportunities he gave them. We had focus. You had a great plan."

"Abbey, I was winging it. I made up the plan as we went along. Sometimes only minutes before I laid out the plan in our meetings."

She said, "Well, your plan was great and you worked your ass off. We all did and it paid off big time."

I said as I hobbled to get another beer, "My ass feels pretty hard worked right now."

Abbey said, "I'd like to take the samples to Ölgii City. I could use a night in a hotel with hot showers."

"Sure. See who wants to go with you. I'll stay here. I need some quiet time to think."

Sumo arrived with a pot of something he began cooking on the stove. I wondered if Walter knew of his culinary skills when he added him to our team. I said, "Do you want to take Abbey and the samples into Ölgii City tomorrow?"

"No. Captain Ganbold wants to go. I'll make a list of supplies and give it to him."

I said, "OK, maybe you can take me fishing." I needed something different to do to refresh my mind. Fishing was all I could think of to do around here that didn't require getting on a horse.

The next morning we got Abbey and Captain Ganbold off with the samples. Hank decided to go with them. After they left I sat drinking coffee and reading in the cool morning air. I was frustrated and mildly depressed. I didn't feel

I was doing a good job. Plus my body was stiff from the five days on horseback. I tried not to think about it and to enjoy my coffee and the sunny morning.

Sumo made himself a second breakfast. I politely declined and refilled my coffee cup.

When Sumo had finished most of his plate of food I said, "Tell me about fishing today. Are we going to catch another taimen?"

"No. Today we fish for lenok trout. The lenok trout is a smaller fish than the taimen. It lives in cold running water and it can weigh over 30 pounds. It is the favorite catch of locals and is also very good eating. In addition to taimen and lenok trout the lakes and rivers in the park are full of osman, grayling, and pike. But tonight I feel like trout.

"They are harder to catch this time of the summer. The best time is ice fishing in the winter. I've caught over a hundred lenok trout in one day during the winter."

Ice fishing in the lakes around Ithaca seemed way too cold for me. I couldn't imagine doing it here in the brutal Mongolian winter.

After he finished eating he gathered the fishing gear and we headed out. Beast followed along sniffing and marking as he went. We walked about a mile up the Tsagaan Gol or White River that comes down from the Tavan Bogd peaks into the lake. Again I was struck by how light on his feet Sumo was. His six foot three, over three hundred pound body seemed to glide along the rocky path.

He stopped and examined the flowing river water. "OK. We will find fish here," he said.

I'm not really much of a fisherman so I just followed

Sumo's lead. We cast and reeled in and then did it again and again. Nothing happened. It was a nice day and it was fun, sort of like throwing pebbles in a pond.

After almost an hour I said, "Shall we try another spot?"

Sumo shook his head. So I cast again and bang, something struck my line. The pole bent and I was so surprised I almost dropped it.

Sumo smiled and said, "Reel it in slowly."

After the fight the fish put up I was a bit disappointed to see it was only a fraction of the size of the taimen Sumo caught the other day.

As I reeled it close to the shore Sumo slipped the net around it. He said, "A lenok trout about eight or ten pounds. It will make a perfect dinner."

He then began packing up the gear. I said, "No more fishing? Just one fish?"

"There are only two of us for dinner tonight, and Beast of course. This is plenty of fish for me to make a most excellent dinner. If you want fish for dinner tomorrow we can fish again. They will be here waiting for you to catch them."

It seemed a lot of time and effort for just one fish and it wasn't even a monster like the taimen. I guess I saw the logic. Why fish for more than you needed? That would be a waste.

So we headed back. Halfway down the river Ranger Batbayar met us. He admired my fish briefly and the spoke to Sumo in Mongolian. He pointed off to where there were several yurts belonging to Kazakh nomads.

Sumo said to me that there was someone Ranger Batbayar thinks we should talk to over there.

As we approached everyone came out to greet us. Sumo was well known as one of the best wrestlers to come from this province. Sumo and Ranger Batbayar spoke to the man who appeared to be the elder of this extended family.

He then called over a boy perhaps twelve years old. The boy and Sumo entered into an animated discussion with much hand waving to indicate direction, size, and who knows what else. At one point the boy made sounds of a goat.

Sumo turned to me. "The boy said that last summer when they were pasturing up the Rashaan River one of the goats ran off. He tracked it to a hillside where he could hear it but couldn't see it. He climbed up and found it in front of a cave.

"He claims the cave is bigger than a yurt and I could walk in the entrance without ducking my head. He went in a little ways and saw paintings on the rocks like the ones tourists come to see. He said he was too scared to go farther in and he had to get the goat back to his family."

I said, "Can he tell us how to find it?"

"I don't think telling us will work. But it sounds to me like it is farther up the Rashaan River than we went. I'd like to try to hire him and his father to guide us there."

I said, "Great. The day after tomorrow would be good by me if they are willing."

Sumo spoke to the family elder. A price was agreed upon and the time was set. Maybe this was the break we needed. If it was beyond where we looked before we needed to go there anyway. This and my fish had brightened my day. I thanked Ranger Batbayar and headed back to camp with a new bounce in my step.

That night Sumo prepared my fish. I always thought it was an old wives' tale that fish you caught yourself tasted better but this fish was good.

I said, "Are the other fish in the lake and river as good as these? Maybe we should catch something for everyone's dinner tomorrow night." Said as if I was a great angler now that I caught one fish.

He said, "The osman is a carp that is only found in this region of the world. The Arctic graylings are common to Siberia, while pike are found all over East Asia. They are OK but not great. The taimen and lenok trout are better.

"We can fish tomorrow and see what we catch."

That seemed like a good idea to me. I went to bed feeling better about things.

The next day we fished. Sumo again caught a taimen. This one was even bigger than the other one. I didn't even get a nibble on my line. I decided fishing wasn't that great after all.

Sumo was cleaning and preparing the fish. I was helping by bringing him a fresh beer when he needed it. The van rolled in and I asked what people wanted to drink. Captain Ganbold smiled and raised a bottle of vodka from the seat next to him. Hank said the beer looked good and I knew what Abbey would like.

After handing Hank a beer and Abbey her wine I helped unload the van. Captain Ganbold and Ranger

Batbayar took several boxes of supplies and headed to the barracks.

Sumo said to Abbey, "Professor caught a most excellent lenok trout yesterday. We had it for dinner last night."

Abbey looked at me and said, "He is a man of many talents."

I decided it was best to change the subject. "Was there any word on the first batch of samples we sent to Houston?"

She said, "The testing isn't complete but they said that we shouldn't get our hopes up."

"That's what I would have guessed." Then I asked Sumo to tell Abbey about our meeting with the Kazakh boy.

When he was finished I said, "We leave in the morning."

She raised her hand with her fingers crossed and got out her iPad. She looked to see if we had identified anything in that area. It was hard to tell from the vague description the boy gave but there were several sites beyond where we went before.

Once again Sumo made an excellent meal. I went to bed satisfied and looking forward to the next day.

The next morning we rode out to the Kazakh family's yurt. The boy and his father had their horses all saddled and were waiting for us. We retraced the track up the Rashaan River we had ridden down three days ago. We rode all day to about where we ended our first trip and Captain Ganbold pick a spot to camp. The best we could tell we were still a two- or three-hour ride from the cave's location.

The next morning we rode about a mile upstream to where a small river flowed down the west side of Mount

Dongoroh into the Rashaan River. The small tributary river was in a valley that ran up the mountainside. Lush grass grew on each side of it and extended up the sides of the valley.

We followed the small river for several miles until we reached a fork. Each side of the fork was not much more than a stream. The Kazakh boy was gesturing, pointing and I had no idea what he was saying.

I looked to Sumo. He said, "The boy says we take the northern fork and we are close. Captain Ganbold decided we should take a break to water and rest the horses. I was happy to stretch my legs."

Abbey came up beside us. "Soon we'll find out if it was worth getting our hopes up."

She pulled out her iPad. "I didn't mark anyplace on this fork of the stream as likely to have sizable caves."

I said, "Keep your fingers crossed."

We rode on up the northern fork of the stream. After a while the father pointed to a spot up the valley wall. The Kazakh boy looked closely and then shook his head no. We rode on. After another hour the boy stopped his horse and looked around. He studied the streambed then looked back and forth on each side of the valley. He was shaking his head and talking to his father.

"What is he saying?" I asked Sumo.

"He said it's not up here. We have gone too far. We need to go back. His father isn't sure."

The boy and his father continued to talk. The boy pointed out features that to me looked just like the rest of the terrain. Finally the father said we had gone too far and must go back but we are close.

All their attention seemed to be focused on the north side valley wall. I took out my binoculars and looked all along that side of the valley. I didn't spot anything.

We turned and slowly rode back. The boy and his father seemed to be studying the streambed and not even looking up at the mountainside. After thirty minutes of slowly walking downstream the boy stopped and got off his horse. He studied the streambed some more then looked up and pointed to a spot on the valley's side.

I turned my binoculars to where he was pointing. I saw nothing that indicated a cave.

Sumo said, "He claims the cave is right up there. He is sure because he was by these rocks in the stream when he heard the goat bleating."

Abbey jumped off her horse, handing me the reins. "Let's go take a look," she said to Sumo.

He said something to the boy and the three of them began to climb up the slope. They were clearly visible climbing up the slope. Then the boy disappeared. Next Abbey disappeared followed by Sumo. I trained my binoculars on the spot. It looked like a continuous rock area of the mountainside.

After ten minutes Abbey reappeared and waved to us to come up. Hank and I got off our horses. The father and rangers weren't interested in climbing.

When we reached the spot where they had disappeared from sight I understood why I couldn't see it from the valley floor. The rock on the down slope side continued up like a wall. There was an overhanging ledge above the cave. The two didn't meet and there were twenty or thirty feet between them. But from below looking up it appeared as just continuous mountainside.

I stepped into the relatively level spot between rock wall and cave mouth. The Kazakh boy was all smiles. Sumo was patting him on the back.

The opening to the cave was indeed tall enough for Sumo to walk in without ducking. It was perhaps nine feet tall and fifteen feet wide. Abbey was standing in the mouth of the cave with a flashlight in hand.

"Let's go, Prof."

I took out my flashlight. We stepped a few feet into the cave and let our eyes adjust. We knew that often the first people to enter a newly discovered archaeological site inadvertently contaminated it and damaged important items.

We stood and pointed our flashlights around the cave walls. Abbey stopped her light on one spot. Through the dust and dirt on the cave wall you could see the outline drawing of a deer or ibex. The boy had been right about the cave containing petroglyphs.

I directed my light to the back of the cave. It appeared to be over a hundred feet in length. There was a chamber that went off to the right about two-thirds of the way in.

We backed out of the cave. I said, "Hank, would you go get the camera equipment? Sumo, let's get the exact GPS coordinates of the cave mouth. Then I'd like you to get on the sat phone back to the University and museums in Ulaanbaatar and see if there are any records of this cave."

Abbey scrambled down the hillside with Hank. When they returned we began to carefully photograph, measure, and sample the cave. As we worked we saw more petroglyphs. This cave may not be more significant than others in the park but it was a find. I just hoped it was a new discovery. But just the petroglyphs we could see made it a worthwhile discovery. The tragedy of the defacing of many of the other petroglyphs didn't appear here. I was keen to see this cave protected.

It was midafternoon when we finished our survey work. Captain Ganbold told us he wanted to go back to the site we camped at last night. That way we could reach our base camp on the lake with one full day's ride starting the next morning.

We reached the previous night's campsite well before dusk. Once we were set up Sumo started to cook and he brought out the vodka bottles. Fortunately Abbey packed wine that she shared with me.

I sat sipping the wine. Abbey said, "You don't seem that excited or pleased about finding the cave."

I answered, "I was just thinking of all the money, time, and energy we spent on satellite photos, geographic surveys, and fancy computer programs. None of these had anything to do with finding the cave.

"In hindsight it seems the most logical thing would have been to go and ask the nomadic herders, who travel up and down this entire area each summer, if they knew of any caves. We have access to all this high-tech equipment because of Walter's company. I feel that all this tech stuff wows me and I stop thinking. What about Hank's idea of looking for the birds and bats that live in caves, why didn't we think of that?"

Abbey said, "I'll tell you why. We were rushed and our goal was to impress the Interior Minister with our high-tech knowhow. We had Walter's requirements and we cobbled something together to fit. Mitch told us our plan was shit."

That didn't make me feel any better.

She went on. "You said let's hope we find a site worth researching. We know how to do that. The BS can stop now and let's apply our trade. Have another glass of wine. Sometimes you think too much."

I said, "Yes. But I was thinking too much about how I hadn't thought enough."

Abbey rolled her eyes and filled my wine glass.

Sumo passed around a plate of fried dough as an appetizer. As I gazed around everyone looked happy. We had found something and maybe it was important. For them it was mission accomplished. I told myself not to be a jerk and spoil it for the others.

I held up my glass to give a little speech. I asked Sumo to translate. In my most authoritative professor's voice I praised the tracking ability of the boy. I said he surely had in him the blood of great Kazakh warriors and a few other nice things that popped into my head. I ended by presenting the boy with a gift of my binoculars.

The boy was beaming, his father was proud, and everyone clapped. Abbey winked at me and much to my surprise I felt happy.

The next day we rode back to our base camp at the end of Lake Khoton. I called Major Campbell, reported what we found, and told him we were going back upriver to work the site in a couple of days. First we would take the samples to Ölgii City for shipment to Ulaanbaatar and then on to Houston.

He asked a few questions about the cave and its location. Then he said he and Professor Cohen would fly to Ölgii City to meet us.

Everyone decided they wanted to go to Ölgii City this time. Ranger Batbayar would stay and take care of the horses. I told him to make sure he took good care of Beast.

We planned to stay three days in Ölgii City. It wasn't really much of a city but three days in a real bed with a hot water shower sounded great to me.

At the hotel I spent most of my time following up on other parts of our project. They seemed on track. I called Ned to see how he was doing on his master's thesis. It was something to do with cyber security. His engineering professors back at Cornell would judge it. My job was to make sure he finished it on time. Abbey had far more computer knowledge than I did and was also overseeing his work.

He told me he was working on it and it would knock my socks off. I reminded him he needed to send a first draft to Cornell by October first. No problem was his answer.

The third day Sumo and I went to the small airport to meet Major Campbell's flight from Ulaanbaatar. When they got off the plane I was surprised to see that Professor Uri Cohen was younger that I had thought, in his midthirties or so.

After introductions he asked me several questions about the cave we just found. Sticking to his cover, I guess.

The next morning we started back to the park. The vans were loaded with supplies. I told Major Campbell we planned to stay up at the cave site for an extended period. He said that would be perfect.

Captain Ganbold drove one van and Sumo the other. I had Professor Cohen ride in the front of the van with Sumo. He could be the sightseeing guide for the professor. I also asked Hank to ride in that van. I wanted to ride with Major Campbell and see if he had any news to share. Abbey took the front seat of the van, Major Campbell and I rode in the back.

As usual Major Campbell wasn't very forthcoming with information. He said he forwarded the information on the cave to Walter, that Walter wanted him to congratulate the whole team, and he hoped to be able to visit the site at some point in the not too distant future.

I pressed him on what else he planned to do. He just said that yes, he and Professor Cohen may have other things they need to attend to. It was all I was going to get so we switched to general conversation.

We stopped at the Syrgal ranger station between the two lakes to pick up equipment we had stored there. While there Captain Ganbold arranged for rangers to bring us more horses. Then we went on to our base camp at the end of Lake Khoton. We set up our base camp again. Sumo and Hank offered to give up the vans to Major Campbell and Professor Cohen but they declined and said they would use the tents they brought. We wouldn't be in the base camp long.

The way Beast jumped around and greeted us you would have thought we were gone for a year not a few days.

We would take tomorrow to organize and pack. Captain Ganbold felt we could reach the cave site in one long day of riding if we left early.

This time we had four packhorses and two additional rangers with us. It was still dark as we started. Dawn soon broke, the rising sun behind us cast long shadows, and the river water sparkled. I felt alive and upbeat. No black mood for me today.

As we rode I watched Professor Cohen. He didn't look uneasy as we rode along at a steady pace. Unless he had been riding recently along with inventing rocket engines he would be sore tomorrow.

We rode three hours before our first short stop and then three more before a lunch stop. With one afternoon stop we arrived at the cave site in the late afternoon. Captain Ganbold picked a spot for the night, saying we would look for the ideal spot tomorrow.

I was stiff. Only the Mongolians seemed unfazed by the long day's ride. I said, "Uri, how are you doing?"

"I'd be lying if I said I wasn't very happy to be off that horse. You looked at home in the saddle."

I answered, "I've been doing this for two months now. Here, have some Advil."

He took them with a smile. No late-night story telling that night. Everyone was asleep shortly after dinner.

Beast again slept in front of my tent. He was up several times checking the horses and sniffing around the camp. He knew his job and took it seriously. I slept better because he did.

When I got up Major Campbell had coffee ready. I had

insisted on bringing coffee. This was going to be our home for a while and I could only take so much tea.

He handed me a mug and said, "What is your plan for the day?"

"Abbey and I will start the 3D mapping of the cave. Next we will do a geophysical survey. Then we will lay out a detailed sampling plan. After that we will begin cleaning and re-photographing the cave paintings. I also want to excavate test pits if we find suitable locations."

He shook his head and said, "What are you going to do after lunch?"

I laughed. "Sites like this cave take years of careful work to fully explore. A lot depends on what we find. One finger bone found in the Denisova Cave not far from here in Siberia led to a newly discovered extinct species of human.

"I'm not sure of our team's skills to perform this type of work or even their willingness to do it."

"They'll do it," he said in his military command voice. Then he softened. "They are all bright, hard-working, and eager. All you and Abbey have to do is instruct them. Anyway it's what you do, teach."

Uri joined us. I looked at him and handed him my Advil bottle. He took it, shook out a few, and offered it to Ian. He shook his head no. I guess British SAS majors have to be tough, even retired ones.

I said to Ian and Uri, "Are you staying with us here or are you going exploring?"

Uri looked at Ian. Ian said, "For now we will stay and help you. If we get bored we may go exploring."

Just two guys enjoying a camping trip without a care in the world.

I said, "Do you want some pick and shovel work to do?"

Ian said, "I plan to help Captain Ganbold and the rangers set up a proper campsite somewhere suitable close by. Then I'm all yours. Actually, I believe I'd rather enjoy the work."

"I'd like to help with your work. If you tell me what to do," Uri said.

I poured more coffee and thought back how much I enjoyed working with Ian in Peru. It hadn't been that way so far this trip. We were in different orbits. I found I was looking forward to the work and the people.

With ten people for breakfast it was rather more of a production. Sumo took the role of head chef and had two rangers assisting him. Captain Ganbold and the other ranger went to attend to the horses. Abbey had Hank helping to unpack the equipment.

I looked at everyone getting what needed to be done without me having to say anything. I must be a great boss.

Abbey came over and said, "How do you want to go about this?"

I thought a minute. "Let's have Hank and Sumo do the documentation of the outside area surrounding the cave mouth, measuring, photographing, and taking soil samples. Hank should know how to do this with only a little instruction.

"You and I will begin the 3D laser modeling of the cave. Uri, where would you like to work?"

"I'll join you two, if I may."

We hauled the equipment up to the space in front of the cave. Abbey went over what she wanted Sumo and Hank to do.

I set the case with the Leica ScanStation C10 at the cave mouth and opened it up.

I said, "We will use the laser scanner to create an accurate three-dimensional model of the cave. In addition to the scanning we will take high-resolution photos of the cave. The high-resolution photos are then superimposed on the 3D model to bring out inscriptions and roughness of the walls."

Uri said, "So after the laser scanning the point clouds are geo-referenced, processed by the software, and converted to a mesh. The point cloud mesh is then used to create a 3D model of the caves. The photos are then draped onto the 3D model."

I looked at him. Abbey was now standing next to us. She said, "Correct except the point cloud is cleaned, simplified, and triangulated before the data is imported into the modeling software."

Uri was scanning the instruction book. He said, "What we need to do first is to determine the setup locations for the total station theodolite so that no part of the cave is missed. I'd just go in a ways, take a back shot to make sure we cover the entrance area, and work to the end of the cave from there. As long as there is overlap the software should seamlessly piece together the 3D image."

I guess this wasn't rocket science and he was, after all, a rocket scientist.

Abbey said, "That is the way I've always done it." She

picked up the theodolite and Uri took the stand. I followed them into the cave.

When I started we did this with optical survey equipment and tape measures. The readings were carefully written in a notebook and then plotted onto paper. With the laser equipment we completed the scans in a few hours.

We took a short lunch break and then continued until about 4:00PM when I said it was happy hour time. We climbed down from the cave site.

Captain Ganbold picked a camp spot a few hundred yards upstream. It was on a level close to the mountainside and protected from the wind by a rock outcropping on the downstream side. There was plenty of grass for the horses and the stream was close by. The whole camp was set up for us.

Abbey and Uri started to download and process the scanned data. After getting everyone a drink I reviewed the data Sumo and Hank had collected. Major Campbell was on his sat phone again.

After a while Abbey came over. "We have a problem. We don't have enough battery power to keep the instruments and computers going. The generators we have are built into the vans and these little solar chargers we brought with us take half a day just to charge a cellphone or iPad. In a day or two everything will be out of juice."

One more thing I hadn't thought of. I waved to Major Campbell to join us.

I explained our problem to him.

He said, "I'll send a couple of rangers back in the morning to get a portable gas generator. With a couple of packhorses they should get it here with enough gas to keep it running until I find a better solution. I'll talk to Captain Ganbold and we will have it sent to the military base tomorrow. So you should have it in two days. What else did we forget?"

I shook my head. "I'll think of it shortly after the rangers leave. Thank you. We have plenty to do for two days even if our batteries go dead."

The next two days were spent much the same as the first, carefully measuring and documenting the cave surfaces.

After conferring with numerous people at the Mongolian National Museum, Mongolian Natural History Museum, and Mongolian National Library, Sumo reported that they found no record of this cave being discovered. That was good news. Just the cave paintings meant the cave was at least a small addition to the archaeology of the park.

In the late afternoon of the second day the rangers returned. They were leading a packhorse and a camel. On the back of the camel was strapped a very old generator. It looked like a fifty-year-old lawn mower engine bolted to some type of generator. There were also several five-gallon jerry cans of gas.

The camel was in a foul mood. When the rangers tried to make him kneel down he bit at one ranger and spit at the other. Finally after unloading everything one ranger led the still complaining camel off to the stream for a drink.

Ranger Batbayar tried to start the generator's engine. It coughed, sputtered, and then stopped. After a few more tries he let out a stream of statements that I took for Mongolian cursing. He then went to get his tool kit.

Everyone had gathered and it was quite entertaining.

Abbey said to Major Campbell, "You don't expect me to hook my laptop and instruments to that thing, do you?"

"Actually, no. The generator, assuming it ever runs, will charge a battery pack that will then charge your equipment. I have Peter Frank looking for a better solution. Until then this will have to do."

Finally Ranger Batbayar got the engine running. He would start it first thing in the morning and charge the battery pack. Then he would turn it off and use the battery pack to charge equipment, computers, and sat phones. When the battery pack ran low he would start the process over again. By prioritizing what got charged and when, we kept everything we needed going.

Once the cave had been mapped, modeled, and photographed we went to the area in the back right corner where there had been a rock slide. Both Abbey and I were dying to know if the cave continued on.

I looked at her and she shook her head. We both knew that we should start at the mouth of the cave and work our way carefully deeper in. Rushing to find hidden treasures had compromised too many archaeological sites.

So next we would carefully clean the areas of cave wall that contained the petroglyphs and then re-photograph them. It would be slow and careful work. I was interested to see how the others would take to it.

Uri seemed the most at ease with the work. He listened to Abbey's instructions and then worked carefully but confidently. Hank and Sumo worried they would do something wrong and damage the petroglyphs. Major

Campbell helped the ranger with the horses and spent a lot of time on his sat phone.

After a long day of tedious work Sumo said he thought fish would be good for dinner so he would go fishing in the stream tomorrow. Hank decided Sumo would need his help. I said a fish dinner would be great. Uri and Abbey just smiled at me.

The next night Sumo was preparing the several lenok trout he and Hank caught. Abbey, Major Campbell, Uri, and I were enjoying a drink and light conversation. I saw Major Campbell look up over my shoulder. I turned and listened. Hank was talking on his sat phone in Navajo. He began making notes on his pad. We were all now looking at him. A call home perhaps? Not likely given the look on Major Campbell's face.

When he finished he came over to Major Campbell and said he needed to speak to him.

I looked at them and said, "Ian, no secrets, Walter said we were to be in the loop."

He said to Hank, "Sit down and tell us what's up."

"Ned says that the Chinese are able to break our encrypted calls in a matter of minutes. He has changed encryptions several times and in less than thirty minutes they can read them. He knows this from the software bug he uploaded to their communication satellite.

"Ned assumes we are now a high priority target of the Chinese because it requires massive computing power to crack the encrypted messages. He said they have cracked the encryptions of the Israelis on the air base also.

"He suggests we evoke the Windtalkers protocol for all

messages we don't want the Chinese to read."

I was looking back and forth between the two of them when it hit me. I now knew why my speaking a few words in Navajo upset Ned. Hank Nez was a Navajo, from the Black Sheep Clan of the Sleeping Rock People.

Chester Nez, a Navajo from the Black Sheep Clan of the Sleeping Rock People, was one of the original Navajo code talkers who served in the United States Marine Corps during World War Two. He died a few years ago. The last of the Navajo code talkers who were used to radio messages in the Pacific that the Japanese couldn't understand.

Windtalkers was the movie about the Navajo code talkers of World War Two starring Nicolas Cage.

I said to Hank, "Don't tell me you taught Ned to speak Navajo? Chester Nez was your grandfather?"

"Chester was my great-uncle and Ned couldn't learn to speak Navajo in a hundred years. One of my cousins is with Ned at the air base."

I went on. "So you speak Navajo on the sat phone and it is encrypted. If the encryption is broken the Chinese only have Navajo. If the Chinese can break the high-tech encryption won't they learn to translate Navajo?"

Uri spoke up. "Perhaps given enough time but the algorithms for breaking encryptions are totally different than for language translation. Plus I believe the Chinese have hacked into the computers of the developers of the encryption programs we are using and have the source codes. I don't see any other way they could break the encryptions that quickly. There is no source code for Navajo."

I looked at Major Campbell. "By the way, I preferred

the 1959 movie *Never So Few* featuring Charles Bronson as the Navajo code talker Sgt. John Danforth to *Windtalkers.* However that was way before Ned's time. So what do we do?"

He said, "Just what we have been doing. All our normal conversation should go on as they are. If we have something the Chinese shouldn't hear we use the Windtalkers protocol but as little as possible.

"Hank, instruct Ned that all routine company business should continue as usual. The data gathered for the government survey and our listening operation should be put on disk drives and sent on company planes to Sudbury or Houston. Create dummy data and continue to transmit it as before via Internet and satellite."

Hank went back to his sat phone.

Once he was gone I said, "Are the Uyghurs in the area with the part of the rocket they found?"

Major Campbell said, "We think so."

I asked, "How do you find them?"

"We don't. They should find us. If they don't it means they aren't interested in dealing with us and we could never find them if they don't want us to."

I looked at Uri and he nodded in agreement.

Abbey said, "Wheels within wheels." Then she poured more wine for us.

Sumo brought over a platter of the trout cut into small squares. He put it on the camp table and issued us each a fork.

Major Campbell, wanting to change the subject, said, "Peter Frank had a few ideas for generating electricity for us. The first was a low-head hydroelectric package power plant. I vetoed that as taking too long to install and being too expensive. Plus it would be hard to maintain or move.

"Sometimes I think Peter comes up with a very elaborate and expensive solution so the one he really wants seems like a bargain. He did come up with an easy to transport and easy to use solar powered system. It is the Yeti 1250 solar generator kit by Goal Zero. It is ideal for lights, phones, tablets, laptops, cameras, and even a TV or a fridge. I believe four of them should be sufficient and when we are done someone in the company can always use them. Plus they are quiet. But we can leave the rusty old gas generator for cloudy days."

Major Campbell liked his gadgets.

The next few days we continued to carefully clean the petroglyphs.

Uri said, "I read that some of the petroglyphs date back to 12,000 BC. How do you tell how old these are?

I said, "The oldest images in the park date from the Late Pleistocene period before 11,700 BC to the Early Holocene period from 11,700 to about 6,000 BC. They extend into the Bronze Age, Iron Age, and Turkic period in the ninth century. Dating them is a real issue. Especially since some of the older petroglyphs were carved over in later times.

"Abbey, why don't you explain how we guesstimate their age."

As we cleaned Abbey explained.

"The real problem is dating petroglyphs earlier than the Bronze Age. For instance how can we determine whether that material belongs to the Late Pleistocene and early Holocene epochs? Scholars have used a number of approaches to the dating of rock pecked imagery with varying success. Some have attempted to infer the dating of stone images on the basis of excavated materials in the immediate vicinity; but there is no necessary connection between the two.

"Some scholars have tried to use the relative darkness of patina and surface weathering in order to judge the age of the image. However this is not very reliable because the patina is as much a function of mineralization of the stone, the slant of the surface, adjoining vegetation, and proximity to moisture as it is a function of age.

"The manner of its execution and subject matter are what we are left with. The techniques used to execute an image are a more reliable indicator of period on a gross scale. Petroglyphs in the park from the Bronze and Iron Ages are occasionally executed with direct, rough blows, but far more typical is an execution indicative of indirect pecking with a finely tipped tool. The direct blows are usually an indication of earlier periods."

Uri continued asking questions and we did our best to answer them. He had an inquisitive mind and the time passed quickly.

As we were heading down to our camp for a mid-morning break we saw three horses heading upstream towards us. The lead horse had a rider, the other two horses were tethered behind.

As the rider approached it appeared something was wrong. The rider was slumped forward in the saddle. Captain Ganbold, Sumo, and Major Campbell walked out to meet the rider, who more fell off than dismounted. Sumo and Major Campbell each took an arm. Captain Ganbold took the horses.

When we arrived in camp they had the rider on a sleeping bag and Major Campbell had one of the medical kits open next to him. Sumo was gently holding the man's shoulders and talking to him.

Abbey said, "He's been shot."

We all gathered around. I looked at his clothing and said, "Is he Uyghur?"

Sumo nodded yes.

It looked as if he was shot in the left side. Major Campbell had the side bandaged and was giving the man an injection.

At the same instant I heard a crack and the Uyghur's head exploded.

Major Campbell and Sumo jumped back, they were both spattered with blood.

I turned around. There were six of them. They all held automatic pistols, wore the same nondescript clothing, and looked Chinese. They moved in closer to us.

Beast growled and crouched at my side. The Chinese man who shot the Uyghur, apparently the group leader, pointed his pistol at Beast.

I stepped forward and said, "No, don't shoot him."

The man pointed his pistol at me. That was too much for Beast, he charged him. The man swung his pistol back towards Beast and fired. Beast went rolling sideways in a cloud of blood and fur.

I screamed, "You didn't have to shoot the dog." I must

have gone berserk. I grabbed a mallet we used to pound in the tent stakes and began to swing in at him over and over. The whole time repeatedly screaming, you didn't have to shoot the dog.

I vaguely remember hearing pop-pop, pop-pop, pop-pop three times.

Next thing large strong hands were holding my arms from behind.

"Stop, Professor, stop." I looked over, it was Sumo holding me.

I looked down at the mallet, it was covered with blood. I looked at the Chinese man, his head was beaten to a bloody pulp. I dropped the mallet, turned to the side, and threw up.

I looked around still in a daze. Abbey, Major Campbell, and Captain Ganbold were holding pistols. The Chinese men were all on the ground bleeding.

I went to Beast and sat.

It wasn't until later that they told me what happened. My first swing of the mallet caught the Chinese man in the wrist and his gun went flying. Abbey caught it in mid-air and shot three of them. Two shots each through their hearts. That was the three double pops I heard. Sumo tackled another and Captain Ganbold shot him. Major Campbell broke the neck of the sixth one. All dead in less than a minute, and they never said one word to us.

I put Beast's head in my lap. His large brown eyes were looking up at me. I said, "You're a good boy, Beast, you're a good boy."

He looked at me, his eyes saying he knew he let me down and he was sorry. I kept telling him no, he was a good boy as the tears rolled down my cheeks.

Major Campbell came over with the medical kit. He poured two packets of the powder used to stanch bleeding into his wound. He gave Beast an injection in the neck then examined and bandaged his wounded hindquarters.

I could feel Beast's breathing slowed. His eyes started to close. "Is he dying?"

Major Campbell said, "No, it's the sedative I gave him. He will sleep. It looks like mostly fur and skin that was shot off. The bullet didn't go very deep into his flesh or hit a bone. He has a fair chance of recovering."

As Major Campbell worked on Beast I noticed Abbey put a new clip in the pistol she caught in the air and retrieved a second pistol that she stuck in her belt. Captain Ganbold was checking each of the Chinese men, I assumed to make sure they were dead.

I jumped as another shot rang out. Abbey went into a shooting crouch and Major Campbell drew his automatic.

An assault-type rifle clattered to the ground behind us, and a seventh Chinese man dropped next to it.

A voice said in English, "Professor Johnson, it's Chad Dillon from the US Embassy. I believe that man was about to shoot your group. I'm coming in. I have a pistol with me."

I looked around. Abbey walked over and picked up the rifle. Major Campbell and Captain Ganbold had their guns out. I said, "Come in, Chad. We won't shoot you. Do you think there are more of them?"

He walked in slowly with his pistol stuck in his belt. "I don't think there are any more. There are seven horses tied up back there."

He looked at the bodies of the six Chinese. "None of you are hurt?"

I said, pointing to the one I had beaten to death, "He shot my dog."

"Well, he got what he deserves then," he said.

I agreed, but I thought his attitude was a bit flippant given the carnage around us.

He went on. "Hi Uri, what brings you to Mongolia?"

"Chad, nice to see you again. I wondered where they sent you after that mess you made in Tel Aviv. Thank you for your good shooting. It would have been rather bad to be gunned down from behind after what we just went through."

Abbey was still examining the assault rifle. Chad said, "It's a Chinese QBZ-95 automatic rifle."

Abbey said, "It has a semi-automatic, automatic, and three-round burst setting. Also it has a very complex recoil buffer system. It doesn't resemble any of the Chinese rifle designs I've seen. I thought the People's Liberation Army used the type 81 assault rifle."

Chad said, "It's relatively new. It was first issued to the Chinese Special Forces. Now it is replacing the type 81. Your grandfather taught you well."

Abbey looked at him sharply. I said, "Chad is CIA. I'm sure they have run all our backgrounds. They probably know more about our history than we remember ourselves."

Captain Ganbold said, "We've got quite a mess on our hands here."

Major Campbell held his hand up and said, "Let's start by finding out what the Uyghur said. Sumo?"

"He didn't say much before he was shot. He just kept

repeating they killed my brother and we have the golden eagle."

I looked at Uri's face, then at Chad's and Major Campbell's. This meant something to them.

I said, "All right. Is the golden eagle what Walter was talking about? No BS. I just killed a man and Abbey killed three."

Major Campbell said, "You tell them, Uri, you understand all this better than anyone."

"OK. It is more what we suspect than we know. We know the Chinese are working on anti-satellite weapons. A few years ago they launched a missile at one of their older satellites and blew it up. It was much the same as an antiaircraft missile. Get close to the target and blow up, blowing up the target too.

"The problem is that when they blew up their satellite they created thirty thousand pieces of space debris. Now the existing debris orbiting in space is already a major hazard for all satellites and the International Space Station. So if you try to destroy a large number of your enemy's satellites that way, there is so much junk in orbit that no one's satellites can function.

"The next area we know the Chinese and others are working on is hacking into the control systems of their potential enemies' satellite systems.

"What we've been able to find out about the golden eagle project is that it is an anti-satellite, satellite system that uses a small laser to damage the enemy's satellite."

I had Beast's head in my lap. I said, "Fifty-nine cents a shot."

Everyone was looking at me like I was crazy, perhaps in shock from my recent experience.

I said, "Rear Admiral Matthew L. Klunder, chief of naval research, said the prototype Laser Weapon System developed by the Office of Naval Research and installed on the USS Ponce has proved cost-effective. The Navy tested it for three months in the Persian Gulf on the USS Ponce and said it worked and cost only about fifty-nine cents a shot."

I stopped. I couldn't figure how I remembered that or why I felt I had to blurt it out now. It was probably the adrenaline still rushing through my body.

Uri looked at me. "Exactly, Professor. However on a ship weight isn't a big concern and you can generate almost unlimited electric power using the ship's engines. In space you don't have that luxury. What we think the Chinese are trying to do is to miniaturize the laser and find a way to repower it between shots. The satellite would maneuver close to an enemy satellite and fire a laser beam just strong enough to damage the electronics of the satellite so it is out of commission. Their satellite would then move to destroy the next enemy satellite.

"There are several ways they could attempt to do this and we don't know what they are trying or what success they are having. If this is the golden eagle it could be a huge help."

Captain Ganbold's walkie-talkie buzzed. It didn't work well in these mountains and he seemed surprised that someone got through to him.

He spoke in Mongolian. Then he said, "Ranger Batbayar is about two miles downstream. He says he's found an airplane part wrapped in a rug. I told him to bring it up here.

He has to unload the supplies from the packhorse to put it on."

Uri said, "Can he lift it? Did he say how big it was?"

"There is another ranger with him. He didn't indicate it would be a problem putting it on the packhorse and bringing it here."

I went to the stream to wash the blood off. Sumo and Captain Ganbold went to retrieve the horses of the Chinese. Major Campbell, Chad, and Uri dragged the dead bodies off to the side and began searching them. Abbey seemed to be standing guard with the assault rifle. Hank stood next to her quietly talking.

Sumo and Captain Ganbold returned with the seven horses. The rest of us watched as they removed the saddles and packs. Major Campbell began dumping out the contents of the saddlebags. Chad and Uri were examining various items.

Uri said to me when I returned, "I heard the rangers talking about Abbey's marksmanship but she looked like a Special Forces expert. That was fast thinking and unbelievable shooting."

Major Campbell knew the story. I said, "In addition to being off the charts talented, Abbey had some unique training. Her grandfather spent his career in the US Marine Corps. He was a gunny sergeant and spent a big part of his career training Marines. For a number of years he helped train the Corps' elite Force Recon units. The ones the media like to call 'the tip of the spear.'

"When he retired from the Marines he and his wife decided to move to Plattsburgh to be near their son, daughter-in-law, and Abbey. They looked forward to retirement together. Unfortunately his wife contracted cancer. She was dead in less than two years. Abbey's parents both worked so Abbey would stay with them after school. When she arrived after school her grandmother would brighten up no matter how much pain she was in. Abbey would read to her and tell her about her day at school. Abbey was only about nine but she could read any adult book. Her grandfather said he couldn't remember a time when Abbey couldn't read. After his wife passed it was his job to watch Abbey. He taught her to play chess. But in about two months she could beat him in ten minutes. She was so quick at learning everything. So he started teaching her the only thing he really knew well, how to be a Marine.

"He told me in all his years training he had few if any who learned as fast as Abbey. In the winter they would go to the shop of a friend of his who was a gunsmith. Abbey would help repair all sorts of small arms. She took apart every gun in the shop, then cleaned and reassembled it. Abbey could take apart and reassemble almost any gun blindfolded. They shot at the range together. She couldn't seem to learn enough. By the time she was fifteen and able to be on her own after school, her grandfather claimed she knew more about being a Marine than he did. But by then she had other interests and activities. She graduated at fifteen and went off to Cornell.

"In Peru she saved both Major Campbell's and my life. However I worry about her. She was forced to kill people there as well. It can't be good for a young woman who never really had any interest in the armed forces or violence. All she was doing was trying to enjoy learning from her grandfather. That training you saw in action today was all learned between the ages of nine and fifteen. Although since Peru she works out more and goes to the practice range with Major Campbell's men."

Hank took out his sat phone, listened and replied in Navajo. Then he said, "Ned intercepted a message that the Chinese are sending six Harbin Z-9 helicopters loaded with commandos to the Altai City airport which is only a few dozen miles from both the Mongolian and Russian border. They are to refuel and be ready for a potential rescue mission."

"Ned figures it will take three to four hours for them to load the helicopters and fly to Altai City. From there they could reach our position in less than an hour."

Major Campbell said, "The Harbin Z-9 can carry ten fully equipped commandos. It cruises at just over 160 mph. It is armed with two fixed 23-millimeter cannon and has pylons for rockets or gun pods."

Captain Ganbold said, "It's one thing to passively eavesdrop on the Chinese from Mongolia and spies caught here are sent home to China a few times a year. But we just killed seven Chinese agents and it looks like the Chinese are willing to stage a major raid into Mongolia to get their golden eagle back. Mongolia is a small country, we need good relations with China."

"What about the Mongolian Air Force?" I said.

Captain Ganbold smiled. "Our air force has ten MI-24 attack helicopters and two MiG-29 fighter jets. All are in

Ulaanbaatar over a thousand miles away. The two MiG-29s aren't currently flightworthy. Plus there is no way Mongolia is going to shoot down Chinese helicopters."

Abbey said, "Let's give it back."

Uri started to protest but Abbey went on. "I'm overseeing Ned's thesis while he is here. It's on spyware. He has advanced his spy software to a point where I believe we could load it on the golden eagle, give it back to the Chinese, and potentially be on the other side of all their firewalls. His software is like your Stuxnet spyware you used to destroy Iran's nuclear-enrichment equipment but on steroids.

"He gave it to me on a memory stick hoping there would be somewhere to use it. You examine and photograph the golden eagle. Then we load the spyware on it and give it back to the Chinese before they come and take it from us. Besides there is no way we would be able to smuggle it out of the country."

Uri said, "I had a briefing on Ned's work from Mossad before I left Israel but tell me how you think this will work."

Abbey went into a detailed technical explanation. I noticed Chad was paying close attention but I doubted he could follow what she was saying.

Uri said, "OK, hopefully I can also download a copy of the golden eagle's software to take with us. We will need a few hours to examine it."

Major Campbell said, "You might not have a few hours if the Chinese sent in those commandos. I would guess they know about where their seven agents were when they last reported. I'm sure they know where we are and they might know Uri is here.

"Captain Ganbold, I suggest you call the Minister's office and tell them you have recovered a Chinese airplane part from a group of bandits. The bandits have been subdued and you would like instructions on what to do with it. Don't encrypt the message, we want the Chinese to hear it. Hopefully the Chinese will decide it is better to have it delivered to them rather than staging a commando raid. It might at least delay the launching of a raid."

I got out my sat phone, took a card out of my wallet, and dialed. I heard one word when the phone was answered. "Da."

"This is Professor Robert Johnson, we met at the National Museum a few weeks ago."

He switched to English. "Yes, I remember, Professor, nice to hear from you.

I hesitated. "Well, I thought you might be interested to know that there are six Chinese Harbin Z-9 helicopters loaded with commandos heading to the Altai City airport. They have orders to refuel and be ready for a potential rescue mission."

"You know this how, Professor?"

I said, "A student of mine over heard a conversation."

"Would that student be Mr. Ned Harris?"

The Russians were probably keeping track of all of us. "Ned is a rather inquisitive young man," I said.

"So his dossier would indicate."

Ned did work for the NSA before joining Falone Advanced Technologies. So the Russians would have a file on him.

He went on. "And why would I want to know this?"

"Altai City airport is close to the Russian border. Plus I thought it was your job to know things."

He said, "So you found it."

"Found what?" I said.

"I hope you are a better archaeologist than you are a liar. Do svidaniya i udachi." Russian for "goodbye and good luck." The line went dead.

They were all looking at me. I held up the card. "My friend at the Russian Embassy from the Federal Security Service. That should give the Chinese one more thing to think about."

Major Campbell said to Hank, "Windtalkers protocol, get my chief of security next to your cousin and have them call you back."

Ranger Batbayar rode in, stopped, and looked over at the pile of bodies. Captain Ganbold told him something, he dismounted, and they unloaded the rolled-up rug. When they unrolled it there was a cylinder just over three feet long and about fifteen inches in diameter. It was some kind of case that would break away when the rocket deployed the satellite.

Uri and Abbey began to examine it.

I said, "When you open the case can you close it again in a way so the Chinese can't tell you examined it?"

Uri said, "No, we won't even put the case back on and hope the Chinese assume the Uyghurs removed it to see what was inside."

As Abbey and Uri worked Chad took pictures. There was going to be a big fight at some point over who got what info. There was no longer much trust between the spy services of Israel and the United States.

Captain Ganbold now had the two rangers strapping the dead bodies of the Chinese to their horses. Once done, he instructed them to take the bodies to the military base at the end of the lake.

Hank picked up his phone and signaled to Major Campbell. I followed him over.

Hank said something into the phone. "Ned says Russian air defense radar started lighting up from Omsk to Altai a little while ago and now air defense radar in eastern Kazakhstan is coming on line.

"The Russians are scrambling fighters from the 6982nd aviation base at Domna airfield in Zabaykalsky Krai. He says that air base has MiG-29 and Su-30SM fighters."

I said, "What, is Ned a one-man spy agency?"

Major Campbell said, "He's getting help from the Israelis. Is my security chief there, Hank?" Hank nodded yes. "Ask him if we have a company jet there capable of a nonstop flight to Sudbury."

Hank spoke into the phone. "He said there is a Boeing 737 arriving at Ulaanbaatar airport in a few hours with equipment for the government contract."

"Tell him to have the plane refueled in Ulaanbaatar and proceed to the air base. Then I want Ned on that plane for a direct flight to Sudbury. He should have a minimum of two armed guards with him at all times. Take him to a secure spot at the company's Sudbury facility and arrange for Elizabeth Walters to go to Sudbury ASAP. Ned isn't to talk to anybody about his work except Elizabeth until it is cleared by Walter or me."

Hank again spoke Navajo into the phone. "Ned isn't very happy about this. He is making quite a stink."

Major Campbell said, "Tell them to handcuff him or put him in a straightjacket if they need to. I want him on the plane to Canada as soon as possible."

I said, "Is Ned in danger from the Chinese?"

"I don't want the CIA to grab him once they figure out what is going on. If Abbey and Uri pull this off it could be the biggest intelligence coup of the century. I'm not sure I even trust the Israeli Mossad not to grab him. I need to call Walter."

I said, "Even the encrypted sat phones aren't secure."

He just looked at me. I guess he knew that.

Now Captain Ganbold was on his sat phone. He looked worried.

He finished his call and came over to us. "That was the Interior Minister. He said they contacted the Chinese ambassador and told him we have recovered what appears to be a Chinese airplane part from a group of bandits. We would be happy to deliver it to them at the border.

"When the ambassador got back to him he said they were sending in a team by helicopter to pick it up along with the bandits. The Interior Minister said he would have to consult with the Defense Minister to get permission for Chinese military aircraft to enter Mongolian airspace and he would get back to him.

"The Russian military has notified our Defense Ministry that they expect a Chinese raid into Russia or Mongolia within hours. The Russians have offered assistance in defending Mongolian airspace if we request it.

"The Prime Minister has called an emergency cabinet meeting. I was told to stay here until they get back to me."

I looked at my watch. It was almost three hours since the six Chinese Harbin Z-9 helicopters loaded with commandos left for Altai City airport. That meant that they could arrive here in as little as two hours. I looked at Abbey and Uri, they were one hundred percent focused on the satellite. I wondered if we were about to start a war.

I said to Chad, who was photographing everything Abbey and Uri were doing, "Perhaps you should call your boss and have the American Embassy warn the Chinese about launching a raid into Mongolia."

Captain Ganbold repeated to Chad what he told us.

Chad walked a distance away and took out his sat phone.

I went over to Abbey and Uri and said, "How is it going? The Chinese commando team could be here in as little as two hours."

Uri said, "Let us keep working. Tell us if and when they leave Altai City airport."

He went back to work.

I said to Captain Ganbold, "Do the Chinese know all the 'bandits' as we are calling them are dead?"

"I don't think so," Captain Ganbold replied.

"I have an idea. The Chinese may believe they are flying in to save and bring home their agents. Have your Minister tell the Chinese ambassador that we believe based on the number of horses that there were nine bandits. Eight are dead and the bodies have been sent to the military base on Lake Khoton. We believe the ninth bandit is dead because of the amount of blood on the horse's saddle.

"With no people to rescue, the Chinese have no reason to send in six helicopters. If they won't agree to us delivering the satellite to the border, compromise by telling them to send in one helicopter. That way there can't be more than ten commandos on board. I'm concerned if they come in with six helicopters and thirty or forty commandos they may try to grab us along with the golden eagle.

"If they do insist on sending in one or more helicopters, your government should request that the Russians send their jet fighters to escort the Chinese helicopters."

Captain Ganbold said, "I'll call. At least the Minister will know we are trying to help."

Major Campbell told Hank to get his cousin and Ned on the line and ask for an update.

Hank spoke and then listened. "Ned says that from the calls he has been able to intercept, it appears the Chinese military is pushing to send in the helicopters ASAP. The diplomats are warning that the Russians are already threating to shoot down any Chinese military aircraft that enter their airspace and that they have offered to assist the Mongolians in defending their airspace."

I said, "Ask Ned for his best estimate of when the helicopters might be ready to depart the Altai City airport."

I waited.

"Ned said they could be ready in as soon as an hour. But no more than two hours. He also said the Chinese know our exact position."

I resisted the urge to interrupt Uri and Abbey to see how they were doing.

I took Major Campbell aside and said, "We may need

to get Uri out of the country fast as well."

"I'm going to let the Israelis do that."

I looked around. "Ian, would you help me change Beast's bandage and see if he needs another shot?"

He nodded and went to get one of the medical kits.

Beast was still asleep. I carefully took off the bandage. The wound looked bad to me but it had stopped bleeding. Major Campbell carefully cleaned it, put on a disinfectant, and bandaged it. Beast stirred a little but didn't open his eyes.

"I'll give him another shot. It's best that he sleeps and doesn't try to move around. It may get noisy around here pretty soon."

I thanked him and sat with Beast's head in my lap for another few minutes.

We heard them before we saw them. Four fighter jets streaked in from the north, they flew directly over our position, and then banked sharply and headed away.

Major Campbell looked up and said, "They are Sukhoi Su-30s, a twin-engine two-seat super maneuverable multi-role fighter for all-weather, air-to-air and air-to-surface deep interdiction missions. It looks like the Russians have sent their top of the line aircraft. I hope they are on our side today."

Captain Ganbold grabbed his sat phone to report the overflight. After talking awhile he said to us, "The Ministry of Defense has just announced a joint training exercise with the Russian Air Force. Joint exercises will be going on for the next several days. We can expect to see numerous over-flights in this area during the joint training period."

"It looks like they are on our side. Joint training, how convenient," I said.

Abbey came over. "What's going on?"

I filled her in and said, "How is your work going?"

"Ned's spyware is inserted in some of the satellite's navigation code. I have no idea if the Chinese will find it or if it will work. Uri is downloading as much of the software as he can. Needless to say there are thousands and thousands of lines of code."

Hank was back on his sat phone. He came over to Major Campbell. "The Chinese are scrambling fighter jets from four air bases in the western part of the country. Ned says it is a show of strength for the benefit of the Russians. The Chinese-run TV stations are calling the sudden, previously unannounced, joint training exercises between the Russians and Mongolian militaries provocative and are calling for them to halt."

Abbey said, "Is this how wars get started?"

"I hope not," I replied.

Uri kept working away. Finally I said to Chad, "Is the US doing anything?"

"I believe they are urging all sides to use restraint. They aren't telling me much," he answered.

We waited. Sumo heard it first. It wasn't the jets, but the whine of an engine. A motorcycle was coming upstream towards us.

It was one of our Tarus-2 all-terrain two-wheel drive motorcycles. Ranger Batbayar was on it. He came roaring up to us.

I said, "How did you get back here so quickly?"

"As soon as we started down with the bodies I radioed to the military base and had them have someone drive up to meet me as fast as they could. When we met I gave him my horse and jumped on the motorcycle."

I noticed he had an automatic rifle strapped to his back.

He continued, "The commander of the base wanted to send his men up here but he was ordered to stay at the base."

Hank was back on his sat phone. "Major, Ned says the helicopters have reached Altai City airport and are refueling. The Israelis are sending several men to the park to pick up Professor Cohen. They hope to be at the park entrance by dark."

Uri asked Abbey to help him put the satellite back together. The Russian jets roared overhead again. My stomach was in a knot. Everyone was quiet.

Chad's sat phone rang. He listened and then put it down. "They told me that the six Chinese helicopters are preparing to take off."

Abbey got up and took Major Campbell aside. I watched her point to several places and Major Campbell was nodding.

Major Campbell came over to Captain Ganbold and said, "I suggest we put the satellite in plain sight over here. The place to land a helicopter is here or here." He was pointing at two level spots near our camp. "The five of us (he was now talking to Abbey, Captain Ganbold, Ranger Batbayar, and Chad Dillon) can take up firing positions along this part on the mountainside. The rest of the people go to the cave behind our positions."

Uri protested. "I'm a fully trained member of the Israel Defense Forces Reserves."

Major Campbell said, "Uri, if something happened to you all this is rather pointless. If worse comes to worst we retreat to the cave and you cover us. I'm hoping if they come they will take the satellite and go."

Captain Ganbold got on his sat phone again. The conversation was short. Then he said, "My government is allowing one Chinese helicopter to enter the country and proceed here to pick up the satellite. Ranger Batbayar and I are to meet the helicopter and deliver the satellite. We are to move you to a safe distance. It isn't clear if the Chinese will comply with just sending in one helicopter or will send all six. If they send more I don't know if the Russians will shoot them down or not. I assume those jets would make short work of the helicopters."

Major Campbell said, "We can cover you from the mountainside, however being out in the open you will be easy targets."

"Put it back in the rug and let's get it into position. Then I want the rest of you in the cave. Stay up there and don't fire unless they come up to the cave after you," Captain Ganbold said.

"What about Beast?" I said.

Sumo said, "I'll carry him up to the cave."

Ranger Batbayar handed Abbey his automatic rifle and a backpack. It was the rifle taken from the Chinese. "If they kill me please revenge my death."

Abbey looked in the backpack and then began to carefully check the rifle.

The Russian jet flew over again. Normally I would find their noise annoying, today I found it reassuring.

Sumo picked up Beast with no apparent effort. He was still out from the shots Major Campbell gave him. I took a blanket to set him on in the cave. We all climbed up to the area in front of the cave.

Hank was on his cellphone. "Ned says the six helicopters are headed this way with an escort of Chinese fighters. If they hold their course they should arrive in about twenty minutes."

I heard jets again and looked up. I said with a little alarm in my voice, "Those are different jets."

Major Campbell turned his field glasses in their direction. "They are Russian MiG-29s. It is an air superiority fighter designed to engage enemy fighters. We could be in for quite a show."

I didn't think that was a show I wanted to see.

Major Campbell went over to Abbey and handed her Captain Ganbold's rifle. It was the same one that Abbey had used against the poacher and in the shooting contest. He took the Chinese assault rifle from her. She didn't protest.

Chad was given Ranger Batbayar's rifle of the same type. All three had automatic pistols as well. They began checking their weapons.

I had a bad feeling about all this. If fifty Chinese commandos came after us we weren't going to stop them. I went and sat on the blanket next to Beast. It was probably best for me to stay out of the way.

As the jet noise faded I heard in the distance the distinct thump-thump sound of helicopters. I listened hard. It was more than one helicopter.

Major Campbell turned his field glasses towards the sound. He said, "There are two." As they came closer he went on. "Harbin Z-9 helicopters, that must be our Chinese friends."

I said, "Two not one. Will the Russian jets shoot them down?"

He said, "It sounds like we will soon find out."

I could hear jets streaking from the north. It was a formation of four Sukhoi Su-30 jets. Remembering what Major Campbell said, I realized these would be the type of jets best suited to shoot down the helicopters.

I said, "Maybe the two sides compromised on two helicopters."

No one said anything. The helicopters kept coming straight in. Two of the jets peeled off left and the other two to the right.

Captain Ganbold began waving a towel at the helicopter to signal his position.

One helicopter slowed and hovered at the flat area Captain Ganbold was pointing to. The other began to circle at about five hundred feet.

The first helicopter landed and the side door opened. Two commandos jumped out with their automatic rifles held at port arms. Next an officer stepped out, went forward, and spoke to Captain Ganbold. After what looked, from here, like formal introductions Captain Ganbold pointed to the rolled-up rug on the ground. The Chinese officer shouted something back to the helicopter and a fourth man got out.

He proceeded to the rug with the officer. They unrolled it and briefly examined the satellite. The officer signaled the commandos to come, roll it back in the rug, and load it on the helicopter. The officer saluted Captain Ganbold, turned, and boarded the helicopter with the fourth man.

As the helicopter began to take off the Russian jets roared in from the east and west. They were much lower now, only a few hundred feet above the circling Chinese helicopter. It seemed in another moment they would meet. Then they pulled straight up going into a vertical climb. After climbing several thousand feet the four jets barrel-rolled and were back in formation. They lit their afterburners and broke the sound barrier as they streaked north.

I realized I had been holding my breath.

Major Campbell said, "That is the most fun those Russian fighter jockeys have had in months and some pretty good flying too."

Epilogue

The next morning Major Campbell, Uri Cohen, Chad Dillon, Captain Ganbold, and Hank started back to our base camp.

Ranger Batbayar, Sumo, Abbey, and I would continue to work the site until Beast had recovered enough to travel.

I decided I would return to Ithaca and teach the spring semester. Abbey would stay here and continue the grant work. In addition to the archaeological study of the cave we had promised the Interior Ministry a whole lot more. Such as a large-scale detailed wildlife management study of the National Park. There would be a great deal for Abbey to oversee.

It turned out her boyfriend was an ornithologist. He had secured a grant to study migratory birds in Altai Tavan Bogd National Park and would arrive shortly.

Captain Ganbold was reassigned by the Interior Ministry, but Ranger Batbayar would continue working on the grant project. I thought again of when Abbey told me the meaning of his name in Mongolian, "firm happiness." That fit Ranger Batbayar when he could be outdoors working with horses and vehicles. His English had improved and I'd noticed that Abbey had picked up quite a bit of Mongolian.

Sumo agreed to continue work on the grant as well. He would accompany me to Khovd Province to review Mitch's work.

We would drive. I wanted a chance to see more of the country and that way I could bring Beast with me.

Not surprisingly Mitch did a comprehensive job. Her report was over six hundred pages. She also had video and audio documentation that was hundreds of hours long. After turning it over to us she planned to go back to Princeton University to finish her PhD.

The Dean of the Cornell Engineering College got a bit of a shock when the FBI arrived in his office. They served him with a warrant from United States Foreign Intelligence Surveillance Court that stated he was to turn over all copies of Ned Harris' thesis work for their review.

Ned remained in Canada working from the company's office in Sudbury. Abbey and I certified that Ned had completed fieldwork enough to grant him the six credit hours he still needed.

A few months later the Dean received a highly redacted copy of Ned's thesis back. The Engineering College decided it would be best to just award Ned his joint BS, ME degree. Ned had them framed and shipped them to his mother.

Back in Ithaca I decided to sell my house in Cayuga Heights at the edge of the Cornell campus and buy a small farm. Beast and I found a suitable one six miles from campus.

Beast had recovered well. Though the fur would never grow completely back on the spot where he was shot. I believe Beast is the only Mongolian dog to make a transcontinental flight on a private jet. I was thinking of writing it up and sending it to the Guinness World Records.

I had a few months before I started teaching the spring semester at the end of January. Beast and I spent the time getting the farm in shape. Friends in the vet school helped me identify two suitable rescue horses. Both were middle age, fit for trail riding, and had a gentle disposition.

Beast had some trouble adjusting to living in a house. I had a large dog door installed so he could go in and out when he wanted to. Once the horses arrived he was better. He now had meaningful work to do. Each day we would take a trail ride. At night Beast would lie at the foot of my bed when I went to sleep. Once he was sure I was settled in he would go out to the barn and sleep with the horses. Two or three times a night he would come in and check on me.

There are no wolves in Tompkins County but coyotes had returned in force. Beast often smelled them and tracked their scent when we were on trail rides. I had no fear that the coyotes would bother our farm, not with Beast around.

However it seemed beneath Beast to hunt mice and they were becoming an increasing problem as the weather got colder. One day, as I was working in the barn, a mouse ran about a foot in front of Beast's nose as he lay on the barn floor. That's it, Beast, we need a cat. Beast thumped his tail twice. OK, two cats then.

We went to the pound and picked out two half-grown kittens that they told me would be excellent mousers. How they knew this I wasn't sure, but we took them. I built a bed for them up on a shelf in the tack room of the barn and installed a cat door into the kitchen.

With my family of four-legged creatures now settled in our farm, I was ready to get back to work. Abbey came back to the States for the month of December. She closed the cave site when the weather became too cold and moved to Ulaanbaatar for the winter where she would work out of the National University until spring.

I would go back next summer with a group of student interns to help work the site for two months. During my time there next summer we would see what, if anything, was behind the rock slide at the back of the cave.

Abbey arrived in Ithaca the second week in December after spending a week with her parents. She stayed at the farmhouse. We would ride each morning and then spend the rest of the day reviewing the test results from the samples taken at the cave.

Based on ash and charcoal remains it appeared the cave had been occupied off and on for over ten thousand years. The petroglyphs alone made the discovery valuable. Time would tell if there were any other meaningful discoveries to be made in the cave.

One day as we were riding Abbey told me about a strange occurrence at the Mongolian National Library. There was a sophisticated break-in in which dozens of rare volumes were stolen. All of them related to ancient medical practices. The investigating authorities assumed the volumes were stolen to order by a collector of such works. The international black market for rare books was strong.

I never heard any more about the golden eagle or Ned's spyware. I did see that Falone Advanced Technologies made an acquisition of a major cyber security firm that worked for both private and governmental clients. The article said the acquisition would allow the company to better protect the data of companies it worked for and expand the range of services it offered.

Notes

Note 1: Public Domain.

Note 2: Painting by el_tazp. Hire him for custom on www. fiverr.com.

Note 3. These photos are being used under the Creative Commons License. Individual photo credits are listed below. They may be reused under the terms on the Creative Commons License.

Photo in Chapter 1
Description: **English:** Eagle hunter looking for corsac foxes in Tavan Bogd National Park.
Date: October 2nd 2012
Source: Own work
Author Altaihunters

Photo in Chapter 6
Description: Go on a journey back to thirteenth century Mongolia with stunning re-creations of Mongolia's grasslands and battlegrounds, complete with archaeological artifacts and weaponry of the Mongol Empire. With the largest collection of Genghis Khan artifacts ever assembled from the conqueror's reign, it tells the story of the man whose innovation, technological mastery, and cultural creativity gave him the reputation of one of the world's greatest yet most misunderstood leaders. The exhibition will also shed light on the influence the Mongol empire had on culture, international law, and finance even to this day.
Date: February 21st 2011
Source: Genghis Khan: The Exhibition uploaded by Russavia
Author: William Cho

Photo in Chapter 7
Description: **Deutsch:** Reiter-Standbild des Dschingis Khan, Mongolei
Date: October 8th 2013
Source: Own work
Author: Steffen Wurzel

Photos in Chapter 8
Russian UAZ-452 van
Description: Français : UAZ, Ulyanovsky Avtomobilny Zavod (russe: Ульяновский автомобильный завод, УАЗ) est un fabricant d'automobile russe basé dans la ville d'Oulianovsk, d'où son nom. UAZ est spécialisé dans la

fabrications de tout-terrain, de SUV, d'utilitaires légers et de camionnettes. Il est considéré comme le 3e membre du Big Three russe, loin derrière AvtoVAZ, et après GAZ.
Date: December 26th 2011
Source: Flickr: soviet mini-van
Author: Ludovic Hirlimann

Russian IMZ-Ural motorcycle with sidecar.
Description: Ural motorcycle with sidecar, shot on local street.
Date: Sept 13th 2012
Source: This file is lacking source information.
Author: Own work.

Photo in Chapter 9
Description: **English:** Bactrian camel in Shanghai Zoo
Date: December 30th 2011
Source: Own work
Author: J. Patrick Fischer

Photos in Chapter 12
Przewalski's wild horse, Mongolian wild horse in Hustai National Park.
Description: Photo of a herd of Przewalski horse in Hustai National Park, Mongolia. Photo by Kelsey Rideout www.rideouts.net. (C) 2006.
Date: December 11th 2006
Source: Transferred from en.wikipedia to Commons.
Author: Kelsey Rideout at English Wikipedia

Tsagaan Salaa petroglyph or rock paintings in Altai Tavan Bogd National Park
Description: English petroglyph at Tsagaan Salaa
Date: July 19 2007
Source: Own work
Author: Altaihunters

Photo in Chapter 13
Gavilán 358, a Colombian light utility transport aircraft.
Description: FAC5062 Gavilán G358M Fuerza Aerea Colombiana
Date: July 4th 2012
Source: flickr.com/photos/aeroprints/7501680174
Author: Aeroprints.com

Photos in Chapter 14
Cinereous or Black vulture.
Description: English: Black Vulture
Date: January 5th 2013
Source: Own work
Author: Juan Lacruz

Ibex, a species of wild goat.
Description: English: Alpine Ibex
Date: November 2004
Source: Own work
Author: Nino Barbieri

Note 4: Photo of Conqueror model number UEV-345 extreme off-road trailer from the company website.

About
the Author

BRADFORD G. WHELER is the former CEO, President and Co-owner of Allan Electric Company. He sold Allan Electric to a New York Stock Exchange listed company. After staying on as President during the transition, Brad retired.

Brad's lifelong love of history, art, books, and the inherent humor in man's nature led to the founding of BookCollaborative.com and the publishing of *MONGOLIA AND THE GOLDEN EAGLE: An Archaeological Mystery Thriller*, as well as *INCA'S DEATH CAVE: An Archaeological Mystery Thriller*; *LOVE SAYINGS: wit & wisdom of romance, courtship, &*

marriage; GOLF SAYINGS: wit & wisdom of a good walk spoiled; CAT SAYINGS: wit & wisdom from the whiskered ones; HORSE SAYINGS: wit & wisdom straight from the horse's mouth; DOG SAYINGS: wit & wisdom from man's best friend; and *SNAPPY SAYINGS: wit & wisdom from the world's greatest minds.*

His community involvements include being a Trustee of Community General Hospital in Hamilton, NY, and chairing their Finance Committee. He is the former Chairman of the Board of Trustees of Cazenovia College, and former Chairman and member of the Board of Directors and Alumni Association and President of the Sigma Phi Society at Cornell University in Ithaca, NY. He is also a former member of the Board of Directors of the Greater Cazenovia Area Chamber of Commerce and several other boards.

Brad played polo on the Cornell University men's polo team for four years and was a member of the Cazenovia Polo Club. In 2012 he was inducted into the Manlius Pebble Hill Athletic Hall of Fame.

He holds a BS and ME in Civil and Environmental Engineering from Cornell University in Ithaca, NY as well as an MBA degree from Fordham University in New York, NY. He is a licensed Professional Engineer.

Brad, his wife, Julie, and their golden retriever Finlay live in Cazenovia, NY and Fort Pierce, FL.

Acknowledgments

A few clarifications: First, this book is a work of fiction. However the regions, cities, archaeological sites, rivers, and national parks of Mongolia are all real. The major historical figures, and experts plus their works are real.

To the extent of my ability I have tried to accurately describe the cultures and landscapes of Mongolia. The same is true with the technology. Most of what I describe exists in some form today. The spyware developed by Ned Harris was made up. But who knows, the NSA may have this type of software.

Any errors are completely my fault.

First and foremost I would like to thank the readers of this book. Thank you for giving it a chance. I hope you enjoyed it.

I would like to thank the following individuals for their direct help with this book.

My wife, Julie, not only encouraged me to write the book, she did the first proofread of the book when it needed a lot of work.

Marcia Abramson for her professional proofreading and editing.

Lorie DeWorken at Mind*the*Margins for her wonderful book design work and producing the ebook files.

My website consultant Brian Hoke of Bentley Hoke Consulting who continually helps with all things web related.

Finally I'd like to thank all those book consultants and experts who help authors and small publishers survive in today's rapidly changing media world.

Buy These Books at a discount on www.BookCollaborative.com

They are also available on Amazon.com and Barnes&Noble.com. You can order them at any bookstore in the US, UK, and Canada for delivery within a few days. All books available in eBook form on Amazon.com.

INCA'S DEATH CAVE
An Archaeological
Mystery Thriller

By Bradford G. Wheler

Twenty-one 5 Star reviews

Adventure, archaeology, technology, and mystery mix to form a breathtaking action-packed tale.

A 500-year-old puzzle catapults an archaeology professor and his brilliant grad student into the adventure of a lifetime in *INCA'S DEATH CAVE*, a new mystery thriller from author Bradford G. Wheler. What happened to a band of Inca rebels who journeyed north in Peru to seek the fabled cave of the true gods – and escape the disease and destruction brought by Spanish conquistadors? They were never heard from again. Did they just melt back into their villages or was something more sinister involved? What trace or treasure did they leave behind?

The ingenious plot of this thriller is full of twists and turns, excitement and adventure, archaeology and technology. Readers will meet fascinating characters they'll never forget: a high-tech billionaire, a quick-witted professor, his beautiful young student, and her still-tough grandfather, a retired Marine gunny sergeant.

Cornell University professor Robert Johnson and his star PhD student are hired by a billionaire entrepreneur to solve a 500-year-old archaeology mystery in northern Peru. But first, they will have to survive corporate skullduggery and drug-lord thuggery. And why, 6,700 miles away in Vatican City, is the old guard so upset? What dark secrets could centuries-old manuscripts hold?

This assiduously researched, fast-paced novel brings the Incas and their ancestors to life against the backdrop of the Peruvian Andes.

LOVE SAYINGS: wit & wisdom of romance, courtship, and marriage

By Bradford G. Wheler

Nineteen 5 Star reviews

Dedicated to love and romance, and featuring art from around the globe, *LOVE SAYINGS: wit & wisdom of romance, courtship, and marriage* is an exciting and vibrant collection of beautiful art and text designed to celebrate the joy, humor, and bittersweet struggles of love. This art-themed quotation book covers topics including Love Through the Ages, Women, Men, Dating, Sex, Children, and more. This collaborative publication has two goals in mind: first, to honor and highlight the power and humor of love through text and artwork, and second, to showcase the talents of new and emerging artists. BookCollaborative.com provides artists with a platform through which they can gain exposure and recognition. Both professional and nonprofessional artists were invited to submit their work to be a part of this art-themed quotation book. The end result showcases 48 artists from countries including the US, UK, Poland, Australia, India, Switzerland, and South Africa. *LOVE SAYINGS* features a variety of art media including paintings, sculpture, and photography. Among the selected artists whose works are featured in *LOVE SAYINGS* is Ninh Le, who lives in the city of Dien Bien Phu, Vietnam. He is a junior high school teacher and finds inspiration in the gentle and romantic struggle of the ethnic people of the Vietnam highlands. Another artist is Kayla Ascencio, who has a wonderfully captivating fantasy art style.

GOLF SAYINGS: wit & wisdom of a good walk spoiled

By Bradford G. Wheler

Seven 5 Star reviews

Lots and lots of wisdom on these pages and a lot of chuckles

By D. Blankenship, Amazon top 50 and Hall of Fame reviewer

I have quite a few books whose subject matter deals exclusively with "golf sayings." I have been collecting these books since I first started playing some 55 odd years ago. Of all the wonderful reading I have on my shelf; all the wisdom, humor and frustration documented in their pages concerning what is probably the greatest game ever invented, this little work is most certainly in the exclusive top five I own.

CAT SAYINGS: wit & wisdom from the whiskered ones

By Bradford G. Wheler

Thirteen 5 Star reviews

Feline Art and Words: For cat lovers and those who attempt to understand them

By Grady Harp, Amazon top 50 and Hall of Fame reviewer

Brad G. Wheler has curated an art and words spectrum devoted to Cats (note the capital C and you'll get the gist of this book!). There is about as much variety of artwork reproduced on every page of this enormously entertaining book as is mirrored in the variety of excerpts of words from the ancients to the moderns. Wheler wisely keeps the reader's interest by dividing his book into chapters: Cats Rule, Wild Cats, Kittens, Humor, Of Cats and Dogs, The Cat Personality, Death of a Friend, Love Of, Cats Vs. People – each topic is generously illustrated with art and comments pertinent to each subsection.

HORSE SAYINGS: wit & wisdom straight from the horse's mouth

By Bradford G. Wheler

Nine 5 Star reviews

Horse Enthusiasts Rejoice!

By Dr. Joseph S. Maresca, Amazon top 1000 and Hall of Fame reviewer

Horse Sayings: Wit and Wisdom Straight from the Horse's Mouth by Bradford G. Wheler depicts the horse in all of its glory together with the continued human interest in the equine. The presentation has pearls of wisdom from horse humor, competition, ancient wisdom, training and many other aspects of horses unbeknownst to the public generally but well known to horse enthusiasts. There are illustrations by 61 artists from 11 countries.

DOG SAYINGS: wit & wisdom from man's best friend

By Bradford G. Wheler

Three 5 Star reviews

A Choice Read, Solidly Recommended

By Midwest Book Review

The simple mutts can be far wiser than they let on. *Dog Sayings: wit & wisdom from man's best friend* looks at a collection of humor and knowledge as well as plenty of art focusing on man's constant canine companion. For centuries, there has been much said about the relationship of man and dog, and much inspiration has been drawn from them. Presented in full color throughout, *Dog Sayings* is a choice read, solidly recommended.

SNAPPY SAYINGS: wit & wisdom from the world's greatest minds

By Bradford G. Wheler

Nine 5 Star reviews

A Top Pick for Anyone Looking for a Solid Collection of Humor

By Midwest Book Review

The best wit and wisdom comes from the best minds. Snappy Sayings is a compilation of quips from countless brilliant minds throughout history, from hundreds of years ago to the modern day. Divided into the many aspects of human nature and the unique quips delivered from these individuals, *Snappy Sayings* is a collection that will lead to hours of entertainment. *Snappy Sayings* is a top pick for anyone looking for a solid collection of humor.

EIGHTEEN 6/10/71: The Poetry of John G. Hunter III

is a collection of poems written by John G. Hunter III and given to Bradford G. Wheler for his eighteenth birthday on June 10, 1971. Each poem is accompanied by a color photograph. The layout and design was done by the renowned Italian book designer Adira Cucicov. Wheler has said many times, "I'm sure I received many fine gifts on my 18th birthday but this is the only one I remember and still treasure."